ENCORE

ENCORE

STEEL BROTHERS SAGA
BOOK THIRTY

HELEN HARDT

WATERHOUSE PRESS

For all cancer survivors, especially my mother, Elise, and in memory of those who lost the fight.

And to everyone who stuck with me through thirty—yes, thirty!—books.

PROLOGUE

Jesse

Emerald Phoenix brings all their own equipment on tour. As the opening act, we didn't have that luxury. We've been renting equipment at each venue. Jake did bring his guitar. But Cage and Dragon—the first night—both said that the keyboard and drums we rented in the UK were better than the instruments we have at home.

I suppose I have to get used to traveling without my guitar. Feels weird being just a vocalist, but Rory and I singing together was what made Emerald Phoenix first take notice of us, so that's the way we will do it from now on.

Brock, Rory, David, and Maddie climb into the limo, and then Brianna and I do.

Of course, Cage and Jake are nowhere to be found. Jeez. They clamber out of the venue, both looking a little haggard.

"Hey, you guys—" Then I stop.

They're here. No reason to give them shit for almost being late.

"What?" Jake darts me a gaze.

"Nothing. So, are you ready to rock Paris?"

"You know it," Jake says. Then he nudges me. "What's with David and Maddie?"

"I'm trying not to think about it," I say back.

We reach the airport, get through security, and head to the gate where the plane is ready.

The plane Emerald Phoenix chartered isn't overly luxurious. But the seating is all wider than a normal plane, and there's only one pilot, one copilot, and one flight attendant.

It's just the band and our guests and significant others.

We get herded on, take our seats, and the flight attendant does her safety spiel. She distributes champagne to anyone who wants it, but Brianna and I just take water.

Ten minutes later, we're taking off.

Once we're airborne, Brianna turns to me and smiles. "I love you, Jesse. I'm so happy to be here with you."

"On such a late flight?" I squeeze her hand.

"On a chartered flight with the man I love. And Emerald Phoenix."

"I love you too."

The air is turbulent, and the plane bounces through the sky. I'm not a frequent flyer, so my knuckles go white around Brianna's hand.

"Easy," she says. "This is normal."

"You don't fly a lot either."

"Not a lot, but I've been on turbulent flights. Going over the Rockies is often like this."

I draw in a breath and let it out slowly. She's no doubt right, but I look across from me to where Brock and Rory are sitting. Rory looks a little green.

"You okay, sis?"

She doesn't reply. Simply nods, her hand clamped onto Brock's.

The air smooths out after a moment, and I breathe a sigh of relief.

"See?" Brianna says. "Everything's cool. We're flying over the English Channel, which are some of the roughest waters in the world. The air pressure is probably a mess."

I have no idea if she knows what she's talking about or whether she's making it up as she goes, but her words soothe me. Slightly.

I take the last drink of my water and look for the flight attendant to ask for another. Where is she? Then I see her up front, buckled into her jump seat.

Okay... Not a great sign.

But the air is smooth, until—

My heart drops to my stomach when the plane falls. Or seems to. It's like that feeling when you're on a roller coaster going straight down.

The turbulence begins again, and—

Brianna lets out a frantic scream as the plane rocks and sways.

I'm trapped. My seat belt restrains me. It's tight. So tight.

A drop.

The roller coaster again.

A shrill sound pierces my ears, and the yellow oxygen masks descend.

Brianna is shaking and screaming. I grab the mask, get it on her as quickly as I can.

Then I panic.

The plane drops, and the overhead luggage compartments fly open. Suitcases drop, one barely missing my head.

Time is fucked up.

Seconds fly by, but I see in slow motion. A haze of debris flying around the cabin, clothes tumbling from carry-ons. Vomit from mouths. Screams. Sobs. Shrieks.

I turn to the woman I love, raise my voice above the commotion. "Don't be scared, Brianna. Wherever we're going, we'll be together."

Then I put on my oxygen mask, grab her, and close my eyes.

CHAPTER ONE

B r i a n n a

I brace myself, gripping Jesse with everything in me.

Don't want to die.

Don't want to die.

Don't want to die.

Please, God.

Please...

Why didn't we just take the train underneath the English Channel? We had to fly this little puddle-jumper to Paris because God forbid the Steels not travel in style.

Except it was Emerald Phoenix who chartered the plane...

And now, it's all over. We're going to crash somewhere in the English Channel, our bodies irretrievable. Our families won't even be allowed to properly grieve us. Our grave markers will stand over empty soil.

And just when things got into a good groove with Jesse.

Tears fall down my face and hit the cold plastic of the oxygen mask.

There's one more bump, and I know this is it. I squeeze my eyes so hard, I fear that my eyelids will rip off.

I hold my breath and yield my soul to the universe—

And nothing happens.

Did it happen? Is this what death feels like? The same as

life?

I open my eyes slightly. I'm still on the plane. Everyone else is still clinging to their seats for dear life.

But the plane is no longer shaking.

I look through the window. It's dark outside, so I can't tell if we're still over the Channel. But we've stabilized and are sailing through a smooth stream of air.

Then a beep from the captain's speaker.

"Ladies and Gentlemen, this is your captain speaking. First and foremost, I want to assure you that our aircraft is now stable and under control. I apologize for the unexpected turbulence we just experienced, which resulted in a significant and sudden loss of altitude. I understand that this was a very alarming experience. What occurred was a rare but very normal event that my first officer and I are trained to handle."

What? I poke Jesse's shoulder. He opens his eyes.

"Holy shit." He slowly releases his grip from me and meets my gaze. "We're okay."

The captain continues his announcement. "The oxygen masks were deployed as a precaution due to the rapid altitude change, and I want to thank everyone for following the safety procedures correctly. Please wait a few minutes before retrieving any fallen suitcases to ensure that our aircraft is stable and it is safe to remove your seatbelt. If you need to access an overhead compartment that has not opened, please be careful, as items likely have shifted during the turbulence.

"Bethany will be moving through the cabin to assist you, check for any injuries, and ensure everyone's safety and comfort. Please remain seated with your seatbelts fastened for the time being, as we may experience more unexpected turbulence.

"Your safety and well-being is our top priority. My co-pilot and I are currently assessing our situation and will keep you informed about our flight status. We might need to adjust our flight plan accordingly, and I will update you as soon as we have more information.

"Please do not hesitate to call Bethany if you need any assistance or have any concerns. Thank you again, and know that we are committed to making the rest of your journey as comfortable and safe as possible."

I look down at my hands. They're still shaking.

I stare ahead, not believing what we just went through. The sounds of the plane became a blur in my brain.

From the void, I hear Jesse's voice.

"Brianna?"

But I can't respond to him. I can only fix my gaze on the back of the seat in front of me.

"Brianna!" Jesse tugs on my arm, pulling me out of my trance. "Are you okay?"

I blink several times, allowing a few more tears to fall.

My God.

I was positive my life was over.

Nothing flashed before my eyes.

Nothing.

It was just...*over*.

Except it's not.

And I should be jubilant.

But I'm...*numb*.

"Brianna..."

I turn to Jesse, look into his dark eyes. He gently removes the yellow oxygen mask from my face.

"I was so scared." My tone is robotic.

"So was I, baby."

The flight attendant, Bethany, who seems not nearly as shaken as we passengers are, walks down the aisle. The stench of vomit drifts toward me, and I swallow back my own nausea.

My left hand is in Jesse's, while my right hand clutches the armrest of my window seat with white knuckles.

Outside, the sky is still pitch black with no lights from below. Either we're above clouds, or there are no boats on the English Channel.

Or blackness has just descended...

No.

I breathe in.

We're okay.

I didn't lose my dinner, and neither did Jesse, but someone did.

As reality sinks back in, I realize the entire episode lasted less than a minute. It felt longer, and yet it also seemed to pass in the blink of an eye.

I swallow.

Bethany stops and smiles at Jesse. "Do you two need anything?"

"I'd love to have the ten years that turbulence just took off my life back," he says.

I can't tell if he's trying to be jovial or if he's covering for how nerve-racked he is.

She nods. "The captain and co-captain are so sorry. There was irregular atmospheric motion, and the wings lost some lift in the process. Everything is fine now, and the captain has the aircraft under control. These things happen sometimes, and the pilot is almost always able to regain control."

I swallow. *"Almost?"*

Bethany's eyes widen. "Forgive me for my poor word choice." She gives a weak smile. "I promise you, I've been doing this flight back and forth every day for the last eight years. As the captain said, the kind of turbulence we just experienced is rare but not unheard of. A plane is always the safest place you can be."

Jesse looks around, eyeing the fallen suitcases and the sheet-white faces of our fellow passengers. "It sure as hell doesn't feel like it."

Bethany nods. "I know. But trust me on this one. Is there anything I can get you?"

"A stiff drink?" he says.

She smiles. "Right away. What would you like?"

He blinks. "Nothing. I couldn't possibly drink. I'm not sure why that came out of my mouth."

"Water then?" she asks.

"Sure." He looks at me. "Brianna?"

I simply shake my head. Anything that goes down is likely to come right back up. I still need to get my bearings.

Once Bethany is gone, Jesse turns back to me and plants a vigorous kiss on my lips. "Fuck, Brianna. I love you so much. If I wasn't sure before, I sure as hell am now."

I nod, gulping. "Me too. Jesse, I don't want to die."

He places his hands over my cheeks. "You won't. You didn't. We're here. I don't think we were ever in any real danger. At least according to that flight attendant."

"It sure felt like it."

"I know it did." He runs his hands through his hair. "Man, I'm glad we don't have a concert tomorrow. The band will need some recuperation time."

"We all will," I agree.

Jesse looks into the aisle. "Our carry-ons are still up in the bin." He nods to Dave, who's across the aisle from him with Maddie in the window seat. "You guys okay?"

Dave nods, but I can't hear what he's saying.

I hope Maddie's all right.

I hope everyone's all right.

What if...

My God...

This would have been like that plane crash decades ago that took out Buddy Holly, Ritchie Valens, and the Big Bopper. I remember Mom and Dad talking about that once, how their parents loved all those musicians. The Day the Music Died, they called it.

All of Emerald Phoenix is on this plane.

And all of Dragonlock, except of course for Dragon himself, who's still in London and will be traveling back to the States soon to begin an intense drug rehab program in Denver.

I nudge Jesse when he's done talking to Dave. "Are they okay?"

"Maddie's shook up. I hope Rory's okay."

"I'm sure Brock has her covered."

He nods and turns back to me. "I can't believe I'm saying this, but I'm grateful that Dave is here. What if Maddie were sitting alone? Had to go through this alone?"

"I don't want to think about it," I say. "I don't want to think about any of it."

He nods, inhaling. "For such a short flight, we sure had a big scare."

I take a deep breath in and sigh. "And I'm the one who told you not to worry. That we were flying over turbulent waters so we should expect air turbulence."

"You were right, baby."

"I didn't want to be *that* right." I rub my forehead. "Did Maddie get sick?"

Jesse shakes his head. "Dave says she didn't. Someone did, though. I saw puke fly through the air when we dropped."

"I know. I can smell it. I'm glad it wasn't me."

"I'm glad it wasn't you, too." He squeezes my hand again. "Do you remember what I said to you when we thought it was the end?"

Most of it's a blur, but I nod. Because that's the one thing I do remember. "You said, 'Wherever we're going, we'll be together.'"

He nods and grabs my hands. "I meant it. From now on, Bree, wherever we're going, we'll be together. We'll find a way to make this work with both our careers." He squeezes my hands tight. "Because the one thing I know for sure after looking mortality in the eye? I don't ever want to be without you." He cups my cheek. "Will you be my wife, Brianna?"

And just for a moment, all the fear and trauma from the last few minutes drifts away. Jesse and I aren't even on the plane. We're floating above it, on our own little pink cloud.

I wrap my arms around his neck. "Yes, Jesse! A thousand times yes."

CHAPTER TWO

Maddie

I swallow, making sure my dinner stays down.

"I don't know how I'll get back home to Colorado," I say to Dave, "because I'm never setting foot on another airplane. Never in a million years. Once this plane is on the ground, my feet are staying on land."

"Don't be silly." Dave grins. "You're pre-disastered now."

Dave is his jovial self, but underneath I see the truth. His complexion has faded to nearly white, and his lips tremble slightly.

"What's that supposed to mean?" I ask.

He shrugs. "You've been through this once, so it's statistically impossible that it will happen to you again."

"The plane didn't crash," I remind him. *Thank God,* I add to myself.

"Which is also highly unlikely," he says. "You're safer in the air than in a car or on a ship, Maddie."

I dig my nails into the armrests. "I don't feel particularly safe."

Dave and I aren't an item, but I'm so glad he's here. So far we've had a sort of friends-with-benefits thing going since he showed up, but Rory and Callie both know how attractive I find him. I wasn't thrilled when I found out Brianna and Jesse were getting together. I didn't see that coming, though maybe I should have. She always hung around him at Murphy's Bar back home. I didn't pay much attention because I was more interested in attracting Dave's attention.

Dave Simpson may not carry the Steel name as the son of Bryce Simpson and Marjorie Steel, but he's every bit a Steel, right down to his gorgeous good looks. He's the prettiest of all the Steel men, but hardly a pretty boy. He's masculine all the way, with dark hair, a rippling muscular body, and long-lashed eyes that sparkle a vivid crystal blue, like the clear sky on a bright summer day on the western slope of Colorado.

I grip my armrests until the plane finally lands in Paris.

A collective sigh of relief echoes throughout the cabin. A few people even clap.

The members of Emerald Phoenix are seated ahead of us, so they deplane first. Once Dave and I walk through the gateway and into the airport, only my cousin Cage and Jake Michaels, the guitarist for Dragonlock, are waiting.

Jesse and Brianna arrive after us, and then Rory and Brock.

Rory is clinging to Brock as if she's afraid he'll disappear into thin air.

"You okay?" I ask her.

She nods slowly. "I'm fine. Just shaken. I'm sure we all are."

Brianna is hanging on to Jesse, of course. She and I have a room reserved at Le Narcisse Blanc, where the bands are staying in Paris, but I'm sure she'll spend tonight—what's left of it—with Jesse.

I don't want to be alone tonight, but I'm honestly not sure I want to be with Dave, either. I like him a lot, but this has been traumatic, and I'm not sure we know each other well enough to be each other's rocks in this situation.

I walk to Bree. "Hey, I hate to ask you this, but could you stay in our room tonight?"

She widens her eyes. "Why?"

"Because I don't want to be alone. That's why. I'm freaked out."

She frowns. "I mean, I am too, but..." She draws in a breath. "Sure. That's fine. I'll stay with you. But then that leaves Jesse alone."

Jesse is talking to Cage and Jake, and he seems to be doing okay. "I could probably get Dave to stay with me, but I'm not sure it's appropriate."

She cocks her head. "Why not? You've already slept together."

"I know. But it's not like you and Jesse. We're not in love."

She smiles. "Maybe you could be."

The thought warms me but also scares me. Dave is only two years older than I am, but he knows what he wants out of life. He has goals. He works with his dad on the financial end of the Steel empire.

Seems like everyone knows who they are except me.

Brianna's a rancher, a cowgirl, who will work alongside her father, Talon Steel, in the Steel orchards. Jesse and Rory, of course, are musicians, their true calling. Donny's a lawyer, and Callie is going to law school.

Then there's me.

Madeline Jolie Pike.

I don't have a clue who I am or what I want to do with my life.

My college major is English. I couldn't decide sophomore

year, and I had to make a choice. I like English. I like reading and writing, and I'm good at it. But I have no clue what I want to do once I'm done with school.

That's me. Always the odd one out, and I'm sick and tired of it.

I turn at a gentle touch on my shoulder.

Dave stands next to me. "Doing okay?"

"Yeah."

"We're all here, so we're going down to baggage claim. You ready?"

I yawn. "I suppose. What time is it anyway?"

"A little after midnight."

I nod and follow Dave and the others through the concourse to the terminal where we get our luggage and go through French customs. It's so late, and apparently we don't look threatening, because we pass right through, getting our passports stamped.

Paris.

This was the part of the tour I was most looking forward to. Just Brianna and me tooling around on the Métro, visiting the sights, noshing on baguettes, and drinking French wine.

We can still do some of that since Jesse will be in rehearsal much of tomorrow—or today, rather. But Dave and Brock will probably join us, and that should make me happy.

Which it does.

Sort of.

I don't labor under any delusion that Dave Simpson will fall in love with me. He's the last of the Rake-a-teers and still very young at twenty-four. Brock's the same age, though, and he fell hard for Rory.

But Rory is Rory—the most beautiful woman in our

hometown of Snow Creek, Colorado.

She's my older sister, and I love her, but envy creeps into me more often than I'd prefer. Not only is she beautiful, she also has the voice of an angel.

Then there's my middle sister, Callie. She's beautiful too, but what truly sets her apart is her intelligence. She's a genius, always has been, and Mom and Dad always knew she'd do great things. She's marrying Donny Steel and going to law school.

Jesse, of course, stands out because he's the only boy in our family, and he's crazy talented as well as handsome.

Then, bringing up the rear, is the baby of the family.

Me.

Maddie, who has no special talents, no special gifts.

Bree told me my gift was empathy, how I feel so much for others. Frankly, I think she was just trying to appease me. My three older siblings are all spectacular, and I...

I'm just not.

A limo is waiting for us, and the driver helps get our baggage loaded up, and then I get into the limo. Dave slides in beside me.

I don't talk as we drive to the hotel.

I don't talk as Brock gets all of us checked in.

I don't talk as he hands me my key card and we walk to the elevator.

Finally, when I get to my room, Dave is still standing next to me.

Finally, I speak.

"Goodnight, Dave."

And I let myself into my room.

CHAPTER THREE

Brianna

Jesse walks me to my room. He grabs both of my hands. "I'll miss you, my gorgeous fiancée."

I kiss his cheek. "I'll miss you too, but Maddie doesn't want to be alone."

"I know." He gazes at the hotel room door. "I could stay with you both."

I chuckle. "That'd be pretty weird."

"It's not like we'd do anything."

I smile and shake my head. "You need sleep."

He trails a finger over my neck. "I'll sleep better after making love to you."

"I know. Me too. But Maddie needs me. This has been..." I sigh. "A fucked-up night."

He nods, frowning. "I wonder who got sick."

"Who cares? I'm just glad it wasn't one of us." I hover my key over the door.

Jesse takes it from me. "First, I want a goodnight kiss." He crushes our mouths together.

I lean into him, melting into his kiss, when—

The door opens, jarring me.

"Oh." Maddie's voice. "Sorry."

Jesse and I break our kiss.

"It's okay, Mads," I say. "We were just saying goodnight."

She blinks for a few seconds. "I changed my mind. I don't need you here, Bree. I'm being selfish."

"No, you're not." I give Jesse a quick kiss on the lips. "Goodnight. I love you."

"I love you too," he says, "and you too, Maddie."

I walk into the room with Maddie, where our luggage has already been delivered by the bellhop.

"Did Dave try to get you to stay with him?" I ask.

"No," Maddie says.

I sit on the edge of my bed. "Are you okay?"

She nods. "I will be. Just a little shaken. It's not like I have a choice in the matter. I'm not in your position, Bree. I don't have a man I can just ask to comfort me."

"Sure you do. If you like Dave, I'm sure he—"

"I do like him, Brianna. I've crushed on him forever, and he's been wonderful. But he's a Steel." She gazes toward the mirror in the room's vanity, frowning. "And I'm just me."

I pick up a pillow. "Do I have to beat you over the head again, Maddie? Why are you back on this train?"

She doesn't reply.

"You listen to me," I say. "And listen good. Our plane came pretty darned close to crashing into the English Channel tonight. I don't care what the pilot says about it being normal. I saw the look on the flight attendant's face. She was scared too. Think of how lucky we are."

She nods. "I know. It's all I've been thinking about."

"Yeah? Then why are you playing the A Steel could never fall in love with me card?"

She purses her lips and scratches the side of her head for a moment. "You know what? You're right. Dave and I will hang out for the rest of the tour, and if something happens, great. And if not? I'm lucky to be alive."

"There you go. That's how you should be thinking." I place the pillow back on my bed. "We're in Paris, Mads. I don't speak a word of French, but we're in Paris!"

"I speak some French."

"Perfect. You can be our makeshift tour guide tomorrow."

"Won't we be on a guided tour?"

I shrug. "I have no idea. Brock said to sleep in a little after the debacle on the plane. We'll meet for a late breakfast slash early lunch at ten thirty."

"Sounds good." Maddie yawns. "You want to use the bathroom first?"

"Go ahead," I tell her.

"Okay, thanks."

Maddie opens her suitcase, grabs her toiletries and pajamas, and heads into the bathroom. A moment later I hear the shower turn on.

Not a bad idea.

I want to wash this day away too. I'm still freaked out, and I wish I were in Jesse's arms, but I'll live.

I lie down on my bed and close my eyes.

★ ★ ★

I'm suspended in air, weightless, like a feather caught in an updraft. The cabin of the plane is dark, and all I hear is the deafening roar of the engines, like mechanical beasts that thrust us through the sky.

But now they're faltering, choking on some unseen obstruction, and I can feel it—the pull of gravity tugging at my bones.

Next to me, Jesse grips his armrest, grips my hand. Is he praying? Is he bargaining to some deity for his salvation?

Then Jesse's gone—disappeared into a void.

The plane lurches to one side, and a collective gasp fills the air. We're on a roller coaster, the tracks creaking beneath us, threatening to collapse. I close my eyes, trying to block out the terror around me, but it's no use. It's already seeped into my soul, flooded every inch of my being.

"Jesse!" I cry out.

But he's gone. No longer there.

Disappeared into oblivion.

The plane shudders again, and —

Downward...

Downward...

Downward...

I plunge into the water, thrashing my arms. "Jesse!" I sputter. "Jesse!"

Until saltwater fills my mouth, and I can't breathe...

Can't breathe...

Can't breathe...

★ ★ ★

My eyes shoot open. Cold perspiration crawls over my face, and I clutch my chest. My heart is racing like a freight train, and I swallow, grabbing the bed linens with the other hand. The nightmare fades like mist, leaving only the echoes of terror behind.

I'm here, in the Paris hotel.

The sound of the shower pelting comes through the

bathroom door. Maddie.

I'm here.

On solid ground.

Not trapped in the air. Not plunging into the English Channel.

I'm here.

Tears well in my eyes. How odd that I haven't cried before now?

There were a few tears on the plane, but I didn't actually cry.

I want Jesse.

I need Jesse.

But I can't leave Maddie.

Where's my phone?

My purse sits on the night table. I rise and grab it, finding my phone. I call Jesse.

"Brianna?" he answers. "Are you okay?"

I take a deep breath, trying to ease my nerves. "I just needed to hear your voice. I had a... Maddie's in the shower, and I was lying on my bed, and... I'm tired. So tired. So I closed my eyes, and it all came back, Jesse. It all came back."

I hear his clothes rustle as he jumps to his feet. "I'm coming."

"No, no. I just wanted to hear your voice. I'll be okay."

"You sure?"

"Yeah. Are you in your room?"

"Actually, no. I'm down at the bar. With Dave."

CHAPTER FOUR

Jesse

"I thought you needed your rest," Brianna says through the phone.

"I do. But I couldn't sleep, and when I got down here, Dave was already here."

"Please try to get along," she says. "We don't need a repeat of Glasgow and London."

I look over at Dave, who's nursing a cognac. "We're good, Bree. Nothing like having your life flash before your eyes to make you realize that petty differences are...well...petty."

"Yeah, for sure. Is Dave okay?"

"He's holding up. How's Maddie?"

"She's kind of getting into herself too much, if that makes sense."

"Meaning..."

She pauses. "It's like... She's going back to feeling like the odd man out. So I gave her a good-natured lecture about how we lived through what could have been a tragedy. She'll come around. She's just feeling like Dave and she might not be anything."

I rise and take a few steps away from the table, out of Dave's earshot. "Do I need to say something to him?"

"Oh God, no. She'd be horrified."

I look back at the table. "Good, because Dave's pretty shaken up. I think he was being strong for Maddie, and now he's letting down a bit. I'm thinking I should call Brock to come down and talk to him."

"Don't do that. Rory needs him. She looked traumatized, and she needs to recuperate to sing."

"I know. But Dave's kind of a mess."

"You want me to come down? He and I are close. Not like he and Brock are, but all of us are close. Like siblings more than cousins."

"No. You stay with Maddie. I don't want her alone."

"I understand." She sighs. "I love you, Jesse. So much. We're going to make this work between us, with our careers and everything. That brush with death made me realize I don't want a life without you."

I smile. Brianna is like the sun coming out from a storm. "It showed me the same thing. We'll figure it out. I love you too. Night, Bree."

When I hear her phone click off, I return to Dave. He's gripping his lowball with white knuckles, and for a moment, I expect it to shatter.

"Ease up," I say to him.

"Is Brianna doing okay?"

"She's good." I frown. "I mean, as good as can be expected. She fell asleep for a minute and kind of relived it."

He swallows. "That's why I'm not in bed. I don't want to be alone with my thoughts."

Before I think better of it, I say, "You want to stay in my room? There are two beds because originally I was rooming with Dragon."

He shakes his head, staring at his drink. "No."

I can't blame him. He and I aren't friends. He's a lot younger than I am, and he's sleeping with my sister, for God's sake.

Still, I made my peace with Brock and—sort of—with Donny.

"Okay, but the offer stands if you change your mind." I take a sip of my drink, swallow, and then yawn.

I'm on edge, but I'm also exhausted.

A good hard fuck with Brianna would ease this tension, but I can't think solely of myself after our near-death experience. I have to think of my sister and what she needs.

Dave finally brings his cognac to his lips and takes a drink. Then he lets out a long, low sigh. "Damn it all," he says.

"I hear you."

"I think I'm one of those people who never thought anything bad would ever happen to him, you know?"

I raise my eyebrows. I'm not sure how he expects me to reply, because that's so not me.

"But then my family's past came to light," he continues. "All those secrets my mom and dad and aunts and uncles tried to bury to protect us. Did Bree tell you all of it?"

"Most of it. She didn't tell me about Dale and Donny's past."

"Fuck." He rubs his hand over his face. "It's horrific."

I breathe in. Out. In again. Take another sip, letting the liquor coat my throat, coat my feelings.

I want to know, yet I also don't want to know.

"She says it's not her story to tell," I say, "and I agree with her."

"Then I'll keep it to myself," he says.

I nod.

"After all that shit came out, and I was forced to realize the Steels weren't fucking charmed, I needed a break. That's why I came here to join you guys on the tour."

"Yeah, I know that."

"Right. I figured it would be the vacation I desired. A respite. See Europe. Hang with Brock and Bree." He shakes his head, sighing. "But you know the biggest lesson in all of this? In my family's secrets? And then tonight's event? It's not to get complacent, Jesse. Not to think you've got the world by the balls. Because you don't. You just don't."

I'm not sure what to say to that. So I say nothing at first, until—

"I grew up resenting the hell out of you guys."

He chuckles, but it's a nervous chuckle. "I know that. I don't think you were alone."

"I'm sure I wasn't. I think I felt it more than most though because of the thing with Donny and me in high school."

"Don is the first to admit that if he'd been on that committee, he wouldn't have been able to choose between the two of you for MVP."

I nod. "Honestly, I agree. Would've been tough. Tough call."

"But you were the quarterback," Dave says.

I nod. "True, but the quarterback isn't always the most valuable player."

"But you were. You and Donny both."

"Who the fuck cares at this point?" And I realize I mean those words with all my heart. Nothing like almost crashing into the English Channel to get your priorities in order.

"Damn, Jesse, you're right about that. When you look death in the face, you realize that nothing really fucking matters. I played football too, and so did Brock. Neither one of us was anything like Donny was, though. The only one who came close was Brock's brother Brad. He was a damned fine player, but he wasn't scholarship material like you and Donny were."

"Donny didn't take a scholarship," I say.

"He didn't. And they offered him the moon."

My heart drops slightly. "Was it because of me? Because he knew I was taking the scholarship to Wyoming, and he didn't want to be in competition with me anymore?"

He shrugs. "You'd have to ask him. He would've done great in Wyoming. But if you want my take, I also think he had his sights set on things other than football. He's always wanted to be a lawyer, so he chose to head to a bigger city to make that happen. He ended up on a partnership track at a major Denver law firm but gave it up to come work in Snow Creek, take his mother's place as city attorney."

I nod once more. I've heard the story. "So they're close?"

"From what I can see, Donny is closer to Aunt Jade than any of her other three children, including the two that actually came from her body. She and Donny have that mother-son thing going. He's such a mama's boy." Dave chuckles.

"Callie says the same thing. I hope it doesn't cause a problem in their marriage."

Dave shakes his head. "No. I've watched Donny go through women since he entered puberty, and I've never seen him as devoted to someone as he is to Callie."

I grit my teeth slightly. "He damned well better be."

"He is. And Brock is the same with Rory. Honestly, Donny and Brock are the best men I know, Jesse. Your sisters are lucky."

I pause for a moment, considering his words. Once I got over the fact that my sisters were both in love with Steel men, I did think they were lucky. But the reason I thought they were lucky is because they'll soon have access to the Steel fortune, and neither will ever want for anything again. My sisters are awesome people, and they deserve that.

It never dawned on me that they might be getting good men in the bargain as well.

"You don't agree?" Dave asks.

"Why would you say that?"

He smirks. "Just the look on your face."

I draw a breath, take another sip of my drink. "I was just thinking about something."

"Anything you want to share?"

"Not really. But I will ask you one thing."

"Shoot," he says.

"I've watched two of my sisters fall for Steels, and I think my youngest one may be well on her way. Do you have feelings for her?"

"Fuck..." He downs the rest of his cognac.

"That's not a real good sign, Simpson."

"No. I mean, it's not a sign at all." He taps his fingers on the empty glass and looks away. "I didn't come here looking for love. I didn't come here looking to sleep with your sister. I came here looking for a fucking vacation. A break from it all. And of course having sex with a gorgeous woman always makes a vacation better."

This time I'm holding the lowball glass with white knuckles. "And...?"

He presses his lips together. "And...I'm still not looking for love. But I'll admit that tonight's events have me thinking about things."

"And is Maddie one of those things?"

"To be honest, yeah. Your sister's beautiful. All three of them are, but Maddie has a...warmth."

"You don't think my other two sisters are warm people?"

He rolls his eyes. "For Christ's sake, Pike. That's not what I mean, and you know it. All three of your sisters are beautiful, smart, and talented. But I've always seen something in Maddie. Something I'm not sure others see."

"And what is that?" I say through my clenched jaw.

"She's a little quieter than the other two. Quieter than my foursome of cousins who she's always hanging out with. She's the most like Angie, so I was surprised that she and Brianna came on this trip together."

"Well, there's a story behind that."

"I figured there was."

"Apparently, your cousin has been in love with me from afar for years."

Dave's jaw drops. "Say what?"

"Yeah, scared the shit out of me when I found out. Especially when I developed real feelings for her. She's so young."

"Same age as Maddie," Dave says.

"I know. She's so young, too." I finally let go of my glass and signal to the waiter. "Can I get another?"

"Deux, s'il vous plaît," Dave says. Then to me, "That's about all the French I know."

The waiter nods. Good thing everyone speaks English here.

"It's more than I know," I tell him.

"So you and Bree..." he nudges.

"I can't explain it," I say. "And I feel weird talking to you about it. Guys don't talk about this kind of thing. At least *I* don't."

"Don't I know it." He exhales sharply through his nose. "But I'll say one thing about Maddie and me—because you're her brother."

I lift my eyebrows.

"I didn't intend for anything to happen with your sister. I thought we would enjoy each other's company while we were here on the trip. She and I talked about it, and I thought we had an understanding."

"Is there more coming, or do I have to kick your ass?"

He chuckles dryly. "You've already tried that, Pike. But yeah, there's more coming." He crumples his cocktail napkin in his fist. "That drop on the plane has me freaked out. Like I said. I've been complacent. You know, when your life is good for so long, and then chaos erupts."

"That's kind of the way of the world, Simpson."

"Right, I get that." He frowns. "But it's never been the way of my world. I never had any worries. About the only bad thing that happened to us before we found out about our family's past was when Aunt Ruby had breast cancer. But they caught it early, and she made a complete recovery. It was like the sun was always shining on us, you know?"

I can't help gritting my teeth slightly. "Oh yeah. I know."

"And now," he continues, "Uncle Talon gets shot, this bitch Wendy Madigan shows up and wreaks havoc, and I find out she's been running a human trafficking ring on our property. It's like some kind of floodgate has opened and we're all struggling to keep above water."

"You guys still have it pretty good," I say.

He casts his eyes to the floor. "Don't think I've forgotten that. We weren't raised to be spoiled brats, Jesse. We were raised to understand our good lot in life, to appreciate hard work and the value of a dollar. But when you never have to worry about anything, well..."

"You kind of forget all of that," I finish for him.

"You knew where I was headed."

The waiter comes with our drinks and sets them down.

"*Merci beaucoup,*" Dave says.

"*Oui, messieurs.*"

I take a sip of my brandy... Or is it cognac? Whatever it is, I take a sip.

"So," Dave says, "I'm not sure I can continue this thing with your sister."

I drop my jaw. "Excuse me?"

His words should have me jubilant, ecstatic. One less thing to worry about—one less Steel in my sisters' pants.

But I fear Maddie will be crushed, and this trip is supposed to be fun for her.

"And why exactly?" I finally ask when he doesn't reply.

He takes a deep breath and sighs. "I'm not sure I know who I am anymore, Pike. When you see your life flash before your eyes, when you realize you haven't done much of anything except be a spoiled rich boy who beds every woman he can, it makes you think."

CHAPTER FIVE

D a v e

Those were the thoughts raging through my head as we were plummeting downward.

I was frightened, yes. Nearly pissed myself.

But after that initial moment of dread, I had this moment—and there was a moment when time seemed to be suspended, and every thought in the world raced through my mind—when I realized how ridiculous my life has been up to now.

Chasing women.

Chasing women with Brock and Donny.

And alone, recently, since Brock and Donny are now spoken for.

But sure, I grew up on the ranch. Learned from my dad about the financial end, but I also worked with Uncle Talon, Uncle Joe, and Uncle Ryan, getting a taste of what each of them did on the ranch.

All of us kids did. Our rounds, we called them.

So yeah, I worked my ass off, learned about the ranch.

Learned to ride a horse nearly as soon as I learned to walk.

I even learned to cook from my mom, who's a gourmet chef.

Went to college with Brock, and while he studied agriculture, I studied business, knowing I'd be working with my father on the business end someday. That's what was expected of me.

So yeah, I did all of that.

Nothing really stood out.

It wasn't my ranch.

Sure, I'll inherit my tenth or whatever when we all get our share, but I'm not my grandfather, Bradford Steel. After I found out about his antics and what he cost my grandmother, I'm not sure I ever want to be him.

Still, I accepted that I was privileged. Born rich, and I would always be rich. Even if our ranch went down, the Steels have enough outside investments to keep us all in a luxurious lifestyle for the next hundred years.

So, yeah. Even knowing my family history is spotted, I still had few worries.

Until I looked my life in the eye, knowing it was coming to an end...

What the hell have I accomplished?

I learned the family business. I got a college degree. I had a cushy position at my father's side handed to me.

Put me in a box with a million other guys who have done that.

Nothing makes me stand out.

Nothing makes David Steel Simpson stand out.

Jesse doesn't respond, and it's not like I expect him to.

Or if he does, he'll probably say something like, "Cry me a river, poor little rich boy," and he'll be right.

Finally I speak. "I've got to make my mark in this world, Jesse. I want to be something more than one of Bradford Steel's grandchildren. I want to be something more than the next CFO of Steel Acres and Steel Enterprises."

"What do you want to do?" he asks.

I bury my face in my hands, run my fingers through my hair. "That's just it. I don't have a fucking clue. And if I don't know that, I sure as hell can't be any good to any woman, and that includes your sister."

"Don't you break her heart," he warns.

I look up at him. "That's why I have to end whatever's between us before she gets too invested. And I think..."

"What?" His voice is pointed, and his expression is far from happy.

I swallow. "I should probably go home. Because I'm not going to find my path in life on a rock and roll tour."

He closes his eyes and takes a deep breath before responding. "Look. I'm the last person in the world who's going to tell you to keep sleeping with my sister, okay? End it if you have to, but do it soon. I don't want her hurting any more than she already will."

I stroke my chin. "I'm not sure she'll be that hurt. She didn't say anything about me coming to her room tonight. I was there right outside her door, and all she said was, 'Good night Dave.'"

"So?"

"She didn't invite me in."

"Did you ask to go in?"

"No."

"Maybe she wanted you to." He shrugs. "How the hell should I know? I don't know how women's brains work. They're a complete enigma to me. I grew up with three sisters, and they all acted nuts at some point or another. Blame it on hormones, on the double X chromosome, or maybe just the Pike genes. I don't fucking know. Just go easy on her. Please.

We've all been through some major trauma."

"Don't I know it." I take a drink of the cognac, let it slide down my throat, warming me.

"But there's something I want you to think about," Jesse says.

"What's that?"

He shrugs. "Your life is far from over. You're twenty-four, and you just lived through something that could've ended us all. I mean, I know the pilot said we were never in any serious danger, but it sure felt that way, and we all thought it was over."

"And…?"

"My point is relax, for God's sake. You're alive, Dave. You're fucking alive. And you're in Paris. Take a few days and enjoy it. Take your well-earned vacation, at least until we leave France. I'm not saying you should sleep with my sister." He wrinkles his nose. "Trust me, I'd rather you didn't. But take a few days without worrying about what to do for the rest of your life. You don't need to go home and figure it out right away. It's impossible anyway."

I meet Jesse's gaze. There's sincerity in his dark eyes, and I think if I hadn't screwed his sister, we might be able to be friends. He's Donny's age, and they were never friends, even though they had so much in common. Maybe they will be now since our families are joining.

"I need to ask you something," I say.

"Sure, go ahead."

"Brock and Donny are marrying Rory and Callie."

"Yeah."

"Are you going to marry Brianna?"

He grins from ear to ear. "Absolutely."

"You're that sure?"

"I am. We fell in love, and I figured we'd enjoy that for a while before making any long-term commitments, mostly because our chosen careers are at odds. If Dragonlock makes it big and we end up going on more tours, even headlining, I'll be traveling a lot. But her heart and soul are there on that ranch with her father. Working those trees. And I don't want to take her life's work away from her."

"But how are you going to make it work?"

He shrugs. "We just will. That brush with death moved me. When I thought my life was over, all I knew was that I wanted her by my side, wherever we were going. It was an epiphany, you know? I didn't have a ring, but I asked her to marry me, and she accepted. We'll make it work because I love her more than anything. Brock and Rory are going to have to make it work somehow, too. I suppose they didn't have this issue when they fell in love, because it was before Rory had even joined the band. She was teaching music in Snow Creek, and she certainly still could have done that while Brock works his ranch. But now they're going to be in the same situation."

"So let me get this straight," I say. "You actually proposed to her?"

Jesse nods. "I did. She says she feels the same way. She's so young, but I have to take her at her word. Believe that she feels what I do."

"She does," I say. "I can see it in her eyes when she looks at you."

He rolls his eyes. "Don't get all poetic."

I take a drink of my cognac. "I just call them as I see them, Pike."

But I'm done talking about this.

Jesse Pike will never understand my life, just as I'll never understand his.

I was born into incredible privilege, but to someone like Jesse, waking up and finding out your family tree is not the pillar of the community you thought it was and then subsequently looking death in the face? It doesn't pack a wallop.

Well, maybe the looking death in the face part. We have that in common.

He doesn't understand that we were always taught that every human being had value. And that we knew how incredibly privileged we were to be born into the Steel family.

But that kind of stuff doesn't sink into a kid's head. Doesn't even sink into a young adult's head. It sure as hell never really sank into mine. Sure, I knew I was privileged. But I never stopped to think about how others lived.

How others might look at us.

Oh, I heard the rumors. *The Steels own this town.*

I never thought it was true, until it was.

Of course it wasn't our family. It was something called the Steel Trust, which was engineered by Wendy Madigan, Uncle Ryan's birth mother.

But still, people knew. The Steel Trust had liens on almost everybody's property in town and around the surrounding areas.

But not on the Pike land.

Jesse must wonder why.

I wonder myself.

I suppose it doesn't really matter. They own their land with no liens other than a mortgage.

Jesse finishes his cognac. "I think I'm going call it a night," he says.

"Yeah. Me too." I hold up my glass. "Just got to finish this."

"You want me to stay?"

"No. I'm fine. Shaken, but aren't we all?"

He nods. "I'm going to check on the girls. Make sure they're okay."

"I appreciate that."

He rises and throws some euros on the table.

"I got this," I say.

He opens his mouth, and I'm pretty sure he's going to balk at that, until he finally nods. "That's kind of you, Dave. Thank you." He walks away.

I'll be damned. That brush with death changed all of us.

CHAPTER SIX

Maddie

Brianna has fallen asleep, but I'm lying in bed awake.

I fear that if I close my eyes, I'll relive the whole thing.

Then I jerk slightly at a knocking noise.

I get out of bed, go to the hotel door, look out the peephole.

I heave a sigh of relief when I see my brother.

I open the door. "Jesse? Everything all right?"

"Yeah." He wraps me into a loose hug. "I just want to check on you two and see if you're okay."

I look back into the room. "Brianna's asleep, finally. But I can't get to sleep. Were you in bed?"

"I had a drink with Dave down at the bar."

My eyebrows shoot up. "Dave?"

"Yeah, sis. That near plane crash has got him pretty spooked."

"He seemed good to me."

"I think he was being strong for you." He pats my arm. "You okay?"

I frown. "I mean, am I? I'm freaked out. We all are."

"I know."

I scratch my arm. "Plus I'm feeling kind of shitty."

"Why?"

"Only about a million reasons, but the main one right

now is that I'm keeping you and Brianna from being together tonight. I'm sure you want to lean on each other after such a horrible thing."

"We're all right." He places his hands on my shoulders. "I'm more concerned about you."

I sigh. "That's just it, Jesse. I don't want everyone concerned about me. Poor little Maddie, always the odd one out."

"That's not what I meant, and you know it."

"Is it, though? I know you'd rather be with Brianna, the woman you love. And I know she'd rather be with you. I'm not blind, Jesse. I see how much you mean to each other."

"Funny, Dave said almost the same thing."

"That he could see how much you love each other?"

"Pretty much. It was weird coming from a guy."

"Not weird as much as it's just very obvious." I sigh. "Now all of my siblings are in love—with Steels no less. Talk about being the odd one out."

"Love isn't something that can be rushed," he says.

I roll my eyes. "Isn't it? All three of you fell in love like lightning flashes."

Jesse cocks his head. "You're right about that. Brianna says the people in her family tend to fall quickly and fall hard. I get it now."

I sigh again. "Do you want to come in?"

He shakes his head. "I don't want to wake Bree."

I hear rustling behind me.

"Bree's already awake," she says.

I turn. Brianna stands in the darkness, her long gorgeous hair flowing around her shoulders, and her nipples poking through her tank top.

Great.

That'll get my brother started.

"Hey, you," she says to Jesse.

"You doing okay, baby?"

"Yeah, I finally got to sleep." She redirects her gaze toward me. "You okay, Mads?"

"I'm still awake, which is how I heard Jesse knocking softly on the door."

"I just wanted to make sure the two of you were okay," he says.

"Haven't you been to bed?" Brianna asks.

"No. I was having a drink with Dave."

"Apparently your cousin is pretty shook up," I say.

Brianna's eyes widen, and she wipes some sleep out of them. "Is he okay?"

Jesse nods. "He is. I think each of us has been affected by this a little bit differently."

"Brianna," I say, "I want you to go with Jesse. I'm okay. I wasn't sleeping anyway."

"No, Maddie. I made you a promise."

I grab her arm. "I'm letting you out of it for tonight. Go be with each other. Comfort each other. Do whatever it is you do when you're together—and no, I don't want the details."

"You sure?" Brianna asks.

"Yeah. Please. Go."

"Are you sure?" she asks Jesse.

A small smile appears on his face. "If Maddie is sure, yeah, of course. I'd love to be with you."

"All right," Brianna says. "Give me a minute. I'll put on a robe and grab my stuff."

A few moments later, Brianna leaves, walking down the

hallway to Jesse's room. They're only two doors down, and I'm okay. I watch them go to the room and close the door behind them.

I'm about to close my own door when I hear the elevator ding, and off steps Dave Simpson.

I'm ready to close the door so he doesn't see me when he looks up and meets my gaze.

Too late now.

"Hey," I say softly.

He walks up to me. "Is this your room?"

I look down at what I'm wearing. "No, I'm just standing here in my pajamas for good measure."

He gives me a weak smile. "Looks like I'm right here, across the hall from you."

"Good. Brianna and Jesse are two doors down." I gesture.

"I thought Brianna was staying with you tonight."

"She was, but Jesse came by to check on us, and I let her go. I have to get through this on my own. I can't be leaning on anyone."

He nods. "I know what you mean."

I blink a few times before speaking. "So... Good night, then."

"Good night." He hovers his key card over the door and opens it.

And I should go back into my room, close the door behind me.

But I don't.

I stand there.

He opens the door, and he closes it, but just as it's about to click, he opens it again. "Maddie?"

"Yeah?"

"I...don't want to be alone."

I scratch my arm. "Neither do I, Dave, but I think maybe it's better if we are."

"There's so much going through my head right now."

"I know," I say. "Me too."

He breathes out slowly. "Maybe we could just...hold each other."

This is Dave Simpson. The last Rake-a-teer standing. And he wants to hold me?

He really is shaken up.

"Do you think that's wise?"

He scoffs. "For Christ's sake, Madeline, I don't know what the hell is wise or not."

I cock my head. "Madeline?"

"Seemed like a *Madeline* moment." He runs his hands through his hair. "I've just been thinking, my whole life is just..."

"What the hell are you talking about, Dave?"

He sighs. "Just come in with me. Or let me come in with you. We don't have to do anything, I promise. That's not what this is about."

Does that mean he doesn't want to have sex with me? Or does it mean that he does want to, but he's not sure I want it? Or he's not sure it's the right thing?

I'm clueless.

"Then what *is* it about, David?"

He smiles then. "Tit for tat."

"Well, you called me Madeline."

"Madeline is a beautiful name. It suits you."

"And David is a...biblical name."

He chuckles. "My mom and dad love it. Except Mom wanted to name me Bryce Junior, but Dad didn't think that would be fair because Henry's older than I am. So then Mom wanted Bryce for my middle name, but then Dad decided he didn't want to use the name his derelict father had given him in any way, so they settled on Steel for my middle name. Then they had to come up with the first name. David was the only one they both liked."

I didn't ask for a dissertation, but I know he's just stalling.

Finally I pull my door open. "Come on in."

He walks through the door. It's still dark in my room because I never put the light on. I didn't want to wake Brianna. I click it on now, my eyes already adjusted because of the hallway.

"You look gorgeous," he says.

I have no makeup on, and I'm wearing a T-shirt and lounging pants. "O...kay," I say.

He smiles. "No, you do. I mean, I've seen you at night before." He narrows his eyes. "But there's something about tonight..."

I roll my eyes. "My hair's still damp. I took a shower. I just wanted to wash this whole night off me."

He nods. "I get it. That's why I stayed down and had a cognac. That was my way of washing the night away."

"Jesse said he had a drink with you."

"Yeah, he came down after he saw you guys to your room. Said he didn't feel like sleeping just yet."

"Talk about awkward."

He presses his lips together for a few seconds. "Actually, it wasn't. We kind of opened up to each other."

I cock my head at him. Again, what happened to Dave? Last Rake-a-teer standing? Jovial David Simpson?

"I guess there's more than one side to me."

I sigh. I hope he doesn't think I was calling him one-dimensional. Best not to try to explain. "What can I do for you?" I ask.

He starts to open his mouth, but I stop him.

"I mean other than sex."

He shakes his head. "I'm not after sex. I'll even sleep in Brianna's bed if that makes you feel better."

He seems to be laboring under the delusion that I don't want to have sex. That's far from the truth. I just don't want to get myself into a place where my heart will be broken. That could easily happen with Dave Simpson.

The look on his face, though, is one of pure agony. It's more than just the trauma of our shared experience.

It's something more. His thoughts are...a mess.

"You want to talk?" Then a yawn splits my face.

He shakes his head and pats my shoulder. "You need to go back to bed. You're exhausted."

"I haven't slept yet, Dave."

"You just yawned."

"I didn't say I wasn't exhausted. Fatigued. Completely tired. But sleep isn't coming."

"Maybe I *would* like to talk," he says, "but it can wait until morning. Let's just try to get some sleep."

I nod. "You can sleep in Brianna's bed if you want. Or you can sleep with me. Whatever you choose."

"What do *you* want?" he asks.

I shrug, trying to appear noncommittal. "I want what you think is best for you. You're obviously shaken up, and if you think it would help to have sex—fuck, whatever—then let's do it."

He raises a hand in front of him. "I don't want you to

think—"

I hold out my hand to stop him again. "David, trust me. I think nothing. I am not harboring any hopes on any of this. Believe me, I know better. Just because all of my siblings have snagged a Steel doesn't mean I have any hopes of doing the same. I like having sex with you. We have good chemistry in bed, and it doesn't have to be anything more than that. I have absolutely no expectations."

He smiles then.

Fucking smiles!

"What the hell, Dave? You think that's funny?"

"No, of course not. I'm smiling because..."

"Why? Spit it out."

"I'm smiling because I was going to say that I don't want you to think that I'm using you as an escape. Because that's not what this is about. If I wanted an escape, I could go back down to the bar and pick up one of the two French women who came on to me before Jesse arrived. One was actually named Gigi. Can you believe that?"

I gulp. "What was the other's name?"

"Simone."

"And were they beautiful?"

"Yes, both blond and both beautiful."

I gulp again. Blond and beautiful, so why would he want my plain brown hair?

He shrugs and continues. "But I'm not there. If all I wanted was to sink my cock into a willing pussy, I could be doing it, Maddie. So if I go to bed with you tonight, it's not just an escape."

I open my mouth to reply, but nothing emerges.

In truth, I don't know what to say. I'm glad that it's not

some escape. But he could mean that he's just seeking solace in the arms—and body—of a friend. A person who understands what he's been through tonight.

Maybe that's how I should think about this as well.

I purse my lips. "So you're saying I'm more than just a fuck."

"Absolutely," he says. "You're more than just a fuck."

I wait for him to elaborate, but he doesn't.

He's not in love with me, and if I'm being honest with myself, I'm not in love with him either. I'm infatuated, for sure. He's gorgeous, funny—usually—and a Steel. Who wouldn't be infatuated?

And he knows his way around my body.

Of course, he's a Rake-a-teer. He's fucked countless women, so he knows how to learn any woman's body quickly.

But at this moment, tonight—technically tomorrow morning already—I can't bring myself to care.

"Let's go to bed." I flick the lights off. "I could use a good, hard fuck, Dave. I think we both could. And you know what?"

"What?" he asks.

"I don't care if it *is* an escape for you, because that's what it is for me."

CHAPTER SEVEN

Dave

I walk in, following Maddie.

My cock is already hard as a rock just thinking about her.

The sex we had was amazing. Probably the best I've ever had.

I'm not really looking for a relationship, and it's certainly nothing we've talked about, but looking your morality in the face makes you think about things differently.

She gets on the bed.

I follow her, leaning over, looking down into her eyes. "You're fucking beautiful." I pull off her lounge pants, peer at her perfect pussy.

There are no lights on in the room, but our eyes have adjusted, and I can see her perfectly.

I pull off my shirt, hover over her, kiss her.

Our lips link together. I move my hands over her gorgeous breasts and then between her succulent thighs.

We kiss for several minutes, our tongues tangling, and then I slide her T-shirt up, exposing her luscious tits. I hold on to one breast, squeezing it, tugging on her nipple while I continue to kiss her.

Then I move my mouth down, over her neck, trailing kisses until I get to her nipple, sucking it, swirling my tongue around it, kissing it.

She moans above me, and I can't take it anymore. I need her. Need to look at her pussy, touch her clit.

I spread her legs, gaze at her full pink lips, at her glistening juices.

I slide my tongue through her folds and then wrap my mouth around her clit, sucking lightly.

"Oh my God..." she sighs.

I tease her clit with my fingers and then replace them with my mouth again, sucking gently, nibbling slightly.

Her hips undulate, and I reach forward, grab one of her breasts again.

I glide my fingers over her nipple, teasing, tugging it, pinching it lightly, as I continue to suck on her pussy.

"God yes," she says. "Put your finger in me, Dave. Please."

I slide not one but two fingers inside her sweet pussy, fingering her, finding her spongy spot, making her squirm.

And then I lick her clit again.

She tastes like magic. Like everything good in the world. About how easy it is to forget.

She lifts her hips, and I continue to slide my fingers in and out of her.

"You taste so good," I say. "God, like candy."

"Yes," she says. "Suck me. Finger me. It all feels so good."

I clamp my lips over her pussy again, suck her clit, and then I remove my fingers and replace them with my tongue, probing her sweetness, tasting the inside of her.

So easy to lose myself in her beautiful body.

And she does have a beautiful body.

Soft milky skin, a pink glistening pussy, beautiful tits with hard brown nipples.

I slide my fingers back in, probing her, sucking her.

I can't get enough of her sweetness, and I want to lose myself in her. Suck her forever.

Except my cock wants more.

So much more.

But I need to make her come first.

"Come for me," I say. "Come for me, gorgeous Maddie."

I shove my fingers deep into her pussy, suck on her clit, and—

"God, yes!"

Her pussy walls clamp around my fingers, and as I piston into them farther, I move up her body, kiss her sweet lips, thrust my tongue between them, letting her taste herself on me.

She breaks the kiss in a moment, pushes me away, and sits up in bed. She pulls her T-shirt over her head and discards it, and then she pulls my legs forward and unbuttons my jeans, sliding them off along with my boxer briefs.

My cock springs out, and she grabs on to it, sliding her hand up and down as she sucks on its head.

Her hair, which is still damp, hangs in waves around her shoulders as she sucks on me, and she looks so beautiful.

She replaces her mouth with her hand, sliding it up and down me, and then she moves over to suck on my balls.

"Fuck," I grit out.

She sucks on them, runs her tongue over them, and then moves back to my cock. Her gaze meets mine as she sucks on me, her dark-brown eyes mesmerizing me. She moves her mouth up and down my cock, replacing it with her hand every now and then, and then using both to get all the way to my base.

I'm long and thick, and no woman has ever been able to deep-throat me, but Maddie comes close.

She moves up then, smiles at me as she meets my gaze, twirls her tongue over the cock head.

My God, I don't want to come, but I'm so ready. So in need of release.

Do I risk coming in that sweet mouth of hers? Or do I stop her and fuck her?

Fuck her hard.

Because that's what we both need.

She slides her lips down the side of my cock, back up over the head again, and then down the other side.

Just watching her is pleasure. A feast for the eyes and the ears. And, of course, the cock.

But then she stops.

Though I let out a whimper at the loss, she climbs on top of me, straddles me, and slides down onto my cock.

I can wait no longer.

I grab her hips, hold her steady, and thrust into her. I thrust upward, upward, upward.

But then she smooths me out, holds my thighs, takes the lead.

She moves up and down on my cock, slapping her thighs against mine, and my God, it feels like paradise.

She leans down, kisses me for a moment, and then sits back up, moving her pussy on my cock, whimpering, sighing, moaning.

She fucks me hard for a few moments, and just when I think I'm about to come—

She slows down.

She slows down, sits on me, moves her hips in a circle so I feel every part of her.

I take the lead then, thrusting inside her as I hold her

thighs steady.

"My God, Maddie... You feel so good. How you fuck me."

She giggles lightly. "I think you're fucking me." She stops me, rises so her pussy lips are teasing the top part of my cock head. And she begins her movement again, slowly moving up and down as she leans into me again and kisses me.

A soft kiss this time. Like an interlude. But I can't take any more.

I sit up, roll us onto our sides, suck her tits, and then climb over her so we're spooning. I sink myself back into her sweet pussy.

She moans, whimpers, cries. And with my hand, I finger her clit as I fuck her.

"I want you to come again, baby. Come for me. I want you to come ten times before I do."

"That's...not...fair..." she says on a sigh as she cups her own breasts, fingers her own nipples.

I lean into her, kiss her neck, and continue thrusting in and out of her.

She takes over for my fingers, caressing her clit, whimpering. I grab her tit, pinch her nipple, all the while continuing to fuck her.

Each time I sink into her, I'm ready to release, but I hold back. Hold back even though she clasps me like no other.

"My God, it's like you were made for me," I grit out.

I increase my thrusts, faster, faster, faster...

But I don't come yet.

When I come, it will be over, and I don't want this to be over. I want to keep fucking. Stay inside this warm cocoon where we're both safe.

I want to give her orgasm after orgasm after orgasm—

"Touch yourself again, baby. So sexy." I squeeze her tit.

She reaches between her legs, sliding her fingers over her clit.

"Come, baby, please."

"Yes," she shouts. "I'm coming again, Dave. Coming, coming, coming..."

I fuck her harder, faster, loving the feeling of her walls clenching around me.

It won't be long now, but I'm not done experiencing her.

I pull out for a moment, crawl downward, slide my tongue between her legs, eating out the juices from her orgasm.

"My God, so delicious..." I shove my fingers inside her cunt once more.

This is what I need. What she needs.

I could go for the easy release. But this... This is fucking rapture.

I drill into her with my fingers, suck her clit.

"So...sensitive..." she whispers.

Then I move us both so she's lying on her back, and I sink back into her as she wraps her gorgeous legs around me.

I move one of her legs over my shoulder, sinking into her even deeper.

She's tight from her orgasm, and my God...

"Damn, you feel good," I say.

"Yes, you too. Your cock is so big. Fills me so perfectly."

I increase the speed of my thrusts, fuck her, fuck her, fuck her...

Again, she slides her hand between her legs as I'm pounding her. Plays with her clit.

A chill runs down my spine. "God, you're sexy. So responsive. I don't think I've ever had a woman be so responsive to me."

Thrust, thrust, thrust...

Then I stop, hold myself inside her, relish the feeling of filling her. I lean down, slide my tongue between her lips.

We kiss passionately for a few timeless moments until—

I have to pull out and thrust back in.

I keep my thrusts slow. I can tell by the dazed look in her eyes that it's making her crazy.

"Oh my God, Dave. I need to come again... Please..."

I slide my arm around her thigh, reach her clit, and massage gently.

She erupts around my cock.

"God, you feel so good," I say through clenched teeth, warring between my body and my brain.

My body wants to come.

My brain wants to keep forcing orgasms out of her gorgeous body.

I shove my cock back inside her, thrusting, thrusting, thrusting...

God, I want to come. Want to release so badly.

Not yet. She's come three times, and I want one more.

"I'm going to pull one more climax out of you, Maddie," I say. "You're going to come for me. And you're going to come so hard that you see stars."

She breathes heavily. "Already seeing stars..."

"Not yet. Not yet, baby. You're going to fucking explode."

I hold back a moment, pull out of her, lean down and kiss her lips, tug on her nipple.

And then I continue fucking her.

CHAPTER EIGHT

Maddie

My body is spent. My flesh is pricked, as if pine needles are poked all over my body. It's a good feeling, a perfect feeling...

And I embrace it.

Embrace the fact that I'm alive, that I'm here in this room with a man I'm wildly attracted to. A man I've fantasized about ending up with.

But then I wash that thought away.

I will accept this night for what it is—a long hard fuck between two people who need each other.

I'm lying on my back, and Dave is perpendicular to me, thrusting his cock inside me, thumbing my clit.

He pulls out of me, replaces his cock with two fingers, hooking them around my G-spot.

I gasp, holding my legs open for him as he leans down, removes his fingers, slides his tongue over me, glides his fingers back in, and then skims his tongue over my asshole. He moves forward then, turning until he's facing my pussy. He keeps tugging on my clit and finger fucking me, leading his cock to my mouth.

I take it between my lips gladly. I want to please him the way he's pleasing me. I want to tell him to come, but my mouth is full of his cock.

He continues to finger fuck me, and I cry out once more.

"Mmm, so good." He moves away from me once more, turning again.

I whimper at the loss of his cock from my mouth, but he slides his wet fingers between my lips. I suck on them, relishing my own flavor, but in a flash he flips me over onto my stomach.

He slides his tongue over my asshole before thrusting his cock into me.

This angle is different, and I feel so much fuller.

I cry out as he fucks me. Hard. Fast. Thorough.

I'm not sure how he can last so long, but he's making it, and I love it.

Faster, faster, faster... His balls slap against my pussy.

Then he leans down, his muscles covering my back, and he tugs on my earlobe, slides his tongue into my ear canal.

I shiver all over. It's all so good, so much...

And then somehow, somehow...

He slides one hand between my legs, kissing my shoulders, his cock still embedded in me.

And I—

I soar to the heavens once more.

I fly over the sights of Paris, beyond the Eiffel Tower and the Arc de Triomphe, past Versailles and the Palais Garnier, into the clanging church bells of Notre-Dame, which reverberate endlessly through my head. When I finally come down, I look over my shoulder, and his lips meet mine.

After a sweeping kiss, he breaks it. "Maddie, Maddie..."

"Yeah?"

"I wish I could give you more orgasms, but I have to come. I have to come."

"God yes, please..."

He thrusts once, twice, three more times, and then stays embedded inside my pussy.

And I feel each pulse.

He stays inside me for a few moments, and then he pulls out, turns me over, leans down, and kisses my shoulders and then my lips.

"My God, Maddie," he says. "You're amazing."

"Just what I needed..." Then I sigh and close my eyes.

★ ★ ★

My eyes pop open to the sun streaming in through the window.

I have no idea what time it was when I finally fell asleep.

But I was so relaxed after Dave and I—

I jerk upward into a sitting position.

"Dave?"

He's not here. He probably went to the bathroom.

"Dave?" I get out of bed and head to the bathroom. The door is closed, so I knock.

No reply.

I open the door, walk into a dark room. "Dave?"

But already I know he's not here.

His room is right across from mine. He probably went back to take a shower and get dressed.

I grab my key, throw a robe around my body, and walk across the hallway to knock on his door.

No response.

I knock again, this time louder.

No response again.

"Where did he go?" I ask out loud.

I go back to my own room, grab my phone to—

Damn. I don't have Dave's number. I can't text him or call him and find out where he is or if he's okay. If he doesn't have a roaming plan, I may not be able to get in contact with him anyway.

I check the time on my phone. Ten a.m.

We're supposed to meet Brock and the rest of the gang of non-bandmembers down in the little café at ten thirty.

I already showered last night, so I just wash the essentials, throw on a little blush and lip gloss, and dress in a long-sleeved tee, jeans, and walking shoes. I don't know if we're doing any sightseeing today. After last night's trauma, Brock's only instructions were to sleep in for a bit and then meet for breakfast slash lunch. Why he didn't say brunch is beyond me.

I brush my hair out and twist it into a long braid hanging down my back.

Then I grab my phone and my purse and head down. It's only ten after, so I'll be early.

I walk into the café, and—

There's Dave, sitting alone at a table with a cup of coffee.

I walk up to him. "Oh, there you are."

"Yeah, I'm sorry. Did I worry you?"

"No, of course not. I just wondered where you were."

He stares into his coffee. "Just down here. Thinking."

"May I join you?"

"Yeah, of course." He stands up and pulls out a chair.

"You're such a gentleman."

"How we were raised."

I like it. I like it a lot.

The server comes toward us. "*Café au lait, mademoiselle?*" she asks me.

"*Oui, merci.*"

She leaves and returns within a few seconds with a cup of coffee, the milk already added.

"I don't normally drink milk in my coffee," I say to Dave, "but when in Rome."

"Actually it's really good," he says. "I'm a black-coffee guy myself, but as you said, we're here. We may as well try everything."

I take a sip, and the milk—not cream—cuts the acidity of the coffee nicely. It's delicious.

I'm not sure what to say. Do I thank him for last night? It was amazing, and I was able to finally go to sleep. But it was what it was.

"I've been thinking..." he says.

"Yeah?"

"I'm wondering if I should just go home."

My eyebrows shoot up.

He doesn't react. "I can see that surprises you. It surprised me as well. I certainly needed a vacation, but so far—other than the time I've spent with you, Maddie—this so-called vacation has been more stressful than ever."

I take a sip from my cup. "I get what you mean. But we're in Paris, Dave. Let's at least see the sights today before you decide."

He nods. "You're probably right. What would you like to do today?"

"Did you get any sleep?" I ask him.

"That was quite a pivot." His eyes smile, but his mouth doesn't. "Yeah, I did. Thanks to you."

"No need to thank me. We both got out of that what we needed."

He looks at me, meets my gaze, and his eyes are... I'm not

sure. He looks like he wants to say something to me, but then he doesn't. Instead, he takes a drink of his coffee.

Our server returns with some croissants, butter, and jam.

"*Merci*," Dave says.

"*Je vous en prie.*" She whisks away.

Dave gestures to the continental breakfast. "Feel like eating?"

I eye the plate of goodies, my stomach growling softly. "Yeah, I do actually. I haven't eaten since dinner last night. Of course, I couldn't eat once we got here after that plane ride."

"Yeah, neither could I." He shoves the plate of croissants toward me. "Please."

I take one and smear some butter on it. Then I spoon some jam—it looks to be blackberry—onto my plate as well.

"Weird breakfast," he says. "They don't do the bacon and egg thing here."

"It'll be fun to try something new," I say.

"Maybe for you." He frowns. "I have to have some protein in the morning, or my energy is lacking."

"I'm sure you can get some."

"Yeah." He signals to the server.

"*Oui, monsieur?*"

"*S'il vous plaît*, I was wondering... Le bacon?"

I sigh. I'll put Dave out of his misery. "Do you have bacon and eggs?"

She smiles. "*Oui, mademoiselle.* Eggs...er...scrambled." Her accent is heavy, but she got the message across.

I look to Dave. "Scrambled? With bacon?"

"Perfect," he says.

"Right away," the server says as she walks back.

"I love bread as much as the next guy," he says, "but if it's all I eat, I'll crash in a few hours."

"Yeah, simple carbs will do that."

"But that's all you're eating."

I shrug. "It's all I want right now. I'll get something else when I need it."

He nods.

I pull my croissant into halves, spread butter and jam on one, and take a bite.

It's warm and flaky, and the butter is delicious. Sweet butter, not salted like it is in the US. The jam isn't too sweet either. It's perfect.

"Good?" Dave asks.

"Yeah, delicious actually. Try it."

Dave takes a few bites of his own croissant, washing them down with his café au lait. "It is good. Still, a man needs meat."

"Here she comes now."

The server sets a plate in front of Dave. It's not bacon exactly, more like strips of ham, and two eggs, sunny side up instead of scrambled.

"*Merci,*" he says politely. Then to me, "I prefer them this way anyway." He takes another croissant and dips it in one of the egg yolks.

The server raises an eyebrow.

"Sorry, do we not do that here?" Dave asks.

"Whatever you like, *monsieur.*" She smiles and leaves.

"They can always tell we're Americans anyway once we talk. Even before we talk, they know us by how we dress," I say.

"What do you mean?"

I point down at my sneakers. "You don't see the French wearing shoes like these very often. They only wear tennis shoes for exercising, not for just walking. It's kind of a tell."

"How do you know? You've never been here, have you?"

"I did a lot of research before this trip," I say. "I was so excited, and I wanted to know everything."

Out of the corner of my eye, I see Brianna coming toward our table.

"Hey," Brianna says. "You two are here early."

I wait for Dave to respond, but he doesn't.

"Just trying to put yesterday behind us," I say. "Where's Jesse?"

"He and Rory ordered breakfast in the room with the band."

"So you won't be seeing him today?" I ask.

She shakes her head. "They want to rehearse most of the day. He and I will have dinner tonight. Then he said he'll be able to see some of the sights with me tomorrow. But he also said that you and I should go ahead and see whatever we want today because he knows there won't be a whole lot of time tomorrow. He'll have to rehearse during the afternoon."

I nod. "What do you want to do today, then?"

"Let's wait for Brock. Maybe we can all agree on what to do."

"Speak of the devil," I say.

Brock strolls toward us, looking like the spitting image of his father, only without the silver temples. All of the Steel men are ridiculously good-looking. Brock's father, Jonah, is the oldest Steel brother. Brock has the same dark hair, same dark eyes, same muscular height and breadth, and same rugged good looks.

Dave's handsomeness is more polished. But there's no doubt—every Steel is runway model material.

"Hey," Brock says. "*Garçon?*" He motions to one of the

servers.

Brianna shakes her head at him. "That's a woman. Garçon means 'young man,' and it's outdated to use it for a server, even a male one. Please don't try to speak French here."

"I think they'd appreciate it." Brock takes a seat after Brianna sits down.

"They do, if you can actually speak French." Brianna laughs. "You, my good cousin, did not inherit the gift of language."

"What's that, amiga?" Brock smiles.

Brianna rolls her eyes at him. "English for you."

"Brianna and I speak enough French to get by," I say.

"Then I guess we'll have to hang with you two today, right, cuz?"

Dave nods. "I guess so."

I can't tell if he's happy about that or not. We certainly had a nice time last night. But he did say he was thinking about leaving.

Something is off with him—something that wasn't that way when he first got here.

Having a near-death experience will freak anyone out, but it seems to have affected David more than most.

Although it affected me pretty badly as well. I don't want to step foot on another plane for a long time. Thank goodness we still have several months of tour left before I have to tackle that.

"I can get us on a guided tour this afternoon," Brock says. "But I think it might be more fun if we just kind of hang out. Walk around, see the sights ourselves. I don't know about the rest of you, but after yesterday, I don't want to be rushed or..." He shakes his head. "Let's just go on our own."

"I'd like that too," Brianna agrees. "Guided tours are great and all, and we can take one tomorrow, but today I think we all need to relax. Go at our own pace."

"Amen," I say.

The server brings a *café au lait* for Brianna and Brock, plus more croissants, butter, and jam.

"How'd you manage to get that?" Brock glances at Dave's now empty plate of breakfast.

"All you have to do is ask," he says. "But I don't recommend you asking."

"I'll take care of it," Brianna says.

She signals to our server and then orders breakfast for Brock and herself in perfect French.

"I'm sorry, Maddie," she says. "Did you want some?"

"No." I rub my stomach. "The croissants were good. I'll just have an early lunch."

"Isn't that what this is?" Brianna asks.

"Nope. It's late breakfast."

Brianna laughs. "Good enough."

Brock takes a sip of his coffee. "So I suppose we should start at the very beginning. The Eiffel Tower."

"I don't think I want to go to the top," I say. "I think I want to avoid heights today. Maybe I'll feel differently tomorrow."

"I agree," Dave says. "Let's not start with the Eiffel Tower."

"The Louvre then?" Brock says.

"Oh yeah," I say. "Let's check out the Louvre."

"You sure you don't want to take a guided tour through the Louvre?" Brock says. "There's a lot to see. You can spend the whole day there."

"We've got almost a whole day," I say. "No, I don't want a guided tour. I want to look at the art at my leisure."

Dave sits rigid beside me.

"Let me guess," I say. "A day at an art museum is not your cup of tea."

"No, not really."

"Then Brianna and I will go," I say.

I won't force Dave to spend time with me.

"Come on, cuz," Brock cajoles Dave. "This is some of the world's greatest art."

Dave takes a deep breath in and lets it out. "Okay."

We talk about nothing in particular until Brianna's and Brock's breakfasts arrive.

Once they're done, Brock rises. "Shall we?"

Brianna rises as well. "Absolutely."

I stand, and then finally, bringing up the rear, Dave gets to his feet.

There's a weird look on his face.

What is wrong with him?

I won't ask.

Not my place.

After all, he's not my boyfriend.

CHAPTER NINE

Dave

Actually, despite my earlier words, spending the day in the Louvre sounds okay. I won't have to do a lot of talking. We'll simply be looking at art. I like art as much as the next guy. I just don't know a lot about it.

But something is nagging at me today. I feel...

Jumpy.

Kind of like a grasshopper's nibbling at the back of my neck and is going to bite through my spine at any moment.

I could give Aunt Melanie a call, except she'd still be in bed right now.

Besides, I know exactly what she'd say.

I'm suffering from some posttraumatic stress disorder. And of course I am. I had a near-death experience last night.

Why are the others handling this so much better than I am? Or are they? The three of them didn't seem to have any trouble eating, though Maddie only ate a croissant.

I knew I had to have some protein this morning. My energy was already lagging, although I did sleep for at least a few hours after my tryst with Maddie. That helped me more than she can even know. It was hard and fast yet long and drawn out, and I'd love to do it again.

"I want to take the Métro," Bree says.

"I think we should," Maddie agrees.

"Okay." Brock pulls something up on his phone. "There's a stop just up the block, and I've got the route to the Louvre on my phone. Are we ready?"

"Ready," Brianna and Maddie say in unison.

I simply nod.

"I'm going to hit the head first," Brock says. "Dave, come on."

"I don't have to go," I say.

"Then keep me company," he grits out.

I shake my head at him. "Okay."

We walk to the restroom on the first floor of the hotel. Once inside, he turns to me. "You okay?"

"Yeah, I'm fine."

He wrinkles his forehead. "We're in Paris, David. Last night was fucked up. But today's a new day. Appreciate it."

"I do."

"Listen," he says, "Jesse texted me last night after he left you. He said you seemed to be a little off. And now that I've seen you, I agree."

"Fuck Jesse anyway."

"Look. I know Jesse has had problems with our family in the past, but he's in love with Brianna, and he'll be a part of our family in the future. He would be anyway because of me marrying Rory and Donny marrying Callie. I think he cares."

"He sure didn't like me sleeping with his sister."

"Would you want him sleeping with Angie or Sage?"

Brick to gut.

Man, do those words hurt. I feel like I should go apologize to Jesse for fucking his sister.

"Jesse's over it," Brock continues before I can reply. "He's over it because he realizes, after last night, that it's so easy to get caught up in the little things that don't matter. So tell me what's bugging you. I want to help you. This has been traumatic for all of us. Do you need to talk to someone?"

"What if I do?"

"Then we'll find someone."

"My French may not be as bad as yours, but I can't speak to somebody here."

"We'll call my mom, then."

"She's not even up yet."

"You think that matters? I'm her favorite son. She'll take my call." He grins.

I look at him and frown. "How can you be so...happy?"

He raises his arms to either side of his body. "Because I'm alive, man. And so are you."

He's right, at that. "I just feel like I shouldn't be here. Like if I hadn't come here, maybe none of this would have happened."

"We were all going to be on that same chartered flight," Brock says. "So whether you were here or not, yeah, it would've happened."

I look to the floor and kick at the bathroom tile. "I was so excited about this trip, you know? After dealing with all the bullshit in our family lately. Then when I got here, and Maddie and I kind of hooked up, it was fun. I'm not looking to fall in love, and I don't think she is either."

He smirks. "Don't be so sure about that."

"What are you saying? She's in love with me?"

"No, I'm not saying that. But all three of her siblings are now with members of our family. I'm pretty sure it's on her mind."

I sigh, rub my hand over my hair. "She's great, man. This thing between us... It's new, but it's great. But that's all it is. It's not love. At least I don't think it is." I drop my hand to my side. "Hell, I don't know."

"Are you feeling something different?" he asks.

"Yeah, but I feel something different with every woman. Don't you?"

"Of course. It's always different with a new lover. But I was pretty sure after a few times with Rory. It was *different* different, if that makes sense. I knew it was something that could blossom into something amazing, and it did."

"I'm not feeling that yet," I say.

But I recognize the lie for what it is.

Because I am feeling something different with Maddie. Something that could bloom into something wonderful.

But right now, I'm not sure I know myself. My head is a mess. It's jumbled with thoughts and horrific images. Of the way my stomach sank to my feet when that plane dropped. The way I had to hold back nausea as I helped Maddie get her yellow mask on before I adjusted my own.

The way I failed to hold back nausea after the fact.

How I...

But I was strong.

I thought of Maddie before I thought of myself.

And now? Now that we're safe?

I'm in my own head.

I'm fucking freaked out.

"We're here, man," Brock says. "Whatever happens between you and Maddie isn't the biggest thing in the world. The biggest thing is that we're alive."

I nod.

Part of me doesn't agree. Because part of me thinks that what's happening with Maddie and me is something big. Something fucking huge. But based on where my head is right now? I'm not good enough for her.

"You ready?" Brock asks.

"Don't you have to take a piss?" I ask.

"No, I'm good. It was an excuse to talk to you."

I go to the sink, look at my face in the mirror.

I look the same.

Same face that looks like a masculine version of my mother except for the blue eyes that come from my father. The dark hair, the classic Steel jawline, the broad shoulders.

And I recognize myself.

Except I don't.

Maybe talking to my aunt Melanie wouldn't be such a bad idea.

Maybe I should just go home.

But I won't. I promised Brock I would stay, at least through Paris. After all, I came here for a vacation. God knows I need one.

Brock washes his hands as well, and we leave the bathroom. The women are still sitting at the table, and they rise.

"All right, Brock," Brianna says. "Where to first, cuz?"

"To the Métro first," he says. "And then, on to the Louvre."

★ ★ ★

At the entrance to the Louvre is the Louvre pyramid, which looks terribly out of place, in my opinion. It's a modern design, constructed with glass panes and metal poles, and it juxtaposes oddly against the historic architecture of the museum itself.

I let out a sigh as I follow Brock, Brianna, and Maddie into the museum. I'm not unlike the pyramid.

That brush with death threw me out of whack with who I am.

Brianna's smile is wide. "Let's start with the Mona Lisa. I've always wanted to see it in person."

"So we're just going to meander around without any plan?" Brock asks.

"Of course not," Brianna says. "The plan is to start with the Mona Lisa. I want to see all the famous works. You know, the ones everybody knows about."

Works for me. I do appreciate art, but I'm not going to get as much out of the Louvre as my cousin Gina would. She's an actual artist. Besides, strolling around a museum isn't going to do much for that grasshopper munching on my spine. I need a good workout. Or another romp with Maddie.

"She's on the second floor, right?" Maddie says.

"Who's on the second floor?" I ask.

"The Mona Lisa." She rolls her eyes. "That is what we're talking about, isn't it?"

I simply nod.

Brock nods as well. "Yep, let's head upstairs."

As we make our way through the magnificent hallways, my mind begins to wander, and I recall the terrifying moments on that plane. The sudden turbulence, the oxygen masks dropping down, and the passengers' panicked reactions. It's difficult not to relate it to the chaos of this bustling museum.

We finally reach the room that houses the Mona Lisa, and the crowd is enormous.

"There she is!" Brianna squeals.

Maddie smiles. "Let's get a closer look."

Brock and the women head closer, and Brock looks over his shoulder. "Dave, you coming?"

I nod and follow them as they approach the iconic painting. I gaze at the Mona Lisa, trying to appreciate its beauty and how the standards of beauty have changed over time.

But her serene smile seems to be hiding something. Some underlying turmoil.

Like I did on the plane, staying calm for Maddie's sake.

Yeah, she's beautiful, but she's not helping me.

I'm staring at her smile when Maddie's voice interrupts my thoughts.

"Dave, are you okay?"

"Yeah, I'm fine."

We move on from the Mona Lisa, and Maddie and Bree continue to discuss the art, but their voices don't permeate my mind. The artwork around me begins to blend together as I struggle to shake off the trauma haunting me.

"Let's check out the Egyptian artifacts," Brock says. "Maybe we'll see some mummies or something."

Brianna swats his shoulder. "There's more to the exhibit than mummies."

We head toward the Egyptian exhibit, and I try to stay engaged in the conversation, but my mind keeps drifting back to the airplane incident. The museum's beauty and the artistry on display do provide some solace, but the memories of that traumatic experience persist. Maddie's here, though, and I want to grab her hand, but I'm not sure if it would be appropriate.

The Egyptian collection is fascinating. A large stone sphinx stands guard at its entrance. T*he Great Sphinx of Tanis,* according to the sign in front of it.

I remember learning about the legend of the sphinx in my world history class in high school. They stood guard in front of important buildings in Ancient Egypt, such as temples. I remember reading about the myth of Oedipus, who had to answer a riddle from the sphinx when he first entered the city of Thebes. If he got the answer wrong, the sphinx would kill and devour him. Luckily, he got it right.

I'm in no danger, of course, of being eaten by this sphinx, but it does seem to present a riddle that I need to untangle. What was I put on this planet to do? Certainly more than just fuck every good-looking woman that spares me a passing glance. Maybe even more than working with my father on the financial side of our business.

After Egypt, we head to some of the most famous exhibits in the Louvre, including the Venus de Milo and the Winged Victory.

The Venus de Milo is captured in marble, and her arms are famously missing. As I gaze at her beautifully sculpted face, I find myself oddly empathetic. The Venus de Milo, without her arms, exudes an air of quiet strength, acceptance, and resilience. She stands here, imperfect yet still captivating, just as I must find a way to stand tall despite the imperfections and trauma that have marked my life.

My life that has been pretty close to perfect up to recent events.

I must learn to embrace my own vulnerabilities and accept that life can be both beautiful and fragile, just like this sculpture. And though my trauma may have left me feeling broken, the statue's silent strength serves as a reminder that I too can find my own inner strength and move forward from the shadows of my recent ordeal. Art, as it should, offers a path toward healing and renewal.

Nice idea, anyway.

I take a deep breath, grateful for this moment of introspection but not convinced anything will change inside me.

Until we get to the Winged Victory of Samothrace.

Though headless, the sculpture's presence is commanding. She's a symbol of triumph, her wings outstretched, as if embracing wind and soaring above adversity. After the brush with death, I've felt wounded, battling my own fears and anxieties.

I'm lost in my own thoughts as the other three chat about the art. Still I stare at the statue. Her graceful form seems to defy gravity, just as I strive to defy the weight of my own trauma.

Maybe art does have healing power. I do feel a little better.

"You feeling okay?" Brock asks me as we leave the museum.

I look over at Maddie. She, all at once, contains the grace and beauty of the Venus de Milo, the stoic and striking stature of the Winged Victory, and a touch of the mystery like the Mona Lisa.

She's a work of art that rivals any other piece in this museum.

And just like the art in this museum has offered me some comfort, so does she.

"Yeah," I say. "I am."

CHAPTER TEN

Maddie

Bright Parisian sunlight greets us when we leave the Louvre.

My stomach lets out a growl, and I find to my surprise that I'm famished. "Can we grab a bite?" I ask.

A moment later, a cozy sidewalk café greets us. It's a brisk day in February, so we stop to see if we can get a table inside. A host greets us and leads us to a table inside covered in a crisp white tablecloth. Surrounding each table are wrought-iron chairs with intricate patterns, and flowers adorn the windowsills, adding a splash of color to the elegant, vintage decor. Adding to the ambience is the window next to us. The view outside of the Parisian street is filled with people strolling by, some carrying baguettes or walking their dogs.

Brianna smiles as she picks up her menu. "I wish we had all day to spend at the Louvre. I could look at art for hours and hours."

Brock peeks out from his menu. "I saw what I needed to see."

I'm not sure what to say. I loved looking at the art, but a whole day? That might be too much for me. I look over at Dave, who's also perusing the menu. "Did you enjoy yourself?"

He clears his throat. "I did. It made me think about some stuff."

"About what?" I ask.

"Just about life in general." He sticks his nose back into the menu.

I miss jovial Dave.

I mean, I get it. We've all been freaked out. God knows I still am. But we're also in Paris, and I want to enjoy it.

A waiter comes by. "*Bonjour*! What can I get for you today?" he says in a slight accent.

Brock sets his menu down. "I'll have the croque-monsieur, please."

"And you, mademoiselle?" he asks Brianna.

"I'll go for the quiche Lorraine, and a side salad."

"Mademoiselle?" He nods to me.

"I'll try the Niçoise salad, dressing on the side."

"*Et monsieur?*" To Dave.

"I'll have the French onion soup and a salad as well, please."

The waiter nods and then takes our menus.

"Crap," Brock says. "We forgot to order drinks."

No sooner do the words come out of his mouth when another server appears. "*De l'eau aujourd'hui?*"

"*Oui, merci*," Brianna says. Then to us, "He's asking if we want water."

"*Gazeuse ou non gazeuse?*" he asks Bree specifically.

"You guys want sparkling?" she asks.

"Plain is fine for me," I say.

"Me too." From Brock.

Dave simply nods.

"*Non gazeuse*," Brianna tells the waiter.

He pours four glasses from a pitcher and then leaves the table.

Our food comes in the next ten minutes, and it looks fantastic. Brock's croque-monsieur is a tantalizing combination of ham, creamy béchamel sauce, and toasted bread with a golden-brown crust oozing with melted Gruyère cheese. Brianna's quiche has a golden pastry crust cradling a velvety filling of eggs, cream, and bacon. Meanwhile, Dave dives headfirst into his steaming bowl of French onion soup, topped with a toasted baguette and a layer of melted Gruyère that rivals Brock's.

I look down at my Niçoise salad. Before me sits a medley of colors and textures. A bed of crisp lettuce with cherry tomatoes, olives, hard-boiled eggs, and seared tuna, drizzled with a zesty vinaigrette. I bring a forkful to my mouth.

"It's delicious!" I say. "It tastes like I'm swimming in the Mediterranean."

Brock chuckles as he wipes some of the béchamel from his chin.

I get no reaction from Dave. Maybe he didn't hear me.

We don't talk much as we finish our meal. Once we're done and have paid up, we head back to the hotel for some much-needed rest.

I don't invite Dave to my room.

He doesn't ask, either. I think we both need a little sleep.

But once I'm inside, someone knocks. I check the peephole. It's Dave.

I sigh as I open the door. "What is it?"

"I was wondering..."

I cross my arms. "No, Dave. Just no. I can't keep doing this. I can't be your escape every time something is bugging you. I thought I could. But I can't."

He grins, and it's jovial...like the old Dave. "I came here to ask you to have dinner with me."

I stand there blinking for a solid fifteen seconds before speaking. "Oh?"

"Yeah."

I scratch my arm. "Why? Because Brock and Rory are having a date? And so are Jesse and Brianna?"

He shakes his head. "Of course not. I thought... I mean, we could have dinner together here in the hotel, as friends, or friends with bennies, or whatever, but I actually thought it would be nice to have an actual date with the woman I..."

I roll my eyes. "With the woman you...what?"

"Damn it, Maddie." He grabs me and kisses me. Hard.

I can't help myself. I open for him, sweeping my tongue into his mouth and tangling it with his.

Is he feeling something?

Am *I* feeling something?

Or is this just a childhood crush?

No.

Not a childhood crush. Jesse thought that's what Brianna was feeling for him, and it wasn't.

We kiss hard for a few minutes until I pull back, releasing the kiss with a smack.

"Does that convince you that I really want to have dinner with you?" he asks.

"Not really." I touch my lips. "It convinces me that you want to come back to my bed."

He shakes his head. "Christ, Maddie, what do I have to do to convince you?"

I frown. "What, all of a sudden you have feelings for me?"

"I've had feelings for you since the beginning," he says. "Despite my reputation, I'm not completely indiscriminate when it comes to the people I have sex with."

"Not *completely*," I scoff. "Wow, that makes me feel better."

He draws in a breath. "You know what? Just forget I asked. Maybe I'll see you down in the hotel dining room for dinner. Maybe I'll just go to fucking McDonald's and have a French Big Mac with French fries. Or do they just call them fries here?"

Despite myself, I can't help smiling. "For God's sake, David, don't do that. We're in Paris. culinary capital of the world. Don't get fast food."

"I already made reservations, Maddie. I want to take you out for an amazing French feast. Why would I do that just to get you into bed? I've already been in bed with you."

He's not wrong. And I probably will let him back in my bed, because he's an amazing lover, and we seem to have awesome physical chemistry.

I *have* been crushing on him for a long time.

So why am I fighting this?

"Look, Dave," I say. "I like you. I like you a lot. And we seem to be great in bed together."

"I'll say," he agrees.

"But I don't want to be the woman you fall for just because you had a near-death experience and you feel like you need to move forward with your life or something."

He doesn't reply at first, and I'm thinking I hit the nail on the head, when—

"I'm not asking to marry you, Maddie. I'm asking to take you to dinner."

And I can't help myself. I burst into laughter.

Because it's all so ridiculous.

He's right. It's just dinner.

"Yes, Dave, I would love to have dinner with you." I shake my head. "I suppose I should apologize. Sometimes I get into my own head."

He exhales sharply through his nose. "Tell me about it. I've been all up in my own stuff since the plane thing. Looking at the art today helped a little."

"How?"

He scratches the side of his head. "Art is bigger than life, I think. Those pieces were crafted so long ago, but they still live today. The people who created them are long gone, but their works still move people. I felt vulnerable in their presence, but in a good way, if that makes sense. As if vulnerability gives us a chance for triumph."

I drop my jaw and look at him in awe.

"Fuck," he says. "You don't get it."

I close my mouth. "No. I do get it, and it's a beautiful thing. That's the whole reason behind art, isn't it? To consider what it means to be human. Vulnerability is a key characteristic of all humanity, and I believe we're all striving for triumph."

He smiles then, reaches toward me but doesn't touch me. "Thanks. You do understand. And I *do* want to take you to a nice dinner. I've told you before, I didn't come here looking to hook up with someone. But I'm glad you're here. I'm glad we've gotten together. Our sex is great, so let's see if there's something else."

I nod. "I'd like that."

"So no more giving me shit, all right?"

"Okay."

"So... You going to invite me in?"

I smile. "As much as I know we'd both love that, no, I'm

not. I really need to relax for a couple of hours before dinner. I don't think any of us got enough sleep last night."

"You're right about that." He leans forward and brushes his lips across mine. "I'll pick you up at six o'clock."

"Sounds good." I watch him walk into his room and then close the door behind me, clicking my deadbolt into place.

* * *

Dave actually booked a limo. A limo in Paris. The driver takes us to a restaurant called L'Ambroisie located on the Île Saint-Louis, in the heart of historic Paris. Parking is apparently limited, so the driver leaves us and will pick us up later.

The restaurant is housed in a beautifully restored sixteenth-century townhouse. The interior is adorned with rich decor that includes opulent chandeliers, elaborate woodwork, and plush upholstery. I've never been in anything so elegant, and I can't help walking through the entrance with my mouth agape.

The inside of L'Ambroisie is surprisingly intimate with a limited number of tables. The lighting is soft and subdued. The decor is muted, with shades of cream, gold, and soft pastels dominating. It screams elegance, sophistication, and affluence.

Part of me feels like I shouldn't be here. I wasn't sure what to wear, and rather than ask Dave, I chose black leggings, an oversized white blouse cinched at the waist with a silver belt, and simple black pumps. While my outfit works, most women are dressed in cocktail attire and some of the men are actually wearing tuxedos.

I sigh.

I don't have any cocktail attire anyway, so what the hell?

Dave is wearing black pants, a dark gray jacket, and a simple blue tie. It's so easy for men to dress for anything.

I glide through a haze as Dave speaks to the maître d' who leads us to a table set with beautiful cream-colored china, crystal glasses, and crisp black linens. The maître d' pulls out my chair for me.

"*Merci,*" I mumble as I take the seat.

Dave sits across from me as the maître d' hands him the wine list.

"*Votre serveur sera avec vous dans un instant.*" The maître d' bows and leaves our table.

Dave's eyes dance. "What do you think so far?"

I dart my gaze around to the other diners. "I think I'm severely underdressed."

"Don't be silly. You'd look gorgeous in a potato sack."

"I kind of feel like that's what I'm wearing." I look down at my plain white blouse.

"Are you kidding?" He burns his gaze into me. "Your look is classic. You fit in anywhere, Maddie. The only one who doesn't believe it is you."

A young woman wearing simple black pants and a white blouse approaches us. "Good evening," she says in heavily accented English. "My name is Giselle, and I take care of you this evening. You would like a cocktail?"

"Actually, I've ordered a special menu created by the chef, complete with wine pairings," Dave says. "So no, thank you."

"Ah, yes. Of course, *monsieur.* I will speak to Chef and return with your amuse-bouche." She scurries off into the kitchen.

Before I can think of something witty to say, Giselle is already back.

"Fois gras on baguette," she says.

Before each of us, she sets a small plate containing a thin piece of toasted baguette covered in something that looks... well, not good.

"What is this?" I ask Dave.

"Fois gras. Goose or duck liver pate."

I resist the urge to wrinkle my nose. "And they eat this?"

"It's a delicacy. Try it. You may like it." He downs his in one bite.

"Why is it so small?" I ask.

"It's supposed to be small." He cocks his head. "Hasn't anyone ever taken you to a nice dinner?"

"Not this nice." I bring the toasted baguette to my mouth and take a tiny taste. The fois gras is creamy and rich, and the flavor is...okay. Since it's so small, I'm able to finish it, but I hope the menu doesn't contain any more liver.

A few moments later, after a busboy clears our plates, Giselle brings the next course.

"Fresh crab meat served with citrus segments, avocado, and a citrus vinaigrette," she says and leaves quickly.

This I can get behind. I love crab. I take a bite, and the tang of the citrus adds a zest to the crab while the avocado adds creaminess. "Wow. This is fabulous."

"Better than the liver?" Dave smiles.

"Much." I take another bite.

"I'm glad you like it. I've never been here before, but I did some research, and this place came highly recommended. I was lucky that they had a cancellation and could get us in."

We finish our salad, and I take a drink of the water that Giselle's assistant brought earlier. "I thought we were getting wine," I say.

"With the main course," Dave says. "Did you want some now?"

"No, that's fine. Just wondering."

The assistant brings a baguette, and Dave offers me a piece, but I shake my head. "I want to preserve my appetite."

"Good idea. You won't leave the table hungry here."

Giselle comes again with our main course.

"Roasted pigeon with a port wine reduction," she says, "with seasonal vegetables and a gratin dauphinois."

I want to ask what a gratin dauphinois is, but I just smile. The seasonal vegetables turn out to be roasted beets and carrots served with leafy kale. The gratin dauphinois is potatoes, and I do a quick search on my phone to find out that they're layered with cream, garlic, salt, and pepper. The top is broiled to a gorgeous brown sheen.

The pigeon, on the other hand, is a perfectly bronzed bird with crispy golden-brown skin, about the same size as a Cornish game hen. The glossy port wine reduction cascades over the meat, mingling slightly with the side dishes.

"This is a feast for the eyes as well as the mouth," I say, looking down at the art on my plate. "I've never had pigeon before."

"Neither have I," Dave says, "but I bet it tastes like chicken."

I laugh. "I don't know where to start. I don't want to disturb any of it."

Before I can think further, though, the sommelier arrives with our wine. "Chambolle-Musigny from *Bourgogne*." He shows us the label. "That is what you know as Pinot Noir. Or Burgundy if you use the French name in English."

Dave nods. "*Merci.*"

The sommelier expertly uncorks the wine and pours a small amount in Dave's glass. Probably just as well. Although our family is in the wine industry, we produce mostly lower-priced table wines as opposed to the fine wines produced by Steel Vineyards.

Dave takes the glass, swirls the liquid, and then sticks his nose inside, just like I've seen my father do countless times. Then he takes a sip, swishing it around in his mouth. He swallows, and then seems to contemplate it for a moment.

"Excellent," he says.

"Very good, *monsieur*." The sommelier fills my glass and then Dave's. He bows and leaves us.

Dave lifts his glass. "To a nice evening."

"To a nice evening." I clink my glass to his and take a sip.

The aroma of ripe red cherries mingles with the flavor of darker fruit. The tannins are mild, and the wine is slightly acidic, which means it will pair well with food.

"An excellent choice," I say.

Dave smiles. "It's delicious, but I can't take credit. The sommelier chose it for me. I don't have Uncle Ryan's or Dale's nose when it comes to wine."

"It's perfect." And I mean it. Even if it sucks with the pigeon, which it won't, this evening is already perfect in my book.

The meal is delicious—Dave was right, the pigeon tastes like dark chicken meat—and when Giselle comes with our cheese course, which includes more baguette drizzled with local honey, I can't eat another bite.

"Try a little," Dave says. "And then of course there's dessert."

"I'm not sure I have room." But to appease him, I take a

bite of brie on one of the baguette pieces. The honey melds into the creaminess of the cheese, and it's wonderful. I end up trying the Roquefort as well, but I stay away from the chèvre. Not a goat cheese fan.

Dessert turns out to be Grand Marnier soufflé served hot from the oven with crème anglaise. The aroma alone opens up a tiny corner of my stomach. I've got to try this.

It's decadent, with orange liqueur as the primary flavor, but egg yolks and vanilla flavor are also apparent, and the crème anglaise brings it all together. Giselle brings a digestif of Calvados, pear brandy from Normandy, that perfectly ends the meal.

I'm truly mesmerized, and my tummy is full of gastronomic delights by the time Dave pays the check—or *l'addition*, as they call it here.

The limo picks us up and drives us back to the Narcisse Blanc.

I float on air as we ascend in the elevator and then get to our respective rooms.

Dave stands next to me and takes my key card, opening my door.

"Maddie, I—"

But I grab his arm and pull him into my room.

CHAPTER ELEVEN

Dave

We rip each other's clothes off in record time.

Our mouths are fused together in a searing kiss, and I can't get enough of Maddie.

Maybe it was the lush Burgundy wine we drank with dinner. Or maybe it was her sparkling conversation. We talked about things other than the plane nearly crashing, other than the concert tour, other than both our families. Most of the conversation revolved around the food and wine we were consuming. We were present in the moment, not thinking of the bullshit we've been through and the bullshit to come. At this point, I can't recall the specifics of what we talked about, only that it made me feel *good*.

Maybe it was the pear brandy, or maybe the lushness of the restaurant itself.

Or maybe...

Maybe I just want *her*.

Maybe I just fucking want her.

We end up on the bed, and she rolls me over so I'm on my back. She climbs on top of me and sinks down on my cock.

No foreplay tonight. I suppose we had enough of that last night.

Tonight she wants to fuck, and I'm totally fine with that.

I reach forward, cup her perfect tits. She has a little more than a handful, and her nipples are dark brown and scrumptious.

She closes her eyes, moves with me, undulating her hips, and then circling while I'm embedded inside her.

Each time my cock hits her anterior wall, I know I'm getting her G-spot, and it makes her go insane.

As I look up at her, her eyelids closed, her dark lashes fanning across her cheeks, her lips slightly parted and swollen, and her body flushed gorgeous pink, I wonder if I've ever seen anything more beautiful.

Her hair bounces around her shoulders, the soft waves hugging her flesh.

No, I haven't ever seen anything more beautiful.

And I've had my share of women. My share of beautiful women.

Maddie Pike is in a league of her own.

Is it because I like her? Because I've actually spent time with her rather than just having the primary goal of fucking her?

Maybe. All I know is whatever this thing is that's blooming between us, I want to see where it goes.

God, I never imagined myself settling down anytime in the near future. But Donny fell, and then Brock...

I was the lone Rake-a-teer, picking up women left and right. Hell, I fucked a couple of women I met at a bar the day before I came here.

That's all a blur. It meant absolutely nothing. Sure, I got my rocks off, but it didn't give me the satisfaction I was looking for.

Fucking Maddie Pike gives me all kinds of satisfaction.

All kinds of satisfaction I never knew existed.

She slides one hand between her legs, fingers her clit, and—

"My God, Dave! So good!"

She clamps around my cock, and though I want to wait, want to love her the way she deserves, like we did last night, I can't help myself.

My balls scrunch up, and I explode inside her sweet heat.

I grunt, groan, grit out her name.

And when our orgasms finally subside, she falls onto my chest, her body fitting against me as if we're two interlocking pieces.

And we fall asleep that way.

* * *

I wake the next morning to the buzzing of my phone. Maddie's limbs are entangled with mine, and I realize it's not yet light out.

Where the hell is my phone?

In the pocket of my pants, which could be anywhere. We undressed in a jumble last night.

I follow the buzzing sound and find my phone. It's nearly on the last legs of its battery.

It's my father.

"Dad?"

"Hey, son. I realize it's early there yet, but this is important."

"What time is it there?"

"Ten p.m. We've got an issue, Dave, and I need you..."

"You need me to what?"

He sighs. "God, I hate to do this to you. You need this trip. God knows we all need one. But this is serious, Dave."

"What is it, Dad?"

He pauses. "I need you to come home."

I drop my jaw. "Why?"

"I can't tell you anything more over the phone," he says. "Please just trust me on this. Dale, Ashley, Donny, and Callie are already on their way home from London, with Dragon Locke in tow. He's going to rehab in Denver, but the four of them are coming straight home after they drop him off. This is serious."

"What about Brianna?"

"She doesn't deal with the business side of our ranch. Uncle Talon and Aunt Jade decided not to ask her to come home, and Donny and Dale agreed with them. That's their call, Dave, but Brock is coming. Uncle Joe just talked to him. He hates leaving Rory, but he understands the seriousness of what's going on."

"How can he understand the seriousness if Uncle Joe didn't tell him?"

"He trusts his father, and I hope you'll trust me."

"Yeah, Dad, of course I trust you." I look at Maddie, still sleeping on the bed.

It's going to kill me to leave her.

I had to go and develop feelings for a woman.

But she's a woman I'll see again. Maddie won't be in Europe forever. Only until the end of the tour.

"All right," I say. "I'll get on the next flight."

"I've already got a reservation for you. You and Brock leave Charles de Gaulle tonight at five p.m. your time."

"Okay."

At least that gives me the day to spend with Maddie. I won't be here to see tonight's concert, but I saw the one in London. It'll be the same concert anyway.

I finally look at my phone for the first time. Four a.m. That's a little over twelve hours to gather the courage to step on a plane again.

At least I can go back to bed, maybe make love to Maddie one more time.

She'll be back in a few months when the tour is over.

"All right, Dad," I say. "I guess I'll see you tomorrow."

"Thanks, son. Honestly, I hate to do this to you, but we need everybody involved."

"Everyone except Brianna?"

"We're going to let her sit this one out if she wants to. She and Jesse just got engaged, and they need to be together."

"Have you told her?"

"I'm leaving that to Brock. She can call Uncle Talon and Aunt Jade if she wants more information."

"You know she's going to insist on coming home."

"She may. And that's her call."

"I'm guessing she'll be on that flight with us tonight."

"She may," Dad says again.

"All right, Dad. I'll see you tomorrow."

"Thanks, Dave."

The phone clicks dead.

What the hell?

I'm numb. Though my heart is beating like a fucking hummingbird's.

Just when I thought it was safe to be a Steel again...

I slide between the covers, wrap my arms around Maddie. My cock hardens as soon as I touch her body, and I reach between her legs.

She's still slick, and I slide into her from behind.

She sighs. "Feels nice..."

I kiss her neck, tugging her earlobe. "It does, baby. God, it does."

CHAPTER TWELVE

Maddie

I wake up, the sun streaming in through my window. I have a vague memory of Dave making love to me in the early hours of the morning.

It was sweet and sexy and perfect.

I roll over to snuggle up to him...and then I jerk upward. "Dave?"

He's gone. I look around the room. His clothes are also gone. I get up and pad to the bathroom, but no Dave. I wrap myself in one of the lush robes, grab my key card, and head across the hall.

I knock softly. "Dave?"

A moment later he opens the door. "Hey."

"Where did you go?"

"Uh...here?" He grins.

"Yeah, stupid question."

"Come on in," he says. "We need to talk."

My heart sinks to my stomach.

I've heard the *we need to talk* line before, and it never leads to anything good.

I swallow. "About what?"

His suitcase is open on his bed, folded clothes ready to be packed.

My heart sinks. "Dave..."

"I'm sorry, Maddie. I have to go home. My father called early this morning. Apparently there's some shit going down, and he needs me home."

"Oh..."

He holds a hand up. "But this doesn't change anything. I'd like to continue...seeing you."

"I'll be in Europe for the next couple of months, Dave."

"I know that. But Brock and I—"

"Brock's going home too?"

"Yeah. Apparently this is a big deal. He wouldn't leave Rory otherwise, and the family wouldn't ask him to."

"What kind of big deal?"

He frowns. "Dad wouldn't tell me over the phone, which means it's a really big deal." He sighs, shaking his head. "Man, and just when I thought I could have a vacation. Now I have to get back on an airplane tonight."

"Oh my God!" I clamp my hand over my mouth.

"What?"

"If he needs everyone home, that means Brianna has to go too."

He cups my cheek. "Actually, no. Uncle Talon and Aunt Jade decided she could stay if she wants. Since she and Jesse just got engaged and all."

"Oh, thank God." Then I clamp my hand over my mouth again. "I don't mean to make this all about me, Dave. I'm so sorry. It's just, without Brianna, there's no one for me to see Europe with. Jesse and Rory will be with the band, and now Brock is leaving. Not that he and I are close or anything, but at least he's not with the band."

"I know, baby. But Bree doesn't have to go."

"I don't want *you* to go either," I say, trying not to whine.

"Believe me, I don't want to go." He brushes a strand of hair off my forehead. "I think what we found together is something... Something worth exploring."

I warm all over. "I think so too. And I never dreamed it would happen."

"Me neither. It was so far from what I came here for."

I cock my head at him.

He shakes his head. "Now don't go taking that the wrong way. I'm glad it happened. And in a fucked-up way, I'm almost glad of that near-death experience we all shared. I think it all helped us get our heads on a little straighter."

"You can say that again," I agree.

He brushes his lips over mine. "I can still spend the day with you. I don't have to be at the airport until around two thirty this afternoon for a flight that leaves at five."

"Okay. What would you like to do?"

"Stay in bed all day?"

"I'd say yes in a heartbeat," I say. "But that wouldn't be fair to you. This will be your last few hours in Paris. You haven't even gotten to see the Eiffel Tower."

He shrugs, frowning. "Honestly, I don't have any desire to see the Eiffel Tower. But I would like to stroll along the Champs-Élysées with you. Maybe buy you a little token of my esteem."

"Your last few hours in Paris, and you want to take me shopping?" I can't help a laugh.

"I think I do. Besides, I can come back to Paris anytime I want. Once whatever this is blows over. Maybe if it blows over quickly, I can get back on the tour and join you."

* * *

A half hour later, Dave and I go down to breakfast in the hotel café. Jesse and Brianna are there, along with Brock and Rory.

"I think you should go," Jesse says, as Dave and I join them.

"I'm so glad you agree," Brianna says. "I don't want to leave you, especially since we've just come so far in our relationship. But if I'm going to prove to my father that I'm an adult and can one day take his place managing the orchards, I have to show him that I'm serious about our family."

"I agree," Brock says. "The only issue is whether I can get you on the same flight with Dave and me."

My heart drops. "Brianna..."

She grabs my hand and squeezes it. "I know, Maddie. I made a promise to you, but this is my family. Something big is going on."

Rory smiles at me. "Jesse and I will be here for you, sis."

"But you guys will be busy taking care of the band. This is your big shot, and you're already working with a substitute drummer. Neither of you can take the time to hang out with me."

Brock raises his eyebrows. "What if I try to get both Brianna and Maddie on that plane tonight?"

Jesse frowns. "This is Maddie's big chance to see Europe. I understand why Brianna has to go, and I agree with her. She needs to be there for her family."

"I don't understand," Dave says. "My dad told me that Uncle Talon and Aunt Jade said you should continue the tour and see Europe, Bree."

"My parents are treating me like a child," Brianna says,

"and I honestly don't blame them. I acted like a child when I was back home. I let my father down by coming on this tour. I should've stayed, worked with him, begun my life's work."

Jesse puts his hand over hers. "But I'm glad you came. I'm so glad we found each other."

Brianna looks adoringly into his eyes. "I am too. Truly. And I was so looking forward to spending the rest of the tour with you. But this is something I feel I have to do."

"I know, and I agree with you," Jesse says. He turns to Maddie. "Tell you what, Mads. What if I promise to bring you back here someday? You won't get to follow the band around on tour, but you'll still get to see Europe. You've seen our set a million times at this point anyway. Maybe we'll get Callie and Rory to come too and make it a Pike siblings trip."

I look around at all their faces.

Jesse is serious, and he's going to marry Brianna, so he'll have the money to bring me to Europe. So will Callie and Rory.

Going home—and being with Dave—has its merits also. Maybe I can finish my last semester of college as well.

"I suppose it all depends on whether Brianna and I can get on the flight," I say.

"Not a problem." Brock taps on his phone. "I just secured your tickets. You leave on the same flight with Dave and me tonight, both of you."

I don't know whether to be happy or sad. I was so looking forward to seeing all of Europe, but it would be fun to return with just my siblings. And I'd like to see if anything can blossom between Dave and me.

I sigh and take a sip of my café au lait in front of me. "All right."

"I hope you understand, Mads," Brianna says. "You know

I'd rather do almost anything than leave your brother or break a promise to you."

I nod. "Trust me. I know. You made your feelings for my brother quite clear. Even before they were reciprocated."

She blushes. "I was that transparent, huh?"

I nod. "Now that I've gotten over the shock of it, I'm truly happy for you two."

Brianna smiles across the table from me. "That means a lot to me, Maddie. And once we figure out whatever's going on with my family, you and I will be together in Snow Creek, and we can hang out. Spend time together."

I force a smile. "I'd like that, Bree."

The server brings our standard continental breakfast, and Dave and Brock order their standard American breakfast to supplement it. I'm good with the croissants. She brought baguettes today as well, which are surprisingly good slathered with butter and jam.

I'm loving French cuisine, and I'd love to explore more of it, but I guess Dave and I can have lunch today during our stroll on the Champs-Élysées.

Then we'll both have to come back here, pack up our stuff, and leave.

I take a bite of croissant, enjoying the flakiness and buttery flavor.

And I wonder how I can be so happy and so sad at the same time.

And then something occurs to me that I've been trying like hell not to think about.

This afternoon... I'm going to have to set foot on a plane. I thought I had a couple of months to get used to the idea of flying again.

Turns out, I have a couple of hours.

My nerves do the chicken dance under my skin, and it's not pleasant.

CHAPTER THIRTEEN

Dave

Maddie and I take the Métro to the Arc de Triomphe that stands proudly at the western end of the Champs-Élysées. It's a monument honoring those who fought and died for France.

"Do you want to go to the top?" I ask Maddie.

She shakes her head. "Let's just walk along the street. That was your original idea, and I like it. We can take in as much Paris as we can before we have to leave."

"Good enough." I grab her hand.

The Champs-Élysées is a wide boulevard lined by trees. I take in the beautiful Parisian architecture and the bustling energy of the locals and tourists who are on the same walk.

This famous avenue is renowned for its luxury shopping, and I want to buy Maddie something special. I don't know if our relationship will continue once we arrive back in Colorado, but it means enough to me that I want her to remember it. We stroll by brands such as Louis Vuitton, Gucci, and Chanel, but I don't take Maddie for a designer fashion girl. She'd consider such decadence a waste of money when her family is struggling.

The street is also dotted with cafés and brasseries. I suggest stopping for a coffee or a pastry, but then think better of it. She said she wanted to take in as much as possible, and we just had breakfast.

We walk by the Théâtre Marigny, and toward the eastern end, we find the Jardin des Champs-Élysées, which turns out to be a green space that offers a refreshing contrast to the urban surroundings. If we were staying in Paris longer, I'd arrange to have a picnic here and enjoy the tranquility amidst the bustling city. We stop to snap a few photos at the Grand Palais and Petit Palais, and then we reach the Place de la Concorde at the end of the Champs-Élysées. It's an expansive square dominated by the hieroglyph-laden Luxor Obelisk—I think back to that sphinx and its riddle back at the Louvre—and surrounded by extravagant statues and fountains.

Time to turn around and go back toward the Arc. Maddie is still staring up at the obelisk.

I place my hands on her shoulders. "Did anything strike you?"

"Strike me?"

"Yeah. I said I wanted to buy you something. You hardly looked twice at the high fashion shops."

She blushes. "That stuff isn't really me."

I shrug. "It could be."

She shakes her head. "I wouldn't feel right spending so much money for something I can get at the local mall for a tenth of the cost."

"Ah...but that one won't have a Gucci label."

She laughs. "So?"

I like this woman. I mean, really, *really* like her.

It scares me a little, especially since my whole world has been turned on its axis recently.

"How about jewelry, then?" I ask.

She twists her lower lip and then lightly bites it.

Bingo.

Maddie likes jewelry.

"Come on." I pull her into the nearest jewelry shop.

The shop is called Luxe Bijoux Paris. The interior is pure opulence, complete with plush carpet, a crystal chandelier, and a marble reception desk where a well-dressed young man sits.

"May I help you?" he asks.

"We're just going to look a bit," I say.

"Of course. Please let me know if I can be of assistance."

The jewelry is displayed within glass cases. Each piece is illuminated by soft, diffused lighting, which accentuates the gemstones' sparkle. Diamond necklaces, emerald earrings, sapphire bracelets, and rare timepieces sit behind the glass.

Maddie's gaze settles on the display of engagement rings. Uh-oh.

But her gaze doesn't linger. She heads straight toward a display of necklaces and bracelets.

"Is there something you like?" I ask her.

She nods but then looks at her feet. "But this is way too much, Dave."

I smile. "Don't be silly. This is our last day in Paris, and whatever happens between us in the future, I want you to have something to remember our time together."

I nod to the man at the desk.

He walks briskly toward us, a big smile on his face. "What can I help you with this day?"

I nod to Maddie.

"The pearl pendant, please," she says. "The one with the blue and red stones."

"*Oui, mademoiselle.* A beautiful piece." He unlocks the case and pulls out the necklace.

"It is set in fourteen karat yellow gold, and it is a cultured saltwater pearl surrounded by rubies and sapphires. *Blue, blanc, et rouge.* Or as you say in the States, red, white, and blue." He places it in Maddie's hand.

"It's such a unique piece." Maddie holds the necklace up to the light. "Did you design this?"

"No, but all our pieces are crafted by individual designers whom we commission. It is one of a kind."

"How much is it?" Maddie asks.

I shake my head. "Don't tell her that. We'll take it."

"Dave..."

"Please, Maddie. Let me do this. We're both giving up our vacation, and I want you to have this necklace."

She nibbles at her bottom lip again, and I wish I were doing the biting.

"Your young gentleman is very generous," the jeweler says.

"Yes, he is." She looks up at me, meeting my eyes. "You sure about this?"

"Absolutely sure. And you know I can afford it."

She scratches her arm. "I wasn't worried about whether you could afford it. I just don't..." She bites her lip. "I'm thinking about what my father would say."

"Yes, your father's a proud man, and I get that. But this is a gift from me."

Finally, she nods. "Absolutely. It's a gift, and instead of bothering you about it, I should be thanking you." She grabs my hands and gives each of them a gentle squeeze. "So thank you, Dave. Thank you from the bottom of my heart."

"I will ring you up at the cash register," the jeweler says. "This will be on a credit card, I assume?"

I nod and pull out my American Express Platinum. The jeweler takes the card, runs the transaction, and then places the necklace in a black velvet box with the jewelry shop's logo on it.

"I think I'd like to wear it," Maddie says.

"Absolutely." I take the box from her.

She pulls her hair up behind her neck, and I clasp the chain, my fingers grazing her soft skin.

She turns around, modeling it for me. "What do you think?"

My God, it's like the piece was crafted for Madeline Pike. Not only do the colors accentuate her features beautifully, but the necklace just... It matches her *spirit*. The pearl at the center was once just an unassuming grain of sand until it ended up by chance in the right oyster, which then turned it over time into a thing of great beauty.

Like the pearl, Maddie and I have been through a lot in the past few days, and we've got a lot ahead of us, too. But everything that we go through only serves to bring out our most beautiful selves. The pearl doesn't realize how beautiful it is for its trouble, and neither does Maddie.

Of course, she's a thousand times more beautiful than any pearl.

The sapphire and rubies sparkle around the pearl, and the light bounces off them onto it, blending into a light lavender. The gold chain brings the whole thing together.

I realize that my mouth is wide open. I close it before speaking.

"It was made for you. It's perfect. The chain brings out the gold flecks in your eyes."

"I have gold flecks in my eyes?"

I smile. "Yeah. You didn't know that?"

She purses her lips. "I just thought they were plain brown. Callie's are way prettier than mine. She has that light amber color."

"Your eyes are perfect just the way they are, Madeline Pike." I brush my lips over hers and then turn back to the jeweler. "Thank you."

"*Je vous en prie.* Have a lovely day in Paris with your lady."

I could tell the jeweler that we're not officially together— at least not yet. But I don't. I like the idea of Maddie being my lady. Without a word, I offer her my arm and escort her back onto the bustling streets of the Champs-Élysées.

By now, our breakfast has worn off. "Let's find a café and have a quick bite," I say. "Then it's back to the hotel to pack, and then to the airport."

My skin prickles as I say the word *airport.* I'm not looking forward to getting on a plane.

CHAPTER FOURTEEN

Maddie

Brianna and I sit at the airport at our gate, neither of us saying a word.

Brock and Dave sit across from us, also not speaking.

Finally Brock opens his mouth. "This is a huge aircraft, just like the one we flew out on. It's not a small chartered plane flying over the choppy English Channel."

Is that supposed to make us feel better? Instead we'll be flying over the Atlantic Ocean, which is way bigger than the Channel.

Brianna grips her cell phone. "I need to talk to Jesse."

"He's in rehearsal," Brock says. "Besides, you just talked to him an hour ago."

She gulps audibly. "I know."

"Look," Brock says, "we all have to just get a grip. We are safer in the air than in a car. We all know that. And besides, our plane *didn't* crash. We *lived*."

"Is Rory okay?" Brianna asks.

"She is. She was pretty shaken up," Brock says, "but we all were. We had a few days to recoup. None of us thought we would be getting on a plane this soon."

I close my eyes. "The first thing I said when we got off the plane was that I was never setting foot on an airplane again."

"How did you think you'd get home after the tour?" Brock asks.

"Honestly, I wasn't thinking that far ahead. I thought I had a couple of months to figure that out. And maybe I'd be over my fear of flying by then."

Brock chuckles. "I suppose there's always an ocean liner."

Maddie rolls her eyes. "Very funny."

"Do you think they give out tranquilizers in the first-class cabin?" Brianna asks.

And I honestly can't tell if she's joking or not.

"Everything's going to be okay, Bree," Dave says. "I don't want either of you to worry."

Dave and I have been intimate, and Brock and Brianna are engaged to two of my siblings. Plus Brianna and I have been friends for years.

Still, I feel like the odd one out here.

Again.

I'm getting on a plane with three Steel cousins, and I'm flying first class again, on their dime.

I haven't even told my mother and father I'm coming home.

They'll be happy I'm home, though. I'll most likely be able to go back to school. At this point, I've only missed a couple of weeks.

But then I'll be in Grand Junction, and Dave will be on his ranch outside Snow Creek.

On the other hand, whatever's going on with his family may not give him a lot of time to spend with me.

Something I hadn't considered before, but I consider it now.

He's not sitting with me. He's sitting with Brock.

I jerk as a voice comes over the intercom. "We are now boarding flight nine forty-seven nonstop from Paris to Denver. Boarding group one, you may board."

We all rise and gather our carry-ons. I force my feet to work as I grip my passport and my phone. I scan my boarding pass and follow Brock and Dave onto the aircraft. Brianna follows behind us.

We get onto the plane, and I check my seat assignment, expecting it to be next to Brianna.

It's not.

It's with Dave, and Brianna and Brock are together with lie-back seats.

"Oh," I say, when I see my seat.

He smiles at me. "I thought it might be nice if we enjoyed the flight together. Is that okay?"

I take a deep breath in. "As long as you don't mind me gripping on to you for dear life."

"If it comes to that, I don't mind if you're on my lap." He smiles.

Some of his joviality has returned. But he's not back to the Dave who met us in Europe before the fiasco on the chartered plane.

"How'd you get through this?" I ask. "You seemed so calm when it was all happening, but then afterward, you were as shaken up as anyone. But now..."

He closes his eyes and breathes in. "I'm trying to focus on gratitude, Maddie. On the second chance we were given. And honestly, going to the Louvre helped me a lot."

"Yeah, you mentioned that at dinner. But you didn't say much more."

He frowns. "I'm not sure it's anything I can put into words

really. Just seeing the works of the great masters, learning about them, thinking about how much more there is to life than any singular incident. Plus, like I said, we're pre-disastered now."

I laugh. Sort of. It sounds more like a joke.

"I'll feel better once the plane is in the air," he says.

"You sure about that?"

"Not really." He lets out a short laugh. "But I'll get a cocktail."

I smile at him, reach over, and squeeze his hand. "Thank you."

"For what?"

"For being here with me. For the necklace. For the last couple of days together. I just want you to know that whatever happens, I appreciate everything. This meant something to me."

"It meant something to me too, Maddie," he says. "And it means something to me. Present tense. This isn't over. Not by a longshot."

"I didn't mean to imply that it was."

He cups my cheek. "Then stop talking in past tense. I'll probably be busy when we get home, dealing with family stuff. But I will make time for you. We'll see how this goes."

I nod.

And then we wait. Being in the first boarding group isn't all it's cracked up to be because we get to sit here and ruminate while everyone else gets on the plane. And it's a really big plane.

Once everyone has boarded, a flight attendant shuts the door.

The plane begins to taxi.

My heartbeat races, and sweat beads on my forehead. I

try to take a breath in, but it's shaky. I hold on to Dave's hand for dear life and bury the other one deep into my armrest, my knuckles white.

The flight attendants' voices, first in French and then in English, are garbled. Jumbled noise coming at me yet going through me.

Taxi, taxi, taxi...

And then I brace myself as the plane accelerates...

"Everything's okay," Dave says above the roar of the engines.

Still, I'm freaked, and when the plane first lifts from the ground, I have to force down nausea.

Then Dave, jovial Dave, leans over to me. "We can always join the mile high club."

And I feel better. So much better.

Not that I want to join the mile high club. Airplane bathrooms are so small and kind of gross.

I close my eyes then. Try to still the beating of my heart as I swallow down the queasiness.

To my surprise, the nausea stays down, and within a few moments we're airborne and leveling out.

I don't dare look out my window. In fact, I wish Dave and I had traded seats so he was by the window.

I close the shade.

I close my eyes again.

Send out good vibes to the universe or God or whomever that the plane will safely bring us home to Colorado.

Half an hour later, Dave nudges me. "They're coming around with cocktail orders. Do you want something?"

"I didn't look at the menu."

"Take a look now, or just order whatever you want."

I blink. "I'd love a sidecar."

"Good enough."

When the flight attendant gets to us, Dave orders. "I'll have a Knob Creek, neat, and the lady would like a sidecar."

"Have you made your selections for your dinner yet?" she asks.

Dinner, right. I haven't looked at that menu either.

"Maddie?" he asks.

"I'm sorry. I haven't looked at the menu. Could you just tell me what there is?"

"Of course, *mademoiselle*. We have a lovely boeuf bourguignon or a chicken Cordon Bleu."

"I'll have the chicken, please."

"Same for me," Dave says, "and a glass of the Burgundy, please." Then he turns to me. "I'm sorry, did you want wine?"

I shake my head. "I'm going to keep it to one drink."

"Sounds good."

A few moments later, my sidecar arrives, and I take a drink of the cocktail made with cognac, lemon juice, and a sugared edge. It's always been one of my favorites. I finish, and when our dinners arrive, I ask for water.

Dave and I don't talk a lot as we eat, which is fine. The chicken is great—another perk of this first-class ticket I didn't pay for. You can't go wrong with tender chicken breast stuffed with ham and cheese topped with a Dijon and white-wine sauce. Still, though, the nerves about the flight are there, and I only finish about half my dinner. Then I close my eyes, hoping to escape my anxiety.

And hoping that my dinner stays down.

★ ★ ★

Someone nudges me.

"Hey, Maddie."

I open my eyes. It's Dave.

"Baby, we landed."

My vision is blurry. I blink a few times to focus. "Are you kidding me? I slept through the whole thing?"

Yeah, I did, because I have to go to the bathroom really badly. I'll have to wait until we get off the plane at this point.

"You did. It was a totally smooth flight. No turbulence at all." He lifts the shade on my window. "See? We're here, Maddie. We're in Denver. We're almost home."

I heave a sigh of relief. The plane is taxiing, and it stops when we get to our gate.

"I can't believe it's over."

He grins. "See? I told you we were pre-disastered."

I give him a good-natured swat in the arm. "Yeah, you did."

We remove our seatbelts and gather our carry-ons. A few moments later we're deplaning. Brock and Brianna are in front of us.

"All right," Brock says. "On to baggage claim and then through customs. I've got a driver waiting to take us home."

"Ugh," I say. "A four-hour drive."

"You'll be comfortable, Maddie. We'll be in a limo."

I've been in more limos since this whole thing began than I've ever been in my life. Crazy stuff.

But I can't think about any of it anymore.

I'm oddly awake, though, probably because I slept through the whole flight.

"What time is it?" I ask.

"It's eight p.m.," Brock says, "Colorado time."

My stomach lets out a growl. "I'm kind of hungry."

"Yeah, we'll grab a bite before we take the long drive home."

Dave whispers in my ear. "I'm kind of disappointed. You were asleep, so we couldn't join the mile high club."

"Dave, that's really kind of gross."

He smiles. "I sort of agree, but it seems like it should be a rite of initiation for one of the original three Rake-a-teers."

I feel a hook catch in my heart. "So you still consider yourself a Rake-a-teer, huh?"

He shrugs. "We'll see. For the right woman, I'm willing to give all that up." He smiles at me again.

CHAPTER FIFTEEN

Dave

I live in the guesthouse behind my parents' main house. Brad has his own place, built on our land, and Angie and Sage, who are still in college, live at home.

They've been called home as well for this big family meeting.

My alarm goes off at nine a.m. I'm exhausted. We didn't get home until well after one in the morning, but the meeting is at ten sharp at Uncle Joe and Aunt Melanie's house.

The entire Steel family will be there, even Diana, who drove home from her architecture internship in Denver.

I don't know what to expect, but I have my suspicions that it has something to do with our newfound cousin, Pat Lamone.

He seems to be the missing link.

The grandson of Wendy Madigan and my grandfather, Bradford Steel, and the son of my new aunt, Lauren Wingdam—he's the product of her rape by three men.

So he's a Steel.

But he's also responsible for drugging Diana her freshman year of high school. And he drugged Callie and Rory Pike, stripped them, and took photos of them in compromising positions.

The photos have been destroyed as far as we know, but

only Pat knows for sure.

Then there's Brittany Sheraton, the daughter of Snow Creek's veterinarian, who helped Pat drug and violate the Pike girls. Her father, Dr. Mark Sheraton, unknowingly helped run a human trafficking business on Steel land in Wyoming.

Uncle Joe and Brock got that shut down a couple of months ago, and Brittany is now in a mental health hospital under constant supervision.

But there are still unanswered questions about her involvement. And about Pat Lamone, who was her boyfriend for many years.

Still more answers to our questions died with Wendy Madigan.

I take a shower and dress in jeans and a white button-down with brown ostrich cowboy boots. I miss my dog, Gary. He's still at Mom and Dad's. They're taking care of him along with their dogs. Now that I'm back, I want Gary with me. I'll grab him later today.

I itch to call Maddie, see how she's doing. It's about a ten-minute walk from the guesthouse to Mom and Dad's house. I'll give her a call on the way.

It's a brisk late January day, so I put on a quarter zip and a beanie hat before I head out. I dial Maddie.

"Hello?" She sounds sleepy.

"Hey, it's me. Just wanted to check in on you. Did you sleep okay?"

"Tossed and turned a little. But I eventually got to sleep. Have you found out what the big deal is yet?"

"No, not yet. I'm on my way over to Mom and Dad's house, and I'll drive with them over to Uncle Joe's."

"Maybe your mom and dad will clue you in."

"They'd better."

"Just so you know, I don't expect you to tell me anything."

"That'll depend on how serious it is and on whether the family wants to keep it just among ourselves at first. But you'll no doubt find out about it anyway. I mean, three of my cousins are engaged to your siblings."

"True."

Is that a touch of resentment in her voice? I'm probably imagining it.

"I just wanted to check in on you. Can I see you later?"

"Yeah, if you have time. Just let me know when the stuff with your family is over."

"Yeah, I'll call or text you."

"Sounds good."

"Bye, Maddie." I'm about to hang up, but I hold on a little longer. "I..."

"You what?"

"I can't wait to see you later."

"Yeah, me too. Bye."

Those weren't the words that wanted to come out of my mouth, but it's way too soon for them.

I mean, *really* way too soon. I've known Maddie forever, but I've only truly known her for less than a week.

I walk the rest of the way to my parents' house, and a panting Gary meets me, wagging his tail and jumping on my chest.

"Hey, boy. I missed you."

He smothers me with dog kisses. I greet the rest of the menagerie and then head into the kitchen where I find my mother and father and my two sisters, Angie and Sage.

"I'm really sorry to ruin your vacation, son," Dad says.

"I know you wouldn't do it if it weren't important."

He nods gravely. "No. Joe wouldn't even tell Mom and me what's going on."

My stomach drops. "You're kidding, right? You and Uncle Joe have been friends forever."

"I know." His voice is solemn.

"Where's Henry?" I ask.

"He's going to meet us there."

★ ★ ★

Talk about a full house.

For parties, we usually gather at Uncle Talon and Aunt Jade's. They have the largest ranch house. But for business, it's Uncle Joe and Aunt Melanie's. They have the largest single room on the east wing of their house, and inside is a massive conference table.

Uncle Joe sits at the head of the table, flanked by Uncle Talon, Uncle Ryan, and my father. The Steel brothers and my dad, their honorary member.

The rest of us are interspersed around the table, including my new aunt, Lauren Wingdam, and her sons, Jack Murphy and Pat Lamone.

I sigh. Well, Pat is a Steel, and we have to deal with that.

I look around.

I can't believe everyone is here.

Uncle Joe and Aunt Melanie, and their sons, Bradley and Brock.

Uncle Talon and Aunt Jade, along with Dale and his wife Ashley, Donny and his fiancée Callie, Diana, and Brianna.

Uncle Ryan and Aunt Ruby, along with Ava and her fiancé,

Brendan Murphy, and Gina.

And of course my mom and dad, Bryce and Marjorie Simpson, my brother, Henry, and my sisters, Angie and Sage.

And the newest Steels, Aunt Lauren, Jack, and Pat.

Diana gazes down at the table, deliberately not looking at Pat.

I stand then, needing to speak. "Why is he even here?" I point to Pat. "Look at how this is upsetting Diana."

"Like it or not," Uncle Joe says, "he's a member of the Steel family, Dave. He's your Aunt Lauren's son."

"And grandson of Bradford Steel," Uncle Talon adds, though he doesn't sound happy about it.

How could he be? Diana is his daughter.

I cross my arms. "We're just going to forget about everything he tried to do to Diana? To Callie and Rory?"

Pat rises. "I was a different person then. I can give you all a bunch of excuses about my upbringing, but I won't do that. I won't waste your time. I'm deeply sorry for all the pain I caused this family"—he looks at Callie—"and your family as well."

"The Pike family *is* our family now," my father says. "Donny, Brock, and Brianna are all engaged to Pikes."

That's certainly not any new knowledge to me, but it hits me like a brick.

Maddie, left out in the cold... And I don't want her to be.

But I erase the thought from my mind for the moment. Right now, I want to know why I was called home from my vacation. I'm sure Brock and Brianna do as well.

Pat takes a seat.

Uncle Joe, the oldest of the Steel Brothers and head of the family, begins. "First of all, Lauren has officially changed her name to Lauren Steel."

Smiles and murmurs.

"Jack has decided to keep his surname of Murphy to honor his father, Sean Murphy."

What about Pat?

But Uncle Joe continues, "We don't have any new information about Dr. Sheraton and his daughter, Brittany, nor have we been able to ascertain anything new about Pat's parents. Why they changed their names, and who may have been responsible for their deaths."

Ryan nods. "I think we can all be in agreement that Lauren's and my biological mother probably had something to do with it."

Lauren nods from the other end of the table. "Yes, I'm sorry to say. My mother was a complete psychopath."

"*Our* mother," Ryan says. "You and I are full-blood siblings, Lauren. You're a member of this family, a daughter of Bradford Steel."

Lauren nods. "Yes, it's difficult to remember that sometimes."

Uncle Joe clears his throat. "We've had our best investigators on the case, and they're digging, but they're coming up empty-handed. I think we may have to accept that the answer died with Wendy Madigan."

"Then why are we here today, Uncle Joe?" I ask. "Because quite frankly, I'd rather be in Europe."

"We know that, Dave." Uncle Joe rubs his chin. "But something happened when Wendy Madigan died—and she's really dead this time."

My stomach lurches. "What?"

"A quitclaim deed was filed at the county recorder's office. A deed transferring all real property here in Colorado to Uncle

Ryan and Aunt Lauren."

"What?" I say. That's our ranch. *Our* ranch, and it's huge and worth a ton.

I'm not alone. Chaos erupts. Uncle Joe lets it go on for a minute until he pounds on the table.

Silence reigns as if a judge has pounded his gavel. Uncle Joe gestures to Uncle Ryan.

"Lauren and I have talked," Uncle Ryan says, "and we have no intention of keeping the property. We're going to transfer it in five equal shares among the five of us."

"Of course," Lauren agrees. "I had no idea I was even entitled to any of it."

"You are entitled, Lauren," Uncle Joe says. "And we will not deprive you of what is rightfully yours. You, and your issue, Jack and Pat, are Steels."

She smiles timidly. "I do appreciate how you've all embraced me. I can't believe my mother did this."

"It was most likely a failsafe," Uncle Joe says. "Wendy was a smart woman—a genius—and when she finally passed away, she likely had things in place. As you know, we found an original deed under Brendan's floorboards that is signed by our father transferring everything to Ryan."

"Apparently there was another," Uncle Talon says. "And this one included you, Lauren. Which means Wendy always knew who your father was, even though she told you he was some fictitious half brother."

"I hate to be a big stick in the mud, Dad," Brock says to Uncle Joe, "but why did we all need to be here for this?"

Uncle Joe clears his throat. "Because the five of us Steel siblings, including Aunt Lauren, have decided to transfer everything to all of our children. In equal shares."

"Wait, wait, wait," Brock says. "You and Mom have two kids, but Aunt Jade and Uncle Talon have four, and so do Aunt Marj and Uncle Bryce."

"That's true. Which is why we need to talk about how the distribution should take place."

"Again," I say. "This couldn't have waited until we got home?"

Uncle Joe clears his throat. "No, David," he says, "because unfortunately, I may not be able to lead the family by then."

I drop my jaw, along with everyone else at the table except Aunt Melanie.

She buries her face in her hands.

"It's all right, Melanie," Uncle Joe says. "That's why we're all here."

Aunt Melanie sniffles and wipes her eyes with a tissue. "I'm okay, Jonah."

Uncle Joe sighs. "I've been diagnosed with brain cancer."

The room goes silent. You could hear a pin drop.

"Unfortunately, the type of tumor I have is called glioblastoma."

Still silence.

"This is not news we took lightly, obviously. I will be starting radiation and chemotherapy to shrink the tumor, and then I'll have brain surgery in about a month with further treatment after that as the physicians deem necessary. However, the average life expectancy after this diagnosis is fourteen to sixteen months."

Oh, God. My heart goes wild, and my mind goes fuzzy. My sisters start to sniffle, and my father, sitting next to Uncle Joe...

His face goes pale as a newly washed sheet.

Uncle Talon pats Uncle Joe's hand. Clearly, besides

Aunt Melanie, he's the only person in the room with previous knowledge of Uncle Joe's news. "So obviously, Joe needs to start his treatment right away, and this is not something we wanted to tell you over the phone. We have to figure out this deal with our property before Joe has his surgery, because at that point, he will need to devote all his energy toward his healing."

"Oh my God, Dad." Brock's voice cracks. "No wonder you needed me home."

"Yes, Brock," Uncle Joe says. "You need to take over."

He nods. "I totally understand. I understand why you couldn't tell me this over the phone." His voice is robotic, as if this hasn't quite hit him yet.

It hasn't hit any of us, though murmurs of sadness echo through the group. Soft weeping, lots of sniffling. We all try to be strong, but Uncle Joe is our patriarch, and this...

This...just isn't right.

He's only sixty-three years old, and he doesn't look a day over fifty. He's in great shape, and he takes care of himself. He still works on the ranch some days.

Uncle Joe clears his throat, and the room silences once again.

"As I said," he says, "the average life expectancy after diagnosis is fourteen to sixteen months." His dark eyes sparkle, and a small smirk spreads over his face. "I will tell you, though, that I do not consider myself average. Approximately one percent of glioblastoma patients last ten years, and the longest anyone has survived is twenty years and counting. I personally plan to blow that record out of the water."

Murmurs of agreement resonate throughout the room along with more sniffles and weeping.

I can't help a smile at Uncle Joe's attitude. He's not known to be jovial at all. That would be Uncle Ryan. So his optimism touches me deeply.

Then I take a good look at my father. His eyes are glazed over. This must be killing him. He and Uncle Joe have been best friends since they were kids. They're like brothers.

And a thought hits me like a brick—how happy I am that it's not my father with this horrid diagnosis. Which, of course, makes me feel even worse because I don't want this happening to Uncle Joe. He's the backbone of our family, and I love him. He's like a second father to me.

"Even so," Uncle Joe continues, "in the event that I don't beat the odds, we need to figure out fair distribution of the property. Brock is correct that Ryan, Lauren, and I only have two children as opposed to Talon and Marjorie's four."

I speak up then. "Honestly, I don't think any of us care, Uncle Joe. I think we'd all give it up if it meant you'd still be around."

"I agree, Dad," Brock says.

"Me too." From Brock's brother, Bradley.

More murmurs of agreement.

Uncle Joe clears his throat. "The fairest thing to do would be to do a per stirpes distribution. Divide into fifths because there are five children of Bradford Steel, and then those fifths go to the children in equal shares."

Uh...what? Sure, I just said I'd give it up if we could keep Uncle Joe, but—

"Which means Pat Lamone gets twice as much as I do?" I say.

"That's not fair, Dad," Brock agrees.

Dale and Donny don't look happy, but neither speaks.

Diana goes red, though.

She stands. "No. No, no, no. Absolutely not. No way will that asshole get twice as much as I do. Or Bree, Dale, Donny, Dave, Henry, Angie, and Sage. No fucking way. Not on my watch."

"Dee..." Aunt Jade says gently.

"No way, Mom. I'll leave this family and you'll never see me again. I swear."

Aunt Lauren wipes her nose with a tissue. "Please. This is all my fault. I don't need anything from this family."

Diana looks down the table at Aunt Lauren. "I have no problem with you, Aunt Lauren. Or with Jack. But I just can't..." She shakes her head and walks toward the door.

Uncle Joe sighs. "You see why I needed you all here now?"

Diana returns and sits down. "I'm sorry, Uncle Joe. None of this is as important as what you're going through."

"Can I say something?" Pat interjects.

Brock shoots him an angry look. "Uh...no."

"This concerns him too, Brock," Uncle Joe says. "And remember, right now, legally, Aunt Lauren and Uncle Ryan own this whole ranch. They don't have to share it with us."

"But of course we're going to," Uncle Ryan adds.

Brock is still red in the face, but Diana has calmed down. I try to remain calm as well. Even with my diminished share, I'll be rich as anything.

"I'd like to say something," Aunt Jade offers.

"What is it, blue eyes?" Uncle Talon asks.

She takes a deep breath. "This family has been through so much. Both in the past and recently. And Diana, darling, I love you and your brothers and sister more than anything, but I honestly think it's time to try to heal from all the trauma we've been through. You're all well aware that whatever your share is, it will be tremendous, and you'll live your lives the way most of you have become accustomed to. I want to be fair, and I think I can say with certainty that we older Steels are done having children."

That gets a soft laugh out of Aunt Ruby, but then her eyes mist over in sadness once more.

"So I propose," Aunt Jade continues, "that we distribute equally to all grandchildren of Bradford Steel. Brock, Brad, Ava, and Gina, are you okay with that? You would all get more with the original plan."

Hmm... She didn't ask Jack and Pat, but who the fuck cares?

Ava is the first to reply. "Of course, Aunt Jade."

Easy for her. She doesn't even use her Steel trust fund.

Gina and Brad agree, and finally Aunt Jade turns to Brock.

Brock darts fire at Pat once more but finally says, "Fine."

"This is a lot to take in," Ava says.

"Is it ever," Brianna agrees.

"Yes," Uncle Joe says. "But I agree with Jade. Let's try to heal from the past. I'll need all my energy to fight this cancer."

Melanie sniffles into a tissue.

"Don't you worry, baby," Uncle Joe says to her. "I've been fighting my whole life, and I don't plan to stop now."

Uncle Talon clears his throat. "There is one other thing while we have you all together."

I grit my teeth and prepare for more bad news.

"Lauren," Uncle Ryan says, "do you want to say this or should I?"

"You, please. It's not something I'd like to relive."

Ryan nods. "Yes, we all understand. As we all know, Pat

is the result of Lauren's"—he clears his throat—"rape by three men. We can't be sure who these men were, but we do know that Wendy had three minions who were rapists. They raped Daphne Steel, and they raped my brother. And many others. Pat is twenty-seven years old, so the timing works out, as all three of them died a little over twenty-five years ago."

My father draws in a breath, his jaw clenched.

And I understand why. One of those rapists was his own father.

This is all part of the horrid past we learned about recently.

But we're back to Pat again? Then I gaze at Aunt Lauren. Her pretty face is twisted with anguish. This is killing her. It's not her fault that Pat did the things he did. She didn't raise him. And now she has to relive the horror of his conception.

"We have a way," Uncle Ryan continues, "to possibly find out who Pat's father is. I've discussed this with Lauren and Pat, and they both would like to discover who he is."

"How?" my sister Sage asks.

"We all have a connection to those rapists," Uncle Ryan continues. "Theodore Matthias was Aunt Ruby's father. Larry Wade was Daphne Steel's half brother, and Tom Simpson was Uncle Bryce's father. So we will take DNA from Aunt Ruby, Uncle Bryce, and either Aunt Marj or Uncle Talon—not Uncle Joe, considering his illness—both of whom are biological children of Daphne Steel. We will compare Pat's DNA to those three samples, and we should be able to tell which one of the men—if any of them—fathered him."

"I have the best DNA guy in the business," Aunt Ruby says. "He'll get us an answer more quickly than anyone else could, and I trust him more than anyone else as well. And even if none of them are a match, Pat is still a Steel by virtue of Bradford

Steel being his grandfather."

Jack swallows and turns to his mother. "Are you sure you really want to know?"

Lauren nods. "I think it will be good for me and good for Pat. Everyone wants to know where they came from. My whole life, I had no idea I was the daughter of Brad Steel. And Ryan, you spent half your life not knowing who your biological mother was. If we can find out, we should."

"God, this is so fucked up," I say under my breath.

My father looks at me sternly. "David, we are all truly sorry about your vacation."

"Oh God," I say, "that's not what I meant. I just... Do you think this could get any weirder? Any worse? Any more horrific? Uncle Joe, we can't lose you. We just can't."

Aunt Melanie wipes her eyes again, and so does Aunt Jade.

"David," Uncle Joe says. "You know I think of you as a son. Bradley and Brock are my biological children, but I regard all of you as our sons and daughters. So believe me when I say this, son. I'm going to fight this with everything I have. But even if I fail, I have two brothers and two sisters who can lead this family into the next generation."

I get choked up at that, and I'm not the only one. Sniffles resound throughout the room. Angie and Sage are nearly sobbing.

"I think we need to adjourn for now," Uncle Talon says. "Tomorrow, Aunt Ruby, Uncle Bryce, and I will go with Pat to see the DNA expert and get our blood drawn. If our suspicions about the rapists are correct, we'll be able to identify Pat's father. In the meantime, Uncle Bryce will begin working on the deed transfers with our attorneys."

"Does that mean we can go?" Dale asks.

"Yes, son. You all can go."

As we all rise, one by one, we give Uncle Joe hugs and wish him well. It makes him uncomfortable, I can tell, but he puts up with it because we're family.

He's been our patriarch since we all came into this world.

And all recent things considered, I'm not sure we can survive without him.

CHAPTER SIXTEEN

Maddie

I spend the morning helping my mother around the house.

"It is nice to have you home, Madeline," she says. "I missed you."

"I would've been in college anyway," I say.

"I know that." She draws me in to squeeze me. "You're my baby. My last little one. We're truly empty nesters now."

"I suppose you'll have grandchildren soon," I say.

She furrows her brow a bit.

"What's wrong?"

"Your brother and Brianna Steel," she says. "I didn't see that coming, and I'm not sure how I feel about it."

I blink. That's strange. She was ecstatic when Callie and Rory snagged Steels. "Then how would you feel about me with Dave Simpson?"

She widens her eyes, and I recognize the look—the ecstatic one.

"There's nothing," I say quickly. I don't want to get her hopes up. "I mean, we're kind of seeing each other. It happened while we were overseas."

Mom frowns. "I didn't even know Dave was there."

"Yeah, he showed up a couple of days into the tour." I bite my lip. "But now something's happening that they all had to come home for, so my vacation got cut short."

"I suppose you could have stayed."

"I could have, and I thought about it, but Jesse and Rory are so busy with the band, and there wouldn't be anyone for me to see the sights with."

"See, that's just it." Mom opens a drawer, takes out a rag, and starts wiping the counter somewhat aggressively. "Brianna Steel made a promise to you, and she reneged."

Ah...so it's Brianna specifically she has a problem with. I place my hand on her arm. "Mom, this is a big family deal for the Steels."

"What's going on?"

"I don't know. Dave didn't know. No one knew. They were just told it was a big deal that they couldn't talk about on the phone and they had to come home."

Mom returns her focus to the counter. "Tell me more about Brianna Steel."

"You know all about her."

She looks up, her eyes pained. "Madeline, I only know I've seen you cry your eyes out over her and the other three."

I cross my arms. "Yes, I always felt kind of left out, but they're family, Mom. And I suppose now Brianna will be part of *our* family."

She drops the rag, her eyes wide. "What?"

"Oh crap, Jesse didn't tell you?"

"Apparently not."

"He and Brianna are engaged."

She bends down and grabs the rag, returning to the counter. "So I'm losing three of my children to that family."

I shake my head. "Wait. You were *thrilled* about Callie and Rory."

"Donny and Brock seem to truly love your sisters. But Brianna..."

"She loves Jesse, Mom. Believe me, I had my doubts at first too, but they're the real thing."

"She's so young."

"She's my age. And it's really no different from Callie and Rory marrying into the Steel family. It's a great opportunity for Jesse as well. Three of your children are going to be rich beyond your wildest dreams."

"Yes, I suppose so." She sighs. "You know your father doesn't like taking Steel money."

"He's *not* taking Steel money. Your children are marrying into it, and all three of them are head-over-heels in love. True love, Mom. This isn't a business deal. When you see Jesse and Bree together, you'll understand."

"I won't get that chance until Jesse and Rory return from the tour."

"No, you won't, but trust me on this." I force Mom's arm from the counter and give her a hug. "Like I said, I had doubts too, but they're so in love. I've never seen Jesse like this."

"Well," she says, "at least I still have my Maddie." She squeezes me in our embrace.

And again, I'm the odd one out.

I love my mother, but what I wouldn't give to be marrying a Steel as well.

* * *

A few hours later, after Mom and I have a quick lunch, and Dad has assured me he doesn't need my help with anything on the ranch, I retire to my room, grab my laptop, and check my email.

My phone rings. My heart flips when I see Dave's name on the screen.

I force my voice a little lower than natural. I don't want to sound like a giddy college girl.

"Hi, Dave."

"Hey." His voice is oddly steady.

"You okay?"

He pauses. "Not even close. Can you come over to my place?"

I check the time on my phone. It's not too late. "I suppose I can. Do you still live in the guesthouse behind your parents' house?"

"Yeah. How far away are you?"

"It'll take me about half an hour, but..." I slap my palm to my forehead. "Shit. I don't have a car, Dave."

"Oh..."

"You could come get me."

"Yeah. I'll come get you. But then we're going to my place, okay?"

"All right."

He hangs up without saying goodbye.

His voice was weird. And he said he wasn't doing well.

Whatever the Steels were called home for...

It wasn't anything good.

CHAPTER SEVENTEEN

Dave

I'm on autopilot as I drive to Maddie's place. The Pike land is adjacent to our land, on a parcel that was exempt from the liens that Wendy Madigan held on all the property in Snow Creek that wasn't ours.

I can't worry about that now.

Uncle Joe...

I don't think any of us ever thought anything would happen to him. He was always so big, so strong. He and my father are so close, like brothers.

This is going to kill my father. I could see it in his eyes today at the meeting. He was holding it together—being strong for Mom and the rest of us—but losing Uncle Joe will fucking kill him.

It will kill all of us.

So much to digest.

Pat Lamone is a member of our family.

Uncle Joe will probably be dead within a year.

It's just too fucking much.

I pull into the driveway of the Pikes' ranch house, exit my car, and walk to the door. I knock softly.

No response, so I ring the doorbell.

Maddie opens the door, and my God, she looks beautiful.

She's wearing simple jeans and a bright-green sweatshirt.

I want to grab her and kiss her.

"Let's go," I say.

"Wait a minute," she says. "I need you to say hi to my mom."

I raise my eyebrow. "Maddie, I can't right now."

She widens her eyes at me. "Dave, please. My dad's out working, but you do need to say hi to my mom before I can leave with you."

Fuck.

I'm going to have to paste on a smile like we're dating.

Which I suppose we are. But pleasing someone's mother right now is pretty low on my list of priorities.

I sigh and follow Maddie through the small foyer into the great room. Maureen Pike is sitting on the couch reading a magazine.

She stands. "Hello, Dave."

"Mrs. Pike."

She narrows her gaze. "Please call me Maureen. Where are you and Madeline off to?"

I'm thinking she's looking for an answer other than *my place to fuck.*

I blink. "We haven't really discussed it."

"Maybe we'll just walk around town and then have some dinner," Maddie says.

I nod quickly. "Yeah, that sounds good."

If walking around town having dinner means fucking like rabbits at my place.

Mrs. Pike crosses her arms. She's not fooled. "That sounds great. When will you be home, Madeline?"

Maddie rolls her eyes. "I don't know, Mom. I'll be home

when I get home."

Mrs. Pike smiles, but her eyes are betraying her true mood. "All right. But if it gets to be too late, please at least give me the courtesy of a call."

"Sure, Mom." She kisses her mother on the cheek. "Bye."

We leave the house, and I open the car door for Maddie. Then I get in on the driver's side.

We're quiet for the first few moments, until—

"I'm sorry about my mom," Maddie says.

I shake my head. "It's okay. I'm just not in the mood for putting on an act today."

"There's no reason to put on an act with my mother. Just be yourself."

"That's the problem, Maddie." He sighs. "Right now *myself* is a mess. It's certainly not someone you want to have talking to your mother."

I place a hand on his upper arm. "You want to tell me about it?"

He takes a deep breath. "I do. But not just yet. Right now, what I need, Maddie, is you in my bed."

She smiles. Sort of. Her lips twitch. It's like she wants to smile but doesn't want to.

"That okay with you?" I ask.

"Yeah." She scratches her arm. "I mean, I love being with you. But at some point, we have to—"

"Talk about us?" I blurt out.

She swallows. "Well... Yeah."

"Sure, Maddie." I tighten my grip around the steering wheel. "We can talk about us. But quite frankly, in order for there to be an *us,* I have to know who the hell I am first. Right now, I just fucking don't."

She bites on her bottom lip, and I keep my eyes straight on the road.

She doesn't say anything else for the rest of the drive.

When I pull into the driveway of my place, she finally turns to me. "David—"

I raise an eyebrow. "David?"

"David, Dave, whatever." She grabs my hand. "I want to be with you. Totally. I'm already wet thinking about it."

"Good, because I'm already hard as a fucking rock."

"But...I don't want to just be a fuck to you."

"You want to be my girlfriend?"

She doesn't reply.

But she's right.

"Maddie, last night I told you that I could give up being a Rake-a-teer for the right woman. I wasn't yanking your chain. Obviously I was referring to you. But man, my life has been turned upside down in the last couple of hours. So could we please just fuck now and talk later?"

She nods slowly. "Sure, Dave. Let's fuck."

I get out of my car, open the passenger door for her, help her out. I hold her hand as we go to the house. Gary is still at my parents' house, so as soon as we're at the door, I flatten her against the wall and crush our mouths together. She opens for me, and I devour her mouth with my tongue, taking her with a kiss.

She wraps her arms around me, and I grind my hard cock into her pelvic bone.

She sighs into my mouth.

I break the kiss then, lift her in my arms, and carry her through the foyer down the hallway to my bedroom.

"Too many clothes," I say.

I disrobe quickly as she watches.

"Strip," I command.

She takes her green sweatshirt off, exposing a lacy red bra.

I suck in a breath. "God, you're fucking beautiful."

She unclasps her bra from the back, tosses it, and her perfect breasts fall gently onto her chest.

Her nipples are already hard and puckered. I want to bite on them, suck on them, nibble until she screams.

But what I need more than any of that is to sink my cock inside her.

I'm already naked, my dick jutting out, ready for action.

She flips off her clogs and then removes her jeans, sliding them over her perfect ass along with her red bikini.

I take a moment to look at her—appreciate her sheer beauty.

But I need more than that. Need to get inside her, fuck her, take a little of today off me.

"Lie on the bed," I command.

She obeys me without challenge, which surprises me, but I know better than to question it now. She's willing to give me what I need, and I'll see that her needs are met later.

I hover over her, look into her warm brown eyes—eyes that draw me in, make me want to give her everything.

And right now, I want to give her my big hard cock.

I dangle it over her clit a few times, making her moan, and then I thrust inside.

God, the sweet suction. The perfect fit.

But my needs overtake me, and I pull out and plunge back in.

I fuck her hard, fuck her fast, fuck her better than I've ever fucked another woman.

It doesn't take long until I'm ready, on the brink—

So I slow down a bit, wanting to last just a bit longer.

But knowing I'm going to explode at any moment.

Because that's what I need. What I brought her here for. For release. Escape.

To run away from the shit that's still going down with my family.

If I thought I needed a vacation before, I really need one now.

I'm going to take it in Maddie Pike's body.

I pull out and thrust back in, emptying myself into her tight cunt.

And with that release, I let go—if only for a moment—all the evil in the world, all the impurity in the world, all the shit in the world.

Everything going on with my family.

Because one day—one fucking day—everything will be right again. As right as it feels coming inside Maddie Pike.

I stay inside her for a few moments, and then I roll over so that we're both on our sides, facing each other, still joined.

"Thank you," I say. "You have no idea how much I needed that."

"I'm happy to help you any way I can. But Dave, I was serious when I said I don't want to be just a fuck to you."

I shake my head. "You aren't, Maddie. I guess we're... dating?"

"You don't sound too confident in that assessment."

I sit up, run my hands through my hair. "Christ. I didn't go looking for this. And you know as well as I do that I didn't go to Europe to follow you there."

"Yeah, you've made that clear," she says dryly.

I scoff. "Don't."

"Don't what?"

"Don't be like that, Maddie. We're great together."

"We're great in *bed*, Dave. We hardly know each other outside of the bedroom."

"That's not exactly true. We spent time together in Europe. We saw Paris together." I finger the gold chain around her neck. Dangling from it is the pearl, sapphire, and ruby pendant I purchased for her in Paris.

She puts her hand over mine. "We did. But before Paris was that awful experience on the plane, and we were both screwed up over that. Now we're home, and something's clearly up with your family again." She sighs. "You're inside yourself, Dave, and you can't be with me if you can't *be* with me."

She's right, of course. But...

"I *do* want to go there, Maddie. Not yet. I want to give you an orgasm first. I want you to feel good."

"Dave." She cups my cheek. "I don't *care* about an orgasm. I care about you. Something has you completely troubled. I can't force you to tell me, but I'm also not going to force you to give me an orgasm if your head's not in it."

"Maddie, giving you an orgasm is hardly a hardship."

She exhales sharply. "You've given me plenty of orgasms, Dave. Right now, you seem to need me. What can I do for you?"

I lie back down on my side. "You did it."

"Damn it." She moves away from me. "I will not be just a fuck to you. Talk to me. Let me help you."

I roll over onto my back, cover my eyes with my arm. "I don't want to lay this on you."

"Lay it on me. Because if you don't, this will be the last time you'll *lay* me."

I remove my arm from my eyes. "You're so much more than a good lay, Maddie. I never meant for it to be more than that, but you are."

She snuggles into my shoulder. "I'm glad for that. And I'm proving to you now that you're not just a fuck to me, Dave. I don't expect you to give me an orgasm when you're clearly bothered."

"God, you don't know the half of it."

"Tell me. Let me help."

I look her straight in the eyes. "You can't tell anyone what I'm about to tell you."

"Of course not."

"It's a lot of things, but the biggest one right now is that my uncle Joe is sick."

She nods slowly. "I'm sorry to hear that. I hope he gets better soon."

I shake my head, feeling a lump forming in my throat. "You don't understand. He has cancer. Brain cancer. A glioblastoma, which is pretty much a death sentence."

She rolls away from me, sits up, slaps her hand over her mouth. "I'm so, so sorry, Dave."

"You know the worst thing about it? I love my uncle, and I feel so awful for him and my aunt, but the first thing I thought was how glad I was that it wasn't my own father."

"That's not bad," she says.

"But it *is*. You've probably heard Brianna say this. All of our aunts and uncles are like parents to us. All of our cousins are like siblings to us. We're that close, Maddie. Joe is the oldest Steel brother. The patriarch of our family. It's like he's the base of our house of cards, and without him, we'll fall."

"The Steels are built on a much more solid foundation

than that," Maddie says.

Are we though? She doesn't know everything.

She knows about Wendy Madigan, about Lauren and Jack, and even Pat Lamone. That has all become common knowledge around town. She knows about Brittany Sheraton, that she's under mental health care now.

She doesn't know about the human trafficking. She doesn't know about Dale and Donny and Uncle Talon. About what Wendy Madigan ultimately cost our family.

She doesn't know about my grandfather, Bradford Steel, who wasn't the pillar of society everyone thought he was. That we were raised to think he was.

And she sure as hell doesn't know about the three rapists connected to our family—Theo Matthias, Larry Wade, and my own grandfather, Tom Simpson. Tom Simpson, who killed himself right in front of Uncle Joe twenty-five years ago. Took his own life rather than face the music for what he'd done. I have the blood of Larry Wade as well. He was the half brother of my maternal grandmother, Daphne Steel, who lived her own private hell inside her head because of him and the other two.

I sigh. "I pray you're right."

She bites her lip. "And you never know. Your uncle may just survive."

"One percent of people, Maddie. One percent of people with this cancer survive for ten years."

"Then there's still hope."

I roll over, facing away from her. "Maybe."

"Dave, I am not going to let you go back to that place." She grabs my shoulders and rolls me back toward her. "You know what everyone loves about you is your optimism, your jovial personality. After that plane almost crashed, I saw you lose that, and then I saw you regain it, now only to lose it again." She places her hands on each side of my face. "You're still you, Dave Simpson. You're still *you*."

She's right, of course.

The family is going to need me more than ever now.

I pull her back into my arms, kiss her lips gently. "You're something else. I think I could fall in love with you, Madeline Jolie Pike."

I think I already have.

But she doesn't push that subject any further, to my surprise. She simply snuggles into me, kissing my shoulder.

CHAPTER EIGHTEEN

Maddie

I know better than to take Dave at his word at this moment. He's in a weird place right now—the high of his release from the orgasm and the low of finding out his uncle is so ill have placed him in a strange emotional limbo.

I don't know Jonah Steel well. My only connection to the Steels—before Callie, Rory, and Jesse got engaged to three of them—was the awesome foursome. All those hours I spent crying, feeling left out of their little Steel clique, and now Brianna is going to be my sister-in-law.

I never saw that one coming in a million years.

But I can't deny how happy Jesse seems. Jesse, who has held resentment toward the Steels much longer than I have.

"No response to that?" Dave asks.

I nuzzle into his shoulder. "I'm not sure how to respond, Dave. What do you say when a man tells you he could fall in love with you? It's not like you said you are in love with me."

He frowns. "To be honest, Maddie, I'm not sure I've ever been in love before."

His confession doesn't surprise me. He was a womanizer, along with Donny and Brock, for so many years. I doubt he was ever looking for love, so he got what he wanted. Lots and lots of indiscriminate sex.

I try not to let that bother me. Clearly Callie and Rory got over it, because Donny and Brock were womanizers too.

It was Rory herself who coined the term *the three Rake-a-teers.*

"And no response to that?" Dave says.

I cock my head. "That you've never been in love before? Is that supposed to surprise me, Dave? You've never been serious about a woman in your life."

He sighs. "You're telling me. Then I went and watched Donny and Brock fall for your sisters. It was the craziest thing ever. Donny's older, so maybe it was time for him to settle down, but Brock? He's my age. I figured we'd both have lots more fun before it was time to start our families."

"I see. And you feel differently now?"

He scratches the side of his head. "When I see Brock and Rory, I do. The two of them are perfect together, and so very much in love."

"It sure made my mother happy," I say.

"That she fell for a Steel?"

"That she fell for a *man.* Rory's been very open about her bisexuality, and she's had relationships with both men and women. Her one and only forever person could've easily been a woman."

"Are you saying your mother's homophobic?"

I shake my head. "No, just traditional. She loves Rory and accepts her for who she is, but I know deep inside she was happy Rory chose a man for her life partner."

"And how do you feel about it?"

I swallow. "I feel...good about it. I love Brock. But I'm mostly happy for Rory because it's always been her dream to be a mother, and that would've been more difficult had she chosen a woman to spend her life with."

"It's not difficult. You can buy that stuff that you need to get pregnant with."

"True, but now she doesn't have to."

"The two of them will make a beautiful kid, for sure," he says.

"God, I know. With Brock's rugged handsomeness and Rory's classic beauty..." I smile.

I smile because I know that makes my mother exceedingly happy. My mother, the former beauty queen, and not one of her daughters were interested in the local pageant scene.

I hate that kind of stuff.

I look back at Dave. He hasn't responded to my last statement.

I'm not sure what to say to him. I've been crushing on him for so long, but I know better than anyone that a crush is not love.

Yet I do feel something for Dave Simpson. Something new and exciting and passionate. I'm almost afraid to put a name to it. Certainly not the L word. Not yet. Especially when he's clearly not ready to go there either.

After all, this has only been going on for a little more than a week.

I could easily be Brianna and say I've been in love with him from afar for the last ten years, but that would be dishonest. I'm not Brianna. I've had a crush on him because he's a beautiful man. So beautiful and so full of joy.

Until now.

But those first two days in Scotland and England, before we had the near plane crash, he was the old Dave. Almost too much so.

Because he was trying to have a vacation from all the shit that has gone down with his family.

I don't want to be just a fuck to him, but I don't want him to go too fast either. Whatever grows between us has to be real. Not some escape for him because his life is troubled.

I'm so young, and so is he. There's no reason to rush into this.

When we first got together in Glasgow, my original thought was that I wanted to snag a Steel like all my siblings had.

But after that near brush with death... And how he reacted...

I want to take it slowly. Or if not slowly, at least not as quickly as all my siblings did.

Because looking your mortality in the face has a side effect. All those things you thought were important?

They're not.

Money? Steel money? Finishing college on time? Figuring out what to do with your life?

None of it matters.

What matters is that you *live*. That you stop and appreciate the little things because life is made up of those little things. You let every second count.

That's what I'm going to do. Every second of my life is going to count from now on. Whether I spend it with Dave Simpson or not.

And right now, although I'd love to immerse myself in his body and have him give me ten orgasms, I'm not going to.

I'm going to just *be* with him.

Show him that I'm here, and that I care.

And yes, I could easily fall in love with him, but I'm not

going to repeat the words he said to me.

It's just not time yet.

"Dave?"

"Yeah?"

"I think I'd like to go home."

He moves away from me. "Did I do something wrong?"

I kiss his shoulder. "No, not at all. But I think you've had a long day. A difficult day. I want you to be with your family. And I think I'd like to be with my family. I have a lot of thinking to do."

"Anything I can help with?"

"You're sweet to ask," I say, "but you have your own stuff to deal with right now. I won't burden you any further."

He smiles. "I don't mind, Maddie. It would be nice to take my mind off my own problems. The problems of my family."

"It's nothing like what you're going through," I say. "Now that I'm home, I'm thinking about going back to school. I can still catch up and finish my final semester on campus."

He's quiet.

Words scramble around my mind as I try to figure out how to continue the conversation—or end it—but then—

He grabs my hand. "I don't... I don't want you to go, Maddie."

"We can still see each other. I'll just be in Grand Junction. No more than a half hour away."

He presses his lips together. "Yeah, that's true. I can't be selfish right now. You need to do what's best for you."

"I think it might be best for both of us," I say. "Maybe we both need some distance. Figure out if what we're feeling is real or just in the moment."

"Yeah, I suppose you're right."

My heart sinks a little. But what was I hoping he'd say? Please don't go? I've fallen madly in love with you, Maddie? I'll do anything to keep you here?

None of that was going to happen.

He has too much on his mind with his family.

All three of my siblings will be forced into the middle of whatever's going on, but I can't force myself into the middle when Dave isn't sure about us.

I also need to make sure what I feel for him isn't just infatuation. That it's something more.

And perhaps going back to school will help me to figure that out.

Dave rises, grabs his jeans, and scrambles into them. "All right, baby. I'll take you home."

"I think that's best for now. Maybe we can see each other tomorrow. Have lunch or something?"

"That depends," he says. "When will you be going back to school?"

I rub my chin. "Probably Monday. I've already sent an email to the registrar. I'm just waiting to hear back if I can get into the classes I want and do the makeup work for the first couple of weeks."

He nods.

I rise from the bed and dress quickly.

We don't talk a lot during the half hour ride back to my home. Always the gentleman, Dave gets out first, opens my door for me, and walks me to the door.

He gives me a quick peck on the lips. "I'll see you soon."

"Yeah. Thanks for today."

"I should be thanking you."

"Why don't we just thank each other?" I give him another

quick kiss and then go inside.

CHAPTER NINETEEN

Dave

When I get home, I don't want to be alone, so I end up going back to my parents' house. Gary is still there anyway, and I want to see my dog.

I walk in. Henry and the girls are in the kitchen, having a snack.

"Where are Mom and Dad?" I ask.

"I think they're in Dad's office," Sage says.

"Thanks."

I don't stop to talk to my brother and sisters, even though I probably should.

Instead I walk down the long hallway to Dad's office. I reach my hand to knock, but then I stop when I hear Mom's voice.

"Everything will be okay, Bryce. One way or another."

Then a choking sob.

And it didn't come from my mother.

My father...is *crying*.

I'm not sure I've ever seen or heard my father cry in my entire life.

I should leave. Give them their privacy, but my feet stay glued outside his office door.

"I don't know what I'll do without him," my father says

through another sob.

"You'll move on. For your family. For your children. You have four children who need you, Bryce."

"Joe has two children who need *him*," my father counters.

"I know, baby. And I know how much he means to you."

"I've known him since before you were born," Dad says.

My mother doesn't respond. She's probably hugging him, stroking his hair, as he cries.

My big strong father, reduced to tears by the illness of his best friend.

Dad and Uncle Joe are brothers-in-law, but I've always known they're so much more than that. They're close like Brock and I are close, only they share no blood between them.

Then my mother's voice again. "He'll fight it. You know Joe. He'll fight this with everything he has."

"One percent, Marjorie."

"Who says Jonah Steel won't be that one percent? He's my big brother too, Bryce. This is killing me just as much as it's killing you."

"I know, baby."

But my mother doesn't break down. This is her big brother, and she stays strong for my father. My father—who's always been the strong one. For her, and for Henry, the girls, and me.

When they've been quiet for a few moments, I knock.

"Who is it?" Mom asks.

"It's me, Mom. Dave."

A few seconds later, she opens the door. "Dave? Did you need something, sweetheart?"

"Just wanted to talk to you guys."

Mom places herself between me and Dad. "Your father

is..."

A throat clear from my father. "It's all right, Marjorie. Let him in."

I walk in. My strong handsome father's eyes are sunken and sad and bloodshot.

"You okay, Dad?"

He takes a deep breath in. "I will be. Mom and I are just having a hard time dealing with Uncle Joe's illness."

"Yeah, I am too."

Mom hugs me.

"It's funny," I say. "I was telling Jesse about how the only catastrophe we've had in this family—before all of the current shit, that is—was Aunt Ruby's breast cancer. We caught it early, and she made a complete recovery. Ava and Gina are now getting annual mammograms, so if anything happens, they will catch it early too. We were so lucky with that."

"Absolutely," Mom says.

Dad just nods.

"And somehow now, it's like the gates of hell have opened, and the four horsemen of the apocalypse have galloped all over our family."

Dad and Mom both just stare at me.

Finally, Mom says, "That doesn't sound at all like my David."

"I'm still in here," I say. "Just seems like the wheel's on the bottom right now for the Steel family."

"Listen, son," my father says. "I'm taking this hard. I can't hide that from you, and I don't want to either. You know I don't have any siblings of my own, and Joe was more than a friend to me. More than a brother-in-law. Other than your mother and you kids, he's the most important person in my life.

I always thought we'd grow old together, sitting on the back porch, smoking pipes—even though we both hate tobacco—and talking about the good old days. But you remember what you've been taught since you were a kid. Remember that you can find gratitude in everything."

"Are you finding gratitude in this?" I ask him point-blank.

He shakes his head and sighs. "I admit it's difficult. But I am grateful for the health of you, your mother, your brother, your sisters. It's bad enough that Joe has to go through this, but if it were one of you..." He shakes his head. "I don't know if I could survive that."

Mom kisses the top of his head. "You would survive it, Bryce, just like you've survived everything else in your life. Because that's who you are. You're a survivor." Then she looks at me. "We all are, Dave. Your father and I, along with your aunts and uncles, tried to give you the perfect childhood. We kept the truth about our family secret so that your childhood could be idyllic."

"It was, Mom."

"Yes, it was." She frowns. "But we ultimately did you a disservice, I think. Training you to think nothing could ever go wrong. That's not how life is, and we're certainly seeing that now."

"I don't begrudge you any of that," I say. "You did what you thought was right at the time."

"Melanie and Ruby were against it. They didn't think we should keep it from you. I look back now, and I wonder why we didn't listen to Melanie." She sighs. "She's a psychiatrist specializing in childhood trauma. We should've been listening to her. Because the problem with secrets, Dave, is that they always come back to haunt you. You just never know when."

"I know," I say. "It must have been damned hard for Uncle Joe to stand there this morning and tell us all of this."

Dad nods. "He's the strongest man I know."

I cock my head. "Stronger than Uncle Talon? Than Donny? Dale?"

Dad nods. "Uncle Talon and the boys went through something so horrific that they can't help but be stronger for the experience. But Joe has carried things—burdens—all these years so his brothers and sister wouldn't have to. I've helped him carry those burdens, ease it for him."

"What are you talking about?" I say. "Are you saying there's something no one else knows?"

"No, that's not what I mean. I..." He chokes back a sob.

Mom rushes to him and rubs his shoulders. "Bryce, honey." Then she turns to me. "Did you need something else, David? Because I think your father and I need to be alone."

"No," I say. "I have a lot of questions, but they can wait."

Mom takes my arm and leads me out the door. "He'll be okay."

"I know. But what about you? This is your brother, Mom."

She nods, swallowing. "I know. I love all my brothers with all my heart, and I can't stand the thought of being without them. But I have to be strong for your father right now, and later, he'll be strong for me. That's what marriage is about, Dave."

My mother's beautiful face is tense, and her eyes heavy-lidded. She's carrying my father right now, something I've never seen. It's always been Dad carrying her when she needed it. I have new respect for my mother. I see a strength in her that I didn't know she possessed.

I give her a hug. "I understand."

Then I leave the office and rejoin my brother and sisters in the kitchen.

Angie and Sage are quiet, which is not unusual for Angie but is for Sage.

Henry's fixing a sandwich at the counter.

"Hey, bro," I say.

"Hey yourself."

Henry and I aren't overly close. We're very different people. He's much quieter than I am. But we're brothers, and we know that.

"You want a sandwich?" he asks.

I'm not hungry, but I nod. "Yeah, I suppose I should eat something."

"That's what I've been telling the girls." He takes two plates over to the table and sets one in front of Angie and the other in front of Sage. "Eat."

Angie and Sage both adore Henry. Something about the oldest kid, the older brother—and he's always treated them more like his own children than his sisters. Big brother to a fault.

Henry fixes a sandwich for himself and for me, and we join our sisters at the table.

I take a bite of my roast beef sandwich. Steel beef, the best beef ever, and it tastes like sludge right now. Even on Ava's homemade bread.

We don't talk, and when we're done, I rise. "I'm going to get Gary and go home."

"Yeah," Henry says. "I was thinking about heading back to my place, but I don't want to leave the girls alone."

"Yeah, Henry, please stay here," Angie says.

"I will, sis. Don't worry."

Neither of them asks me to stay.

That's okay. But I'm not sure I want to be alone either. I was hoping Maddie would spend the night, but she's acting weird.

Everyone's acting weird.

And I just have this huge feeling of foreboding.

Maddie told me this afternoon that the Steels were built on a solid foundation.

But more and more, I feel like the house of cards is about to fall.

CHAPTER TWENTY

Maddie

Mom and Dad are ecstatic when I announce that I'll be going back to college beginning Monday. Everything worked out with the registrar, I got my scholarship back in place, and they found a single room for me in one of the dorms.

Angie, Sage, and Gina are living in the sorority house, where I would be if I hadn't forfeited my spot to go to Europe.

"This really couldn't have worked out better, Madeline," Mom says. "I know it's a shame that you didn't get to see Europe, but this way you'll graduate on time and get back to your own life."

"I suppose so. What about all the weddings?"

"I haven't gotten your sisters to nail down a date yet. We were talking about it, but now there's Jesse and Brianna to consider, I suppose." She sighs. "I just don't know how we're going to afford all of this."

Dad grumbles behind his newspaper.

My father's the only man on earth who still reads the newspaper every morning—on paper and not his iPad.

"A small wedding here on the ranch," he says.

"That may not be what the girls want," Mom says. "And their fiancés can certainly afford—"

Dad folds his newspaper down sharply. "Stop it now,

Maureen. You know how I feel about taking money from the Steel family."

My mother and father have been going at this since Callie and Donny got together. My mother is a proud woman, but she has champagne tastes on a beer budget. She always has.

And then my father, even prouder, who's had to rein my mother's tastes in over the years. He refuses to take a cent of Steel money.

That's just going to have to change, because Callie and Rory should be able to have the wedding they want. After all, their in-laws-to-be can certainly afford it.

"Dad..." I begin.

"Yes, Maddie?"

"I know the Steels are a sore subject with you, but I'm just wondering. That Steel Trust thing, apparently run by Wendy Madigan, didn't have a lien on our property."

"No, they didn't," Dad says.

"None of us have been able to figure out why."

Dad raises his eyebrows. "Why didn't you just ask me?"

"Well... I guess I wasn't sure that you would know."

He puts his newspaper down. "Madeline, your mother and I own the property. Of course we would know."

"The truth is, Maddie," Mom says, "we bought this property back when Jesse was just a kid. You weren't even born yet. We actually bought it from the Steel family. It was property that another family had been using as a ranch, leasing it from the Steels."

"And..."

Dad clears his throat. "There was no lien on it because it was owned by the Steels themselves."

"So..."

"The Steels own all their property outright," Dad says. "I wouldn't have purchased any property subject to a lien anyway. That's bad business. Frankly, I can't believe so much property changed hands over the years with that lien in place."

I have no idea how to respond to that, and Dad's tone indicates that he's not interested in discussing the matter any further, so I decide to change the subject.

"I'll need one of you guys to drop me off tomorrow night," I say.

"Of course, Madeline," Mom says. "Your father and I will both go."

"That's not necessary. Maybe I can get a ride with Angie and Sage or Gina."

"Aren't they at school now?" Mom asks.

I shake my head. "All the Steels, even the youngest ones, were called home for that big meeting. I figured you knew."

"The Steels don't make it a priority to share their business with us," Dad says.

"No, of course not. I just figured Callie had told you. She was there."

Mom glances at Dad. "She hasn't said anything to us."

"Then you don't know Joe is sick?"

Dad's eyes widen. "Jonah is ill?"

"Callie knows, and Rory and Jesse no doubt know by now as well. I'm sure Brock and Bree called them."

"Caroline Rose." Mom sighs. "I guess I need to give her a call."

"Anyway," I continue, "it's some kind of brain cancer. Dave told me what it was, but I can't remember the name of it."

"How bad is it?" Dad asks.

"It's pretty bad. Basically only a one percent survival rate."

For once, both my parents are speechless.

"Isn't it strange, Maureen," Dad says, "how we never imagined anything bad could happen to that family?"

Mom rises and hugs Dad, who's still sitting in his chair. "I love you, Frank."

"I love you, Reenie," he says.

My parents do still love each other after all these years. They certainly don't see eye to eye on everything. Mom, for example, never quite came to terms with Rory's bisexuality, but Dad accepted it with no questions asked.

My father is an amazing man. He's in excellent health despite a heart attack last fall. But he does have one Achilles' heel. His pride.

He wouldn't allow the Steels to help us when our vineyards burned down, and I understood then.

Now, three of his children are engaged to Steels, and he still won't take their money.

I don't know whether to be proud of him or to resent him.

"Anyway," I say, "I don't think the girls are going back to school anytime soon. At least not for another couple of days, so Daddy, if you could take me, I'd appreciate it."

"Of course, Maddie."

Today is Saturday, and I'm supposed to have lunch with Dave. Or at least he said so. I haven't heard from him since.

If he doesn't text me, that's okay. I need to get my stuff packed up and ready to go back to school anyway.

Since I'll be in the dorms, I'm going to need bedding and everything else for my room. I really lucked out getting a single room.

I give Mom and Dad a kiss and go to my room to begin packing.

I get a lot done, start a few loads of laundry, give my room a good cleaning, and by then it's lunchtime.

I look at my phone.

No text from Dave.

Well, that's that.

I lie down on my bed, wanting to cry.

But I don't.

CHAPTER TWENTY-ONE

Dave

I take Gary and head over to Mom and Dad's house in the morning. I want to check on everyone, and I meet them for breakfast.

Dad looks a little better this morning, though he's still not himself by a longshot.

Angie and Sage are still sniffling, but Henry is good. Mom is good.

This is Mom's big brother, and she's taking it better than Dad is.

I can't believe I never saw how strong my mother is, but as I look back, I see it was always there—that gentle strength, so different from Dad's. Mom is the only daughter of Bradford and Daphne Steel, full sibling to Uncle Joe and Uncle Talon.

We know so little about our grandmother, Daphne Steel, but we do know she went through a lot in her life and spent most of her adult life in a world of her own making to escape the pain of her past.

But there's no doubt in my mind that she loved her children, even Uncle Ryan, who biologically wasn't hers. She never knew about Lauren, who grew up with her birth mother, Wendy Madigan.

I'm supposed to have lunch today with Maddie, but I'm

not sure I'm up to it. I feel like getting outside today, and for the first time since I was a kid, I wish I worked with Uncle Joe and Brock on the ranch. I could use a day of hard physical labor.

There's no reason why I can't, though, is there?

I don't want to bother Uncle Joe, given what he's going through.

But I know Brianna and Uncle Talon can use some help in the orchard, and working with trees seems more my speed than working with animals whose fate is to end up on someone's dinner plate.

After breakfast, I take Gary and head back to the guesthouse where I change into work clothes.

I text Brianna quickly.

> *Hey, Bree. You and Uncle T need some help in the orchards today? I feel like I need an outside day.*

The three dots move almost instantaneously.

> *Dad's not working, but yeah, come hang with me. I'm in the orchards today, so great timing.*

* * *

Brianna's dressed in flannel and jeans, her long brown hair pulled back in a braid that hangs nearly to her ass, and she has working cowboy boots on her feet. She's in the orchards, supervising no fewer than fifty ranch hands who are pruning the fruit trees.

"Hey, Dave," she says as I approach. "I'm filling in for one of the foremen today who caught some kind of crud. Feel like pruning?"

"Isn't it early for that?"

"Then I've really fucked up, haven't I?" She laughs. "Early February is a perfect time for pruning in Colorado. As long as the weather is cooperating, of course. Right now, it's easy to see the dead or diseased branches and get rid of them. Then we can shape them correctly to improve air circulation, sunlight penetration, and tree health, which will lead to better fruit production."

I can't help widening my eyes. Here's my cousin, one of the flirty awesome foursome, but damn, she knows her stuff.

She points to a pile of tools. "Grab some pruning shears if you want to try it. But you'll have to put on some gear."

"Are you going to prune?" I ask.

She shakes her head. "Not today. I'm going to do some soil testing. Check for nutrient deficiencies. Then I'm going to start mulching."

"What's that?"

"We apply a layer of organic mulch around the base of the trees to help conserve soil moisture, regulate soil temperature, and suppress weed growth. Mulching also adds organic matter to the soil as it breaks down."

"Need help with that?" I ask.

"Always." She tosses me some leather work gloves. "For later. We'll do the soil testing first."

And we get to it. And with every chore I help Brianna with, the weight of the world seems to pull me down a little less.

Something about manual labor...

Brianna feels it too. I can see it in her face.

She doesn't mention Jesse, and I don't mention Maddie. We don't mention anyone, especially not Uncle Joe or Pat Lamone or anything else related to our family.

Clearly, we don't want to talk. We want to work.

When the sun begins to set in the west, I glance at my watch.

It's nearing five o'clock, and damn...

I was supposed to have lunch with Maddie.

I pull my phone out of my pocket.

There's one text from her.

Only one.

Are we still having lunch today?

It came at about eleven thirty this morning.

And I didn't bother responding. Not on purpose, of course, but I needed to give my mind a rest. I needed to work my body today. I haven't even looked at my phone, and with the sounds around me, I didn't hear it ding.

"Hell," I say.

"What?" Brianna asks.

"I have a text from Maddie. She and I were supposed to have lunch today, and I totally spaced it."

Brianna frowns at me. "Dave, please don't lead her on if you don't intend to pursue a relationship with her."

I look up from my phone, scowling. "Jesus, Bree. How is this any of your business?"

"It's my business because Maddie is my friend and Jesse is her brother. I can't bear to see her get hurt."

"It's not my intention to hurt her or anyone."

Brianna cocks her head, narrowing her eyes at me. "Could you be honest with me about one thing?"

I shrug. "Sure. I guess."

She crosses her arms. "What the hell do you mean you guess? You can or can't. Yes or no, Dave."

"Fine." I sigh. "I'll be honest."

I know what she's going to ask.

"Do you have any feelings for Maddie? Feelings that could evolve?"

I close my eyes, run my hands through my sweaty hair. "This isn't something guys talk about."

She scoffs. "Do I look like I give a damn? She's my friend. And because of our stupid family business, she lost out on her trip to Europe."

"Uncle Joe's disease is not stupid family business."

"I know that, and you know that's not what I'm talking about. I'm talking about Pat Lamone and all this other crap. Wendy Madigan. Doc Sheraton and Brittany. All of it." She shakes her head. "Do you know how hard it was for me to leave Jesse?"

"The family said you didn't have to come home, Bree."

"And you know how much that pisses me off? Acting like Brianna's just the youngest of the bunch so we don't really need her? I hated it." She pounds a fist to her chest. "This is my family too, and I'm just as much a member as any of the rest of you. So yeah, if you and Brock were needed here, then so was I. That doesn't change the fact that I hated leaving Jesse. But I'm here. You're here. And so is Maddie. And I want to know. Do you feel something for her?"

"I don't know."

But the words are a lie, and my cousin wastes no time on

calling me on it.

"That's bull," she says.

"Fine. It's bull." I take a deep breath and let it out. "Yes, I'm having feelings. I've always liked her and have been attracted to her. I wouldn't have... You know... If I didn't." I shake my head. "You know how weird it is to be talking to my female cousin about this?"

She rolls her eyes. "Get over it. We're having this talk whether it's comfortable for you or not."

At this point, I'm too exhausted to fight with her.

Brianna and Uncle Tal do their share of work inside to run the orchard business, but they're also used to working the land. Used to the outdoors. Me? This isn't what I normally do. Sure, I'm in good shape. I keep my muscles up at my home gym, run a few miles every day, but I'm not used to eight hours of hard manual labor.

"Yes," I finally say. "I'm feeling something. After that near brush with death on the plane, I realized that I didn't want to lose her."

She walks up to me and pokes me sharply in my ribs. "Then don't fuck this up, Dave. Maddie's been through a lot. Did you know she's decided to go back to college?"

"Yes." The thought of her not being here sends waves of sadness through me. Of course, she'll only be in Grand Junction. That's not much farther than the trip between our houses. "If she wants to go back to school, of course I support her. This way she'll be able to finish up her last semester."

"Yeah, I think it's a good thing. Angie, Sage, and Gina are home right now, but they'll be going back to school too. Not tomorrow with Maddie, but probably later in the week. Maybe next week."

"Our family business screwed everything up," I say. "But even if it didn't, we'd all be home to support Uncle Joe."

Brianna nods. "I hate that this is happening to him. He's so strong."

"I know." I lean in and lower my voice. "I watched my father cry over him. I don't think I've ever seen my father cry."

"They're very close," Brianna agrees. "And I'm sure there are things we don't even know."

"God, can there be anything else we don't know?"

She bites her lip. "I'm afraid there might be. Things seem to crawl out of the woodwork in our family. But all we can do right now is hope and pray that Uncle Joe can get through this."

"One percent chance, Bree."

She sighs. "I know. But at least it's a chance."

I nod and grab my phone, ready to call Maddie.

CHAPTER TWENTY-TWO

Maddie

My heart jumps when I see Dave's phone call.

Damn it. Why do I have to be so happy to see that it's him? I can't believe he blew me off today.

I'm trying to be understanding. His family is going through turmoil, and that's what I should be focused on. I should do my best to sympathize with what he's going through.

Still, though, an explanation isn't an excuse, and the fact remains that he didn't come through on our lunch plans.

"Hi," I say into the phone.

"Hey, Maddie."

"What do you want, Dave?"

"I'm so sorry..."

"About what?" I ask.

I want to hear him say it. See if he's actually sorry.

"You know what. We were supposed to have lunch, and I forgot."

I pause a moment, trying to formulate a smart-ass comment, but I come up with nothing.

Eventually, I simply say, "Oh."

"I don't really have an excuse, except that I was working with Brianna in the orchards. I felt like I needed a day in the outdoors, you know? A day of hard manual labor. The kind I haven't had since I was a kid. I just sort of fell into it, I guess. I completely lost track of time, and it wasn't until the sun was setting that I even realized how long we'd been at it."

"I see."

"Do you? I can hear from your tone that you're not pleased, and I can't blame you."

I sigh. "Dave, what's going on with your family is just shitty. I wish I could do something about it. I truly do. I hate that you're hurting. I hate that Brianna's hurting. I hate that my sisters and Jesse are hurting because their fiancés are hurting. It all just sucks, Dave, and I'm so sorry. Especially about Joe."

"That's kind of you."

I scoff. "Kind of me? Well, here's some news for you. I'm a kind person, Dave."

"Never said you weren't."

"But that doesn't change the fact that you blew me off. I understand why it happened, but if you want to actually see if something will work out between us, you need to meet me halfway."

He pauses before responding. "You're right, Maddie. There's no excuse. Even with all the bullshit with my family—"

"I know, Dave. And I'll let this one slide given the circumstances." I sigh. "I feel awful that you feel so badly about this. I care a lot about you."

"I care about you too, Maddie."

My instinct is to push him further. Make him tell me exactly how he feels about me. But I'm also afraid I'm not ready for that answer, whichever way it goes.

So I clear my throat. "I'm heading back to campus tomorrow. I talked with my advisor and the registrar, and it's not too late to complete my final semester of college."

"I know. I'm glad it all worked out for you."

"It just seemed like the right thing to do."

"I totally understand. I need to go home and shower, but would you like to have dinner after? I'll take you out somewhere. Make up for screwing up our lunch date."

"Are you sure you're up for it after working hard all day?"

"I wouldn't have offered if I weren't," he says. "I can pick you up in about an hour and a half if that works."

I take a look at my watch. That would be around six thirty. "All right."

"Who's taking you to school tomorrow?"

"My dad."

"Tell him he can save the gas. I'll take you."

"Are you sure?"

"I'm beginning to feel like an echo here. But I wouldn't have offered if I weren't."

There's a hint of his usual joviality in his voice, which makes me smile. "All right. If you'd like to, I think I'd like that."

"Good. I'll see you in an hour and a half at your place."

"Where will we go?"

"Did you want to go somewhere specific?"

"No, I'm just asking so I know what to wear."

"Just wear whatever you want," he says. "You always look beautiful, Maddie."

"Okay." That was no help at all.

"I'll see you soon. Bye."

"Bye." I end the call.

★ ★ ★

I decide on simple black leggings, midcalf boots, and a wine-colored sweater that covers my ass.

I pin my hair up into a messy bun and accent my ears with silver wire earrings.

And that's it. Just a little bit of makeup.

It's a look that will work for everything but the finest restaurant, and I doubt that's where Dave is taking me.

Not at this point, anyway. He would've needed to make reservations earlier, although as a Steel, he could probably get in anywhere at the last minute.

Still, I don't think that's what he has in store for me tonight. My guess is Lorenzo's or something here in town.

I'm still in my room when I hear the doorbell.

I leave my room and walk out toward the house's entrance. My mother is answering the door.

"Hello, David." She's smiling. That's a good sign. "Please come in. I'll get Maddie."

"Thanks, Mrs. Pike."

"Please, it's Maureen."

Yeah, Mom has that *I want all my children to marry a Steel* look on her face.

I hate to tell her that she may be barking up the wrong tree with me.

But you never know.

"I'm here, Mom." I walk toward Dave.

His eyes are wide. "You look great."

I feel a spurt of blood rush to my cheeks. "Thanks. So do you."

He's wearing black jeans, black ostrich cowboy boots, a white button-down, and a gray blazer. No tie.

"What time will you be home tonight, Maddie?" Mom asks.

"I don't know, Mom."

"We won't be late, Maureen," Dave says.

"Great." She gives a wide smile. "You two have a nice time."

We walk out of the house, and Dave opens the passenger side door of his Jaguar.

Once he's seated beside me, I say, "Sorry about that."

"About what?"

"About the curfew interrogation from my mother."

"That's no problem."

Except it is a problem. Or maybe the problem is that Dave said we wouldn't be late. Which means he's not taking me to his place to...

It doesn't matter. I'm leaving for school tomorrow. Maybe I'll meet someone new.

Except I won't. I already know all the guys in my class. All the older guys are gone, and I'm not really interested in checking out the younger guys.

I sigh. "So where are we off to?"

"My place," he says.

I widen my eyes. "I thought we were having dinner?"

"We are. I ordered lasagna from Lorenzo's. It should be there by the time we get back. And I've got a bottle of Dale's finest Italian blend."

"I see." Though I'm not sure why he's dressed for going out.

"Is that okay? Was I being presumptuous?"

"No, it's fine. But you did tell my mom we wouldn't be out late."

He shrugs. "You won't be. I'll make sure you get home by midnight or earlier."

"Okay."

He stops the car then. Right in the middle of our driveway. He turns and looks at me. "Maddie, do you want to spend the night with me?"

"I..."

"Because I'd love to spend the night with you," he says, "but you're leaving tomorrow. I don't want to start something that neither of us can finish."

His words astound me.

I take a deep breath, then sigh. "I guess... I just don't know where you're coming from, Dave. Clearly we're attracted to each other, and we have great chemistry between the sheets. But your family is going through some major upheaval, and I'm about to go back to college. I just don't know where either of our heads are."

"I feel the same way," he says. "I have a lot of feelings for you—feelings I never thought I'd have, at least not until I was older—but I want to make sure that this is the real thing. I don't want it to be something false, a bond that stems only from our shared trauma."

His words have both a positive and a negative effect on me. Because in truth I agree with him. I want feelings that are real, feelings that will stand the test of time. And he's right. We've both been through a lot. But we certainly had chemistry before the plane almost went down.

"I understand."

Though, to tell the truth, a part of me doesn't.

"I'm glad." He starts the car again.

★ ★ ★

The bag containing the takeout from Lorenzo's is sitting on Dave's front stoop when we enter. He grabs it, unlocks his door with the code, and we go in.

I follow him into his kitchen, where he sets everything on the table.

"What can I do to help?" I ask.

"Not a thing. I've got the table set, and the wine is open, decanting."

I look at the table. He even has glasses of ice water sitting there.

He pulls out the takeout, which includes a large pan of lasagna, a loaf of garlic bread, and Italian salad.

"Please, have a seat."

I sit down, and he serves me a plate full of food. Once he serves himself and takes a seat, I wait.

"Go ahead," he says.

I say a silent *thank you* for the food, and then I bring a forkful of salad to my mouth.

Lorenzo's Italian food is wonderful. I don't go to town to eat very often. My family just doesn't have the money for those kinds of things.

"Delicious," I say after swallowing.

"I'm glad you like Italian," he says. "One of my favorites, and Lisa does it like nobody else. Even Aunt Marjorie says Lisa beats her with Italian food."

"Your family's not Italian," I say.

"We're not Greek either," I say, "except for Aunt Ruby on her father's side. But my mom can sure make a Greek feast."

I nod. "Yeah, I remember the food at your aunt and uncle's anniversary party. It was great."

Then I clamp my hand over my mouth.

That party didn't end well either. Ryan Steel was rushed to the hospital on suspicion of a heart attack. Turned out it wasn't a heart attack, but no one really knows what happened. The Steels kept it quiet.

Callie told me it was a panic attack, but I'm sworn to secrecy, so I can't say anything to Dave about it.

That was the beginning of what would turn out to be the big upheaval in the Steel family... And for all the citizens of Snow Creek.

We don't talk a lot while we eat, and once I finish my rather large slice of lasagna, my belly is nice and full.

I drink the wine, which of course is way better than any of the wine my family makes. Ryan and Dale Steel are artists, whereas my father makes wine that's accessible to the masses. Table wines that are good with everything and easy on the pocketbook.

Of course, this season he's made no wine because of the fire.

Ugh.

Just what I don't want to think about.

"You want any more?" Dave asks.

"God no," I say. "I couldn't eat another bite."

"That's a shame, because in the freezer I have some of my mom's vanilla bourbon ice cream made with brown sugar."

I rub my stomach. "It sounds amazing, but I can't."

"Okay. Maybe later."

"Sure."

I suppose now he's going to try to seduce me into his bed. I'm certainly not averse to the idea. Just sitting with him, I'm already hot and horny as hell.

I'm not sure if it's the best thing, since I'm leaving

tomorrow.

But instead of rising, bringing me to my feet, and kissing me senseless, he takes my hand, brushes his lips over the back of it, and then looks me straight in the eye.

"Maddie, we need to talk."

My heart plummets.

Here it is—the classic brush-off. It's never a good thing when a person says those four fatal words.

"All right." I keep my countenance balanced. No way will I let him know how disappointed I am.

He kisses my hand again. "I like you a lot."

"I like you too, Dave."

"And I'd like to continue seeing you. After you go back to school."

My eyes widen in shock. "Oh?"

He cocks his head at my reaction. "Did you think I was going to say something else?"

"I... Well... Yeah. You said the standard break-up line. *We need to talk.*"

He raises an eyebrow. "That's the standard break-up line?"

"Oh, come on, Dave. You were one of the Rake-a-teers. Surely you know how to brush a woman off."

He frowns. "Actually...I don't."

"Come on, you must've brushed off a million of them in your day."

He chuckles at that one. "A million women? You must think I'm much more of a Lothario than I am."

Then I giggle. "Lothario? Really?"

"Hey, it's a word."

"Yeah, if you live in the nineteenth century."

He chuckles, but then his face gets serious again. "To be honest, Maddie, I've never used that phrase before with a woman. I was never serious enough about a woman to even have to make an excuse for brushing her off."

I cock my head. I'm not sure whether to be flattered by his words or pissed off. I choose flattered.

"But it's like we said before," he continues. "I want to make sure that the feelings between us are real and not just the result of everything we've been through."

I nod. "I agree with that."

"So in a way, it's good that you're leaving. Going back to school. It will be more difficult for us to see each other, but we'll be able to see whether what we're feeling is real."

"Sure. I get it."

"Good."

"So next weekend, then, I'd like to come to Grand Junction," he says. "And take you on a real date. Not just dinner but dancing afterward. A big night out."

"I'd like that."

"Good, then." He pulls out his phone and opens the calendar app. "Saturday night. A week from today. It's a date."

"Absolutely."

"So what time do you need me to take you to school tomorrow?"

"Dad and I were planning to leave around two."

He scrolls through his phone. "Yeah, I think I can make that work."

"Is there a problem?"

"No. We have another big family meeting scheduled at Uncle Joe's house. Ten in the morning. But I should be able to pick you up by two to take you."

"You might want to bring your truck," I say. "I've got a lot of stuff. I'm not sure it will all fit in the Jaguar."

He smiles. "The truck it is."

Then he rises finally, brings me to my feet, and pulls me to him for a kiss.

CHAPTER TWENTY-THREE

Dave

My cock has been hard since I picked Maddie up, but I was determined to go slowly, to make sure she knew I didn't want to jump into something that neither of us is prepared to finish.

But I am still David Simpson.

I still love sex.

I still love fucking a beautiful woman.

And Maddie's kisses...

They make me feel so much more than any other kisses.

I was never one for kissing. Always wanted to get into the good stuff, get my cock into a pussy.

Fuck and fuck and fuck some more.

With Maddie, I want to go more slowly.

I want to actually make love.

God, *make love.*

I always hated that phrase. I preferred *fucking*.

But with Maddie? I want to make love to her.

But still... I worry...

Because this is still new to me, so different. Am I actually feeling something? Or is it just the trauma, and I'm looking for something stable in all of it?

And then I wonder... Does it even matter?

Feelings are feelings, and they're all valid. No matter

where they come from, they are still real.

I slide her into my arms, pick her up, and take her to my bedroom.

I lay her gently on the bed.

"I'd like to fuck you now," I say. "I'd like to fuck you, and it won't be pretty. I'll be getting out some aggressions, and I want you to do the same. Use my body, Maddie. Use it for what you need."

"I'm happy to fuck however you want to fuck," she says. "I like a good hard fuck as much as the next person. We've done both, Dave, and I love it all."

"All I could think about as we were sitting and eating dinner was how much I wanted to sink inside you. Sink my cock inside your pussy and lose myself in your beautiful body."

"Then do it." She narrows her gaze, her eyes smoldering. "I won't stop you."

She lifts her burgundy sweater overhead, revealing a black lace bra, her tits lusciously squeezed into it.

"You have the most beautiful set of tits I've ever seen," I say.

And that's saying a lot, though I don't tell her that. I've seen a lot of tits in my life. I like them all. Big, small, medium, perky, saggy. I don't care. If they're tits, I love them.

But Maddie's are in a category all their own.

Just big and perky enough, with brown nipples that harden when I look at them.

"Take off that bra," I grit out. "Let me see those tits."

She slides her hand behind her back and unclasps the bra. It falls to the bed, her tits released.

As I suspected, her nipples are already hard, begging to be sucked.

And yes, I will suck them. But not before I fuck that beautiful pussy.

I remove my jacket, unbutton my shirt. I sit down on the bed and remove my boots and then my jeans and underwear.

My cock is hard and ready, and it springs out, already dripping with pre-come.

"Let me suck your cock," she says.

Damn.

I need to get inside that pussy, but inside that little mouth might be just as good.

"I know you want to fuck me," she continues, "and I want that too. But I haven't sucked your cock enough, Dave, and I want you in my mouth."

She crawls forward on the bed, sits down as I'm still standing, and licks the tip of my cock.

I shudder.

Damn.

Her lips are hot and her mouth warm. And as she slides her lips over my cock, I close my eyes, ready, so ready, to explode inside her mouth.

She pulls back then, sucks on my head, and then slides her lips over my cock.

She adds her fist, getting all the way down to the base and back, base and back, base and back—

I pull away. "You've got to stop, or it will all be over too soon."

She lifts her eyebrows.

"It's a good thing, sweetheart. But I need to get in that pussy. I need to get in and come inside that tight little body of yours. And then I promise you... I'll make love to you all night long. Slow and sweet and however you like it."

"I like it any way you like it," she says. "Any way with you is wonderful."

She leans back on the bed. I pull her legs up and plunge into her pussy.

God, sweet heaven. The suction overtakes me, and again, I'm ready to come. I hold myself in check, force my balls to chill.

And when I think I've got a handle on it, I pull out and push back in.

Only to erupt.

Fuck...

I've never come this quickly, not with any woman.

But with this woman... This woman who offers herself to me so freely. Says I can do whatever I want to her.

I'm lost in her body.

Lost in her as I soar to the sky on my orgasm.

I open my eyes, look down at her tits, so pert and beautiful and lovely.

And I soar higher.

The orgasm flows through me and around me, and its intensity is something new, something almost divine.

When the contractions finally ease, I pull out of her. Then I gaze at her. Take in her beauty. Her red lips slightly parted, her gorgeous tits falling gently to the side, and her nipples, peaked and turgid, ready for my lips.

"You're amazing," I say.

"So are you."

I can't help a sarcastic laugh. "Two thrusts and I come? That's not an amazing lover, Maddie."

"You did what you said you were going to do. And before that, you let me suck your cock when I asked you to. I don't expect anything other than that, Dave."

"You should. You should, because you're worth everything, Maddie. You deserve more than a quick fuck."

She shrugs. "I told you. I like a quick fuck."

I grin. "I hope you like a long slow fuck too, because that's where we're going next."

CHAPTER TWENTY-FOUR

Maddie

I want to tell him that he doesn't have to do this. That I'm happy with the quick fuck I just got. That I don't need an orgasm tonight, and I don't need to suck his cock anymore. That I'm here because I want to be here—not simply for the sex.

But on the other hand, he's offering... So how can I refuse?

"Suck my nipples, Dave. Please."

He moves up my body, hovers on top of me, his cock tickling my clit.

"Your breasts are so beautiful," he says. "I could do nothing but gaze at them and be happy."

"That's nice, Dave, but get your mouth on them. Now."

He doesn't need to be told twice. He clamps his lips around one nipple, and electricity surges through me.

That quick fuck he gave me has me in the mood, and I don't want nice and pretty this time. I want him to cover my whole body with his mouth and bite me. Mark me. As if this is our last time on earth.

Because honestly, I leave for school tomorrow. With everything going on with the Steel family now, with Jonah's illness and everything else, I don't know how much of Dave I'll see.

Sure, he made a big deal about taking me out on a date

next Saturday night, but is that going to happen?

What I need is to find myself. To be Maddie. Not try to emulate the awesome foursome, and not try to snag a Steel just because all my siblings did.

I need to find out who I am.

To accept that my life may not include Dave Simpson.

I have to be okay with that.

But right now? Right now, I want something nasty. Something to remember. I want orgasm after orgasm after orgasm, and it's starting with his lips on every part of me.

I close my eyes, surrender to the moment. I let my body go, let it be my guide, and let it guide Dave as he sucks on my nipple, pinches the other one, making me insane.

He slides his fingers over my body, trailing them over my sensitive abdomen to my clit, where he massages gently... And then not so gently.

He sucks on my nipple.

"Harder," I grit out. "Suck it harder."

He obeys quickly, and in that next moment, he thrusts two fingers inside my pussy.

As his thumb rubs my clit, his lips and teeth work my nipple...

"God, yes!"

The orgasm catapults through me, making my flesh buzz, my skin heat.

It ricochets throughout me, from my pussy outward and then inward, as if my entire body is on fire with a thousand sparklers.

Dave drops my nipple and meets my gaze.

"Look at me, Maddie."

I open my eyes.

His eyes are on fire. "Look at me when you come. Tell me I made you come."

"You made me come."

"I did that. Tell me. Say 'Dave, you made me come.'"

I meet his gaze head on. "Dave, you made me come. Now make me come again." I close my eyes and throw my head back on the pillow.

He grins. "Your wish is my command. I want to suck those nipples. Suck them until they're sore."

"God, please..." I breathe out.

"Then I'm going to eat that pussy, Maddie. I'm going to suck every bit of juice out of you until you're screaming at me to stop."

"Won't happen in this lifetime," I whisper.

"Don't be so sure about that. I can eat pussy for a good long time."

He goes back to my nipples, sucks on the other one, twisting the first one with his fingers.

Then he adds his teeth... God, what perfect teeth. He nibbles on me, bites me, and then nips so hard that I jerk, my hips rising, my back arching.

And it's good. All so fucking good.

He drops the nipple. "You like it a little rough? I didn't know you had it in you, Maddie."

"I can take whatever you can dish out," I say through gritted teeth. "I want it all tonight, Dave. Every single fucking thing."

He groans above me, nibbles on my nipples again, moves to the other one, and gives it a sharp bite.

My God, the currents are sliding through me, like electricity sparking across a tidal wave. Only instead of electrocuting me, it's setting me on fire, flames skittering across my flesh all the way down to my pussy.

Dave Simpson is a god in bed. He can fuck me sweet and gently, and then hard and fast. And he can do what he's doing now—make my body burst into flames with the pleasure and pain he inflicts.

I want to roll over, tell him to spank my ass, but do I want that more than I want him to eat me?

No.

When he's finally done with my nipples, he trails his lips over my chest and abdomen, nipping as he goes. Harsh bites, and some sucks, which I'm sure will leave a trail of hickeys.

And I relish that. Relish being branded by him. This is what I need right now. Knowing it may be the last time we're together.

He spreads my legs, inhales, and then dives into my pussy.

"God, you taste good." He slides his tongue over my opening, up to my clit, and then he puckers his lips around it and sucks gently.

I'm ready to go again, but he puts his fingers back in my pussy, fucks me that way. I've always loved finger fucks. I'm not overly experienced, but the little I do know about my body is that fingers work for me even better than a dick. I love the good burn of a cock, but something about fingers... Fingers that know where to hit the right spot.

And right now, I want those fingers.

I want... I want all of them.

"I want you to fist me," I grit out.

He groans, but it sounds more like a low growl. "God, that's hot. You sure?"

"I wouldn't say it if I wasn't sure." I moan. "I want your

hand inside me, Dave."

"My hands are pretty big, Maddie."

"All the better."

He slides his tongue over my clit again, and then inserts three fingers, stretching me.

He rubs my interior, finding my spongy G-spot within a nanosecond. I feel him scissoring his fingers inside me, curling up against my G-spot, and my God, I'm ready to explode again.

"Don't come yet," he commands. "You tighten up when you come, and that'll take longer, if this is what you really want."

"God, yes. I want everything you have, Dave. Give it all to me."

He works his three fingers inside me as I arch my back, lift my hips to accommodate him.

"I'm going to add the fourth now," he says. "God, you're so fucking hot." He slides in the fourth finger, and yes, it's tight, and God, it's awesome.

I want his whole fucking arm inside me.

I feel myself opening for him, wanting to let him in. Aching to experience something with him that I've never experienced with another.

And I know now that whatever happens between Dave and me, I'll never ask another man to do this to me.

This is for Dave only. I'm sure I'm far from the only woman he's ever fisted, but that's okay. I can live with that.

He'll be the only man who does this to me.

He works me, smooths my pussy muscles as I feel more juices slide out of me.

He hasn't sucked my pussy, and that's okay. We have all the time we need tonight.

"You ready? I'm going to add my thumb."

"I'm ready," I grit out. "God, do I want this."

I gasp when he slides his whole hand inside me.

So different from a dick. It stretches me, stretches me so wide, and once I get used to the fullness...

"My clit, Dave. Suck my clit. I need to come."

He works his fist inside me for a few beautiful seconds, and then he moves his lips to my clit.

With only a few swipes of his tongue, I'm soaring again.

"My God, this is hot," he says. "You're pulsing around my whole hand, Maddie. Damn..."

"God, yes!"

So full. So fucking full, and I'm flying. Flying on this wave of nirvana and pure passion.

I let go, go, go...

"Fuck, I can't wait."

I whimper when Dave removes his hand from my pussy, but in a flash his cock is inside me again, and he's fucking me, fucking me, fucking me...

He releases again after about five thrusts. My orgasm is still going, and we come together.

We come together.

And I know...

Whatever happens...

This is something I'll never forget.

CHAPTER TWENTY-FIVE

Dave

I stay inside her for a few moments, and I'm in awe of how tight she still is even after I had my whole fist inside her.

I move onto my back, wiping the sweat off my forehead with my hand. "My God..."

"That was amazing," she says. "I can't believe how amazing it was."

"You're telling me. You're the first woman who ever let me do that."

She jerks into a sitting position, looking down at me. "Seriously?"

"Yeah."

Her eyes are wide and oh-so beautiful. "I can't believe that. I mean, you're a Rake-a-teer."

I caress her face. "I don't think I am anymore."

She cocks her head. "What do you mean?"

"I meant what I said before. I want us to date."

She doesn't say anything for a moment, and I can't quite read the expression on her face.

Finally, "So you meant that."

"Of course I did. I don't say things I don't mean."

She looks down. "I guess I just thought..."

"Thought what?"

"That...with everything going on with your family and your uncle Joe. With me going back to school... I just figured..."

"That I didn't mean what I said?"

"It's not that. I just figured you were probably letting me down gently."

I sit up then and take her into my arms. "Maddie, I don't say things I don't mean. And if I were going to let you down gently, I would do just that. I would let you down gently."

She presses her lips to my neck. "Are you sure this is what you want?"

I pull away, meet her gaze. "Yeah. We'll see where it goes. I didn't expect to develop feelings for you the way I have. But I can't say I'm upset about it. I would like to see where we go. But I am using caution because of what's going on with my family. I don't want to mistake a desire for escape for something more."

"I understand," she says. "I don't want to do that either." She brings her hand around the pearl pendant I bought her. "Because when I decide to love someone, it's going to be forever, Dave."

Her words take me back just a bit, and she bites on her lip, as if she's rethinking whether she should've said them.

But after the initial shock, I feel the warmth.

And in that moment, I want to be the one she's going to love forever.

I erase the thought from my mind. Donny, Brock, and Brianna fell in love with Pikes quickly. Seems to be the way my family does things.

I have to admit, spending the rest of my life with Maddie Pike certainly doesn't sound like a chore. But I need to make sure it's for real. And I need to figure out my own life as well. I'm not sure if working with my father is what I need in the long term.

"I promised you a pussy licking," I say.

She smiles then, lies back down on the bed. "I know you're not one to break promises."

"No, I am not. Give me just a sec." I get up, walk to my bathroom, wet a washcloth with warm water, and bring it back. I clean her and then toss the cloth to the floor.

"You sure?" I ask. "You may be sore after that."

She grins. "I will never be too sore to have my pussy licked. I want it all tonight, Dave. I may even let you fuck my ass."

I raise my eyebrows. "Now that's something that requires a lot of trust, Maddie."

"Don't tell me you've never done it before."

"Oh, I have."

"And you had trust with all those women?"

"For that act, yes. You can have trust without having love behind it. But I want more with you, Maddie. I want your complete trust. Let's leave that for now. We've both experienced something for the first time tonight."

"How do you know that was my first time being fisted?" she asks innocently.

A brick hits me right in the head. I don't know that. I was just assuming.

"It wasn't?"

She smiles then, and her whole face lights up. "Just joshing with you. Yes, that was the first time."

"I don't know a lot of women who want something like that," I say.

She blushes. "It's always been a fantasy of mine. It was amazing, but it was rough, and it's not something I want to do every time."

"If you ever want to do it again, I'm game." I spread her legs. "Right now I'm going to eat you until you scream."

"God, please..." She arches her back.

I slide my tongue over her glistening pussy. She's still wet, of course, and her juices taste like a tangy strawberry. I go slowly, savoring her, moving from her pussy to her inner thighs, kissing her, sucking her flesh. I'm leaving little marks on her, even though it's not something I've usually done with women. I want to mark Maddie. Mark her as mine.

I slide my tongue gently around her clit, and she lets out a small gasp.

"I want to come again, Dave..."

"You will. But I'm taking my time with you, Maddie. Getting your pussy ready to come again."

"My pussy is ready to come."

"Maybe, but anticipation will make it even better." I slide my lips over her clit. "Besides, with a dessert this delicious, I want to take my time."

And take my time I do. I lick her like I'm licking an ice cream cone, slowly, but just quickly enough that it doesn't melt. I slide my tongue into her pussy, taste the inside of her, and then I slide it over her folds, around her clit, and over her inner thighs once more.

She moans, groans, and then—

Her hands are in my hair, pulling and tugging, forcing my face into her pussy.

"Ready to come, Dave. Please... Don't do this to me any longer!"

I can't resist her pleas. I slide my tongue back and swirl it around her clit, sucking it gently between my lips, increasing the pressure until—

"God, yes!"

Her pussy pulses around me, and I'm getting hard once again.

But I don't fuck her this time. This is for her. This orgasm is all for Maddie.

When she finally lets go of my hair, I slide up her body and kiss her lips, forcing my tongue between her lips into her mouth. She kisses me back eagerly, no doubt tasting herself on me.

We kiss enthusiastically for a few more timeless moments, and then I roll us on our sides.

"I don't want you to leave," I say. "Spend the night with me, Maddie. And then we'll have amazing morning sex."

She opens her eyes and smiles. "I'd love that..."

And I know a *but* is coming.

"But...I told my mom I'd be home."

"You're twenty-two years old."

"I am, but I told her I'd be home, and I'll see you in the morning anyway. This is my last night before I head back to school, and I want to spend it in my own bed."

"I understand, but I'd love to sleep with you snuggled against me."

"I'd like that too. Maybe next time."

"All right. Would you lie with me for a few minutes at least?"

"Of course." She snuggles up to my shoulder and tangles her legs with mine.

And for these few seconds, I experience perfection.

★ ★ ★

For a moment when I wake up the next morning, I forget that Maddie went home. I actually feel the other side of the bed, looking for her beautiful body.

But I took her home last night at her request.

It's early now, and I get out of bed to let Gary out.

I shower quickly, grab some breakfast, and head over to Mom and Dad's house, where we'll all go together to Uncle Joe's for the big meeting at ten.

Once I get there, Henry is in the kitchen. "Hey," I say. "Where are the girls?"

"Still getting ready."

"What do you think this is about?"

"I asked Dad this morning." My brother takes a drink of coffee. "Apparently, Pat Lamone's DNA results are in."

My eyes go wide. "This quickly?"

He nods. "Ruby's guy is quick. That's how we found out that Jack Murphy was related to Brendan and Sean so quickly."

I nod. "Wow."

"Of course, they don't know what the results are. Apparently only Aunt Ruby knows, and they asked her to let us all know today at the meeting."

"This is all kinds of fucked up," I say.

"You're telling me, brother."

Angie walks in then, her dark hair bouncing. "Hey," she says.

Angie's quieter than Sage, but she's usually a little more jubilant than this. Who can blame her, though? All we can think about is Uncle Joe. I don't think any of us really gives a rat's ass about who Pat Lamone's father is and if he's related to us in some other way.

We already know he's a Steel, through Lauren. What does

the rest matter?

Angie grabs a cup of coffee. "Has Sage come down yet?"

"I'm right here." Angie's twin enters. Her eyes are red and swollen.

"Hey, sis." I grab her in a hug. "You doing okay?"

She wipes her eyes. "Every time I think I am, I start to cry again. What are we going to do without Uncle Joe?"

"We'll get along, just like we always have," Henry says. "After all, no one will live forever."

"I know." Sage grabs a cup of coffee.

A moment later, Mom and Dad enter.

Dad is still a mess. His eyes look worse than Sage's. He clears his throat. "Everyone ready?"

"Sure," I say.

Though none of us are ready for any of this.

A tear drops from Sage's eye. "Daddy, why does this even matter? Who cares who that guy's father is?"

"It matters to him," Dad says, "and like it or not, he's one of us now."

"Let's go," Mom says.

CHAPTER TWENTY-SIX

Maddie

Having breakfast with just Mom and Dad seems so strange. Rory and Jesse are in Europe, of course, and the tour is going really well. We all want them concentrating on that and not the problems back here.

Callie, of course, as Donny's fiancée, was invited to the big Steel meeting at ten o'clock today.

I have no idea what it's about. I didn't ask Dave. I don't want to horn in on anything, and I know Callie won't tell me either, unless she's been told it's not confidential.

I'm not a member of the Steel family. My three siblings are, but I'm not.

I have to learn to be okay with that.

"More eggs, Maddie?" Mom asks.

I rise and take my empty plate to the sink. "No thanks, Mom."

"You have everything packed up?" she asks.

"Just a few more things I need to get together. Oh, by the way, Dave asked if he could drive me to school this afternoon at two."

Dad lifts his eyebrows and looks away from his paper. "Oh?"

"Yeah, I kind of told him he could. I hope you don't mind."

"No, of course not." Mom smiles.

She's no doubt hoping to get another Steel-in-law out of this.

Dad cocks his head. "Anything we should know about, Maddie?"

"We're dating," I say, "but I wouldn't expect anything. Dave has made it clear that he's not one to fall in love quickly, even if the rest of his family seems to be."

Mom's shoulders slump.

Yeah, I was expecting that.

"Sounds like he's a sensible young man," Dad says. "I have no doubt that Donny, Brock, and Brianna love your sisters and Jesse, but it did happen awfully fast."

"Apparently that's how it happens in the family," I say. "Except for Dave."

"You just turn on your natural charm," Mom says. "He'll come around."

I resist rolling my eyes. "I like him a lot. I may even love him, but I don't want him to"—air quotes—"*come around* unless he feels the same way."

"How could he not?" Mom asks.

"Mom," I sigh. "You just don't get it, do you? I'm not Callie or Rory or Jesse. There's nothing special about me at all."

My mother doesn't reply at first. She's no doubt trying to think of something to say.

But my dad rises, comes to me, takes both my hands in his, and forces me to meet his gaze. "Madeline, I don't want to hear you say that ever again. You're perfect just the way you are, and you are just as special as your sisters and brother. It's not easy being the youngest, and it's not easy following three siblings who are all amazing. But you're not in their shadow, princess.

You never were. You are *you*. You're beautiful and smart and talented."

I scoff. "I don't have a smidgen of talent."

"Of course you do. Perhaps you just haven't found it yet. You're an excellent writer. I read all your papers from English class."

My dad is trying to be nice, but my papers are simply college papers. Sure, I get straight As. Big deal. I'm an English major. I'm not going to law school like Callie.

"You're going to find your place in life," Dad goes on. "Maybe your siblings found it earlier than you did. Maybe they knew what they wanted earlier."

I close my eyes, rub my temples. "It just all came so easily for them."

Dad laughs then—a great big raucous laugh.

I wrinkle my forehead. "What?"

"Do you hear yourself? Jesse has been trying to make it big for years. He's thirty-two and only now getting his chance. Rory wanted to be an opera singer, but that didn't work out for her. She taught for years until she found her true calling with Jesse and the band."

I shrug. "They went for creative jobs. They knew going in that it was going to be tough. Either of them would have done fine in a more traditional job, like Callie. She always knew what she wanted to be."

Dad frowns. "Callie knew she wanted to be a lawyer from day one, but after college, she couldn't go straight to law school because we just didn't have the money. She's twenty-six and going now."

My jaw drops.

My dad is right. How did I forget all that?

"You're so young," he continues. "Twenty-two years old, Madeline. Your ship will come in. Don't be so eager. Let the good things come to you when you're ready to receive them."

Mom joins us, cups my cheek. "Your father is so much wiser than I am, and he's right. I'm glad you're going back to school, and I'm glad you get to finish your final semester on campus. I know you're bummed that you didn't get to continue the European tour, but things happen for a reason. I believe your father's right."

I look at my feet. "Maybe."

Mom tips my chin back up, and then looks at my dad, beaming at him. "I don't know how you do it, Frank. I don't how you're able to keep such a good outlook after everything we've been through. But I'm glad you are, because I don't know what I would do without you."

Dad gets to his feet and hugs my mom. "You'll never know, Reenie."

I step away from my parents then. This is a moment for them, and I want them to have it.

Because I already got what I need out of this moment.

A different outlook.

And maybe, just maybe, that's all it takes.

CHAPTER TWENTY-SEVEN

Dave

Everyone is sullen and quiet as we're seated around the big conference table at Uncle Joe's house.

Uncle Joe clears his throat. "Thank you all for coming again. First thing I want to say is that I'll start my treatment next week. It will be a combination of chemotherapy and radiation." He forces out a chuckle. "Always wanted to know what I'd look like bald, and now I have the chance."

Aunt Melanie breathes in deeply.

"My doctors say that otherwise I'm in excellent health. If anyone can beat this, I can. Although we know the prognosis is terrible, I'm choosing to look on the bright side. My physicians have also informed me of some experimental treatments, and as you know, money is no object for us, so I may be a good candidate for them."

"We've all got your back, Joe," Uncle Talon says.

Murmurs of ascent drift through the room.

"I don't want any of you worried about me. We've got some great things going on in our family." He scans the table, stopping for a moment on each of his children, nieces, and nephews. "We've got four weddings to look forward to. Brianna, Brock, Donny, Ava, you've all found wonderful partners to live the rest of your life with. I plan to be around for all of those weddings and for a grandchild or two, so stop the weeping. I want to be surrounded by love and happiness. That will help me more than anything."

Aunt Melanie grabs his hand, smiling. "I love you so much, Jonah."

Uncle Joe squeezes her hand and kisses it. "And I love you too, baby. We're going to get through this."

Aunt Melanie nods.

"I'm going to turn it over to Ruby, who I believe has the DNA results for Pat."

"Honestly, I haven't even looked at them yet." Ruby holds up a manila envelope. "Tucker delivered them to me late last night. "

"Please don't keep us in suspense," Lauren says. "I'd like to know who fathered my son."

Pat sits next to her. His face is pale, his lips trembling. He raises his hand. "Can I just say something?"

"Sure," Uncle Joe says.

Pat swallows. "I know I haven't been the best person in life. I'm truly sorry for what I put you through, Diana, and you too, Callie, as well as Rory."

I look at Brock. His jaw is clenched.

"I wouldn't blame you if none of you wanted to speak to me again," he says, "but I appreciate that you've opened your family to me. I will do what I can to make up for my past transgressions."

"We know you will, son," Uncle Joe says.

Son? He really just said *son*?

But then I look at Uncle Joe and realize what's happening. He's looking at his own life, considering it may be over sooner than he anticipated.

He's not here to hate anyone. He's here to extend love.

And perhaps the rest of us should do the same.

"I don't know you very well," I say to Pat, "but I want to be the first to welcome you to the Steel family. Your past may be spotted, and you may have hurt members of the family, but I believe in second chances."

I look around then, waiting for someone to offer agreement.

Brianna speaks. "I agree with Dave. We should give him a second chance. He's our cousin."

Brock takes a deep breath and then mumbles, keeping his gaze fixed on the table. "I saw a little bit of a different side of you when you were caring for your grandmother in the hospital. As much as I hate what you did to Diana, Callie, and Rory, I've been looking at things differently lately. At least, I've been trying to." He sighs. "I'll try harder."

More murmurs of agreement.

Pat swallows. "This means a lot to me. I know we may never find out why my parents changed their names and mine, or why they and my little sister died, but I'm glad to know I have another chance in life and a new family."

Lauren squeezes his hand.

"I'll get back to it, then." Aunt Ruby slides her thumb under the envelope and pulls out papers. "We took samples from Bryce, Talon, and me to see if Pat shares DNA with any of us." She scans the paper, and her eyes widen. Then she looks at Pat. "Seems you and I are half brother and sister, Pat."

Jaws drop.

"So Theodore Matthias is the father?" Uncle Joe says.

"Apparently," Ruby says.

Lauren closes her eyes. "So it was one of those three,

which means..."

"Which means it is clear that our esteemed mother orchestrated it." Ryan clenches his teeth. "My God, I'm glad she's finally dead."

"Me too," Lauren agrees.

Uncle Ryan tents his fingers in front of his pale face. "All this time, I had a sister. I wish you had been able to grow up with us, Laur. None of this would've happened to you."

Uncle Talon shakes his head. "We sure as hell don't know that, Ry."

Lauren shakes her head. "Please. I don't want a bunch of people feeling sorry for me. I healed from that trauma long ago. Everything that happened brought me here, to this family. For that I'm truly grateful. And I'm grateful for both of my sons." She turns to Pat. "Pat, I'm sorry I couldn't keep you. It was too traumatic at the time. But you're here now, and I have a second chance to be a mother to you. I hope you'll let me."

Pat gives a weak smile. "Thank you for that. I was alone in the world for a while, and I got involved with some bad people. I'm not using that as an excuse. I own the bad things I did. And I don't know that I can ever make up for them, but I will try. That I promise you."

Uncle Ryan nods but then glances at Aunt Ruby. "Baby? Are you okay?"

Aunt Ruby's lips are turned down into a frown. Is she upset that Pat is her brother? Can't say I blame her, but—

"I'm fine," she says, breathing in deeply. "It's just... This will sound ridiculous, but I have such feelings of ambivalence about my father. He was a despicable human being, but I thought he was trying to change at the end. He saved my life that day. And now... Now I see he was never really any different at all." She turns to Lauren. "I know it helps you and Pat to know, but I'm so sorry."

"You know I don't blame you for your father's actions, Ruby," Aunt Lauren says.

"Of course I know that. It's just... I was hoping there was some good in him."

"He saved your life, baby," Uncle Ryan says. "He didn't have to do that, but he did. It's okay to feel what you're feeling."

Aunt Ruby simply nods.

Brock frowns. "So let me get this straight. Theodore Matthias, Ruby's father, is also Pat's father."

Aunt Ruby nods, sniffling. "Yes."

"So you and Pat are half-siblings," Brock continues, "and Pat is the grandson of Brad Steel."

"That's the way it works," Aunt Ruby says.

"Is our family the most fucked-up family ever or what?" Brock then says.

That gets a laugh out of everyone. A laugh we all need.

"Son," Uncle Joe says, "when you're right you're right."

Pat is quiet as the rest of us talk among ourselves. Then he raises a hand again, as if he's in a classroom.

Uncle Joe nods to him.

"Do you think my grandmother, Wendy Madigan, knew who my father was?"

Uncle Ryan fields that one. "Most likely. She knew everything and didn't bother to tell us. Plus, she died before we were able to get all the information out of her. She probably knew what happened to your parents, Pat. Why they changed their names."

Pat looks to the floor. "When my parents had their own child, the one that was their own flesh and blood, I kind of became an afterthought."

Lauren pats his arm.

"It's no excuse for how I lived my life, though," Pat says. "No excuse for pulling the stunts I did back in high school, and no excuse for helping Brittany Sheraton pull the stunts she pulled. I honestly didn't know she was so mentally and emotionally compromised."

"None of us did," Uncle Ryan says. "But we do now. She's getting the help she needs. As far as we know anyway. As far as her father goes, I believe at heart he's a good man. He was angry at us for not bringing him in full-time on the Steel payroll as one of our veterinarians. But I honestly don't think he would've been helping Wendy if he'd known what he was actually doing. For all he knew, he was working for the Fleming Corporation."

Ava shakes her head. "The whole thing makes my skin crawl. All those liens, and I was the beneficiary. I don't want her dirty money. Gina, Jack, Pat—divide it among yourselves."

"No, Ava," Uncle Ryan says. "You take your share. Your grandmother put you through hell, and you deserve something for the trauma you suffered."

"But I don't want it, Daddy."

"Then give it away, sweetheart. Choose a charity."

Gina speaks up then. "I don't want mine either."

"Neither do I," Jack says.

Even Pat agrees. "If I'm going to turn over a new leaf, I can't take her dirty money either. Ava, since she left it to you, why don't you choose a charity?"

"I think that's a great idea, sweetheart," Uncle Ryan says.

Ava finally nods. "All right. I'll do that, but I'll make the donation in all four of our names, not just mine."

Uncle Ryan nods. "Good for you, sweetheart, and you

too, Gina, Jack, Pat. You'll be well taken care of for the next several lifetimes without any help from my mother." He shakes his head. "My damned mother. I suppose, Lauren, we should at least be happy that she's now acknowledged you as her child. The quitclaim deed we found underneath Brendan's floorboard listed me as the sole beneficiary of all the Steel properties."

"She was something else," Lauren says dryly.

"I wish Dad had gotten to know you," Ryan says. "I honestly don't think he knew he had another child."

"No, he didn't," Lauren agrees. "I was always told that my father was Brad Steel's half brother."

"And I was the only one who knew about the half brother," Uncle Joe chimes in. "And now we come to find out he probably never existed in the first place."

"Was there anything that my mother couldn't pull off?" Lauren shakes her head. "How did one person become so powerful?"

"Through intelligence—genius-level intelligence—and shrewdness, money, and investigative knowledge," Uncle Ryan says.

"That's right," Uncle Talon says. "It's so easy to forget, given everything else, but she was a damned good investigative reporter in her day."

"True," Uncle Joe agrees. "She was the one, Tal, who covered your heroics when you came back from your military tour."

Uncle Talon nods. "She's the one Jade and I went to for answers before we knew who she truly was. Sometimes I wish we could go back to those days, but then I realize we needed to know everything." He frowns. "Though it irks me that some of the secrets still died with her."

Through all of this, I'm listening with one ear.

They continue speaking, but I stop listening. We know all we're going to know, because Wendy Madigan is dead. Now what we need to do is get the Steel holdings back into their proper hands. The deed that was recorded covers only real property, and the Steels own much more than that. I should know, as I've been Dad's right-hand man since I got out of college.

And it hits me then.

What I've been looking for.

I don't want to work with Dad anymore. I'm tired of the grind. I majored in business to please him, but working outside with Bree for a day made me realize I want to be working on the ranch. Helping *that* side of the business.

How will I tell him, though? He's about to lose his best friend and brother-in-law. I can't put any more on his plate.

I erase that thought only to think of Maddie and how much I'm going to miss her.

I wish she weren't leaving, but I understand why she has to. She needs to find herself.

I won't tell Dad today that I want to change my focus. He'll need me as we work with our attorneys getting all the property in order. But afterward...

As these thoughts are running through my head, Uncle Joe finally stands. "I think we can adjourn for now. Bryce and Dave will be working on the paperwork with our attorneys this coming week, and I... Well, I'll be in Grand Junction, starting my treatment."

"And I'll be with you," Uncle Talon says.

Uncle Joe shakes his head. "Tal, Melanie will be with me.

You don't have to be there."

Uncle Talon places a hand on Joe's shoulder. "You're my big brother, Joe. I'm going to be there."

Uncle Joe looks at Uncle Talon, sadness and guilt in his eyes.

I've talked to Brock about it. Uncle Joe still feels some guilt from all those years ago for not being able to help protect Uncle Talon.

"Please, Tal," he says. "This is something I need to do alone. Just my wife at my side." Then he looks at Bradley and Brock. "And I don't want you two there either. I can't bear for you to see me that way."

"Dad..." Brock begins.

"Do me this favor," Joe says. "Please."

Those are the last words spoken at the meeting. We all rise and get on our way.

CHAPTER TWENTY-EIGHT

Maddie

I'm ready by the time Dave comes by with his truck at two o'clock. I've already said my goodbyes to Mom and Dad, but Dad comes out and helps Dave load the truck. They shake hands afterward.

"What was that about?" I ask when Dave gets in beside me.

"What? Shaking your dad's hand?"

"Yeah."

"It's kind of what guys do, Maddie."

"I know that." I twirl my hair around my finger. "I just mean it seemed kind of strange."

He shrugs. "I'm not sure what's strange about it."

He's quiet then.

"How did your meeting go?" I finally ask.

"It was eye-opening. Seems Pat Lamone is not only my cousin, he's also Aunt Ruby's half brother."

"What?"

He takes a deep breath in and holds it for a few seconds before letting it out. "I don't know how much you know about my family. A lot of it is public at this point. The stuff about the liens on the property, the fact that Wendy Madigan controlled them. But there's so much more to our family, Maddie."

"I'm sure my siblings all know."

He shakes his head. "I'm not sure Jesse does. He and Brianna haven't been together long enough for her to tell him the whole story. But Callie and Rory probably do." He presses his lips together. "It's not pretty, Maddie. Please don't make me talk about it now."

I nod. I feel like I'm being pulled in two different directions with him. On the one hand, I want to respect his wishes. Let him keep it inside. But on the other hand, I want him to talk to me. Lean on me.

We don't talk much more during the half hour that it takes to get to Grand Junction. We drive past the sorority house where I was supposed to be living. I lived there the first semester, but since I said I wasn't coming back, they gave away my room. So I'll be living in the dorms, but I'll still be a member of the sorority and be able to take part in their events.

I clear my throat. "Dave?"

"Yeah?"

"Next month is the Valentine's Day dance at the sorority. I was wondering if you might be my date."

He nods slowly. "Sure, Maddie. If we're still doing this by then."

My heart sinks again.

Didn't he tell me only days ago that he could fall in love with me?

"What do you mean if we're still *doing this*?" I ask.

Then he stops. Right in the middle of the road on the way to the dorm.

He turns and looks at me.

Is he waiting for me to speak?

Finally, he says, "I don't know what to think anymore."

I jerk backward, my heart nearly stopping. "What the hell are you talking about, Dave?"

He rubs his forehead. "It's ridiculous, really. I'm trying to deny what I know I'm feeling for you. I don't want to be the Steel that falls in love quickly. But, damn it, Maddie. You're all I think about. I'm tearing my hair out over this."

I sigh in relief. "I don't think that has to be a bad thing."

He runs his hand through his hair. "It's all so fucked up. Everything with my family, and I just wanted a goddamned vacation."

I grab his hand. "And you did have one. It wasn't very long, but you got to take in some good sights." I take the necklace out from under the sweater I'm wearing. "And you got me this beautiful souvenir, something I'll cherish forever."

"And it led me to you," he says.

I feel blood rushing to my cheeks. "That too. We've had a good time since we got back, your uncle's news notwithstanding. And who knows? Maybe we can go back to Europe again sometime soon. Make a real trip out of it."

"Maybe on a honeymoon?" he asks.

My jaw drops.

"God, I can't believe I blurted that out."

I rub at my temples, tamping down the joy his words ignite in me. "Dave, I'm getting some really mixed signals here. First you tell me we may not still be together on Valentine's Day, and now you're—"

He grabs me and crushes our mouths together.

We can't get too close because we're both wearing our seatbelts, but his kiss is ferocious, all lips, teeth, and gums. And I love it. I love every minute of it.

But finally I pull back.

"I'm sorry," he says.

"No, don't be sorry. It's just my seatbelt was digging into me."

He smiles. "It's stupid, Maddie. We hardly know each other."

I stop myself from rolling my eyes. "You didn't say you love me, Dave. You just intimated that we might have a honeymoon. You didn't even say we would be together."

"I know. I'm not sure how it even came out of my mouth." He blinks for a few seconds, staring at the open road through our windshield. "But... I can't deny it, Maddie. I love you. You're all I've thought about since that first night in Glasgow."

Oh my God. He said it.

It was buried under a lot of word salad, but he said it.

How do I respond?

"I think I was rejecting the whole idea. Thinking that I would be the one Rake-a-teer who would always be a womanizer. Who never wanted to settle down. Hell, I'm only twenty-four."

I swallow. He just keeps talking. Doesn't give me a chance to say it back to him.

Do I want to say it back to him?

Maybe I misheard him. What did he just say?

Something about only being twenty-four.

"So is Brock," I say.

"Don't I know it. He's going to have a field day with this."

He slowly turns his head to face me, his eyebrows raised. "What?" I ask.

"You didn't say it back, Maddie. How exactly do you feel about me?"

I think I want to say it back. Actually, the more I think

about it, the more sure I am that I want to. Truly I do.

But something stops me.

I don't want to throw myself at Dave just because all my siblings fell for Steels, and now I have the chance to have one myself. I want to make sure that my feelings are real, and I won't know that until we've been apart for a little while.

"I like you a lot, Dave," I say, "and yeah, I could easily fall in love with you."

He stares at the steering wheel. "But you don't *love* me."

I place a hand on his arm. "I didn't say that. I've never been in love before. I feel the same way you do about it. I'm not exactly sure who I am yet or what I want to do with my life. I want to make sure I don't get caught up in the romanticism of it all. Caught up in the envy I have for my siblings because they all snagged Steels."

"Yeah, but none of your siblings snagged *me*." He waggles his eyebrows.

Indeed, David Simpson is the best-looking Steel if you're looking for classically handsome.

And I am.

I lean in and kiss his cheek. "Let's just get me to school. Then you'll kiss me goodbye, and we'll see each other next weekend. We have a date. I think I may be ready to say it then."

"You say it whenever you're ready, Maddie. I won't rush you."

He starts the truck then, and we drive to my dorm room. Luckily, the vacant single is on the first floor, so we don't have to drag things upstairs or into an elevator.

The room is sparse and very small, but it has all the necessities. A bed, a dresser, a closet, and a desk. The walls of course are white cement blocks, and I don't have my own bathroom. I'll have to use the one down the hallway. But at least the floors aren't coed in this building, so I won't have to worry about running into a guy in a towel.

I voice this to Dave, and he says, "Damn right you won't. If you had guys on your floor, I'd have something to say about that."

I shake my head, but I can't help a small smile. I am both slightly annoyed and slightly touched by his sentiment.

He helps me get moved in and stays while I put the linens on my bed and get my clothes in the closet and in the dresser.

"I have to go to the bookstore," I say. "I start classes tomorrow, and I have to pick up my books."

"Why didn't you just order them online?"

"Because I decided to do this like three days ago. I'll pick them up at the bookstore. You want to come along?"

He kisses my lips slightly. "I think I'm going to let you get settled in. I'll go home. I'm needed there. Dad and I have a lot to do right now. But I'll see you Saturday. I'll text you with the details." He kisses me once again and then trails his finger over my cheek. "I do love you, Maddie Pike."

Then, without waiting for me to reply, he turns and leaves.

* * *

My alarm goes off at six thirty the next morning.

The numbnuts that I am, I signed up for an eight o'clock class. I have only one more general requirement that I need to get my degree, and this was the only time that I could get my science requirement and still fit in all the other classes I wanted.

So I'm off to biology, something I'm not even remotely

interested in, at eight o'clock in the freaking morning.

After biology, I have poetry and then Spanish.

That's all for today.

Tomorrow, I have another English course—creative writing—and then watercolor.

I already have my fine arts requirements on my transcript, but I've always wanted to try watercolor.

I don't expect to be any good at it, but who cares? It's time to try new things and figure out what I was put on this earth to do.

I am only twenty-two, so if I don't know what to do with my life, it's not the worst thing in the world. Just because my siblings all knew doesn't mean I have to know. Rory didn't even get it right the first time.

Biology class is finally done, but then I have to go to a lab before poetry class to make up what I missed the first few weeks of classes.

I walk in, and the only other student in the lab is a tall man with brown hair and light-green eyes. He looks up at me and smiles. "You must be Madeline Pike."

"Guilty," I say. "Call me Maddie. And you are?"

"I'm Dr. Carmen's lab assistant, Grayson George." He holds out his hand. "I'm here to get you up to speed."

"That's kind of you, but you don't have to. I'm perfectly capable of doing the work on my own."

"Dr. Carmen asked me to do it"—he eyes me up and down—"I'm pretty glad she did."

My cheeks warm. And I find myself...

Feeling...good. I'm pretty sure I love Dave, but it's nice to have some male attention. Grayson must be a senior like I am, but I've never seen him before. Of course, I don't hang around with the science geeks much.

"Am I the only one who saved her science requirement for the last semester?" I ask.

He chuckles. "You'd be amazed how often it happens. Some people seem to be afraid of the sciences, but they're nothing to fear. I find them incredibly interesting."

"You'd get along well with my friend," I say. "She's going to med school."

"Who's your friend?"

"Angie Simpson."

"Oh yeah, I know Angie. She's Sage's sister. One of the"— air quotes—"Steels."

I have to laugh. "Yeah, I live on the ranch adjacent to them. Of course, it's tiny compared to theirs."

"Since they own almost the entire state of Colorado, I would imagine yours is tiny." He laughs. "Let me show you what we need to do."

We go through the labs quickly, and his hands brush against mine more often than they should.

When we're finally done, I've missed my poetry class.

I double-check the time on my phone. "Oh my God, I didn't even realize the time."

"See? Science is fun."

"I missed my poetry class, and I've already missed a couple of weeks."

He smiles timidly, a small patch of pink on his cheeks. "Must be the company."

I return his smile. "I *will* say that you made biology not so bad."

He raises an eyebrow. "Just not so bad?"

"That's about all I can muster up," I say. "Since I missed

poetry, I'm going to head to lunch."

"Would you like some company?"

"I was just going to the cafeteria. I have a meal plan with my scholarship."

"So do I. I take all three meals there. It's not gourmet, but it's paid for." He winks at me. "Come."

CHAPTER TWENTY-NINE

Dave

I'm sitting with my father the next morning. Uncle Ryan and Aunt Lauren are also here, as their signatures are needed on the transferring documents. The attorneys have drawn everything up for the real property to be split equally among all of Bradford Steel's grandchildren with life estates for the older Steels, but there's other property to take into consideration as well. We have investments in everything—from precious metals to foreign currency to Fortune 500 companies to real estate all over the world.

Steel Acres Ranch is but one portion of our portfolio. The ranch and the vineyards are subsidiaries of Steel Enterprises, which is itself a wholly owned subsidiary of Steel Holdings, all of which falls under our umbrella corporation of Steel Companies, Inc.

My cousin Donny, when he first learned of our family's past, asked me how our family became billionaires by raising beef, apples, and peaches.

My answer was, of course, that we didn't.

The ranch is our life. It's what we all enjoy doing, but it's only a minute portion of our portfolio.

Still, when he asked me, my own curiosity was piqued. Just where did all this money come from? So I delved into some research. It was our grandfather, Bradford Steel, who took his father's already very successful ranch and made it into what it is today. He made enough money that he could increase his holdings by diversifying his investments.

But it was also Bradford Steel who brought Wendy Madigan into our lives, who made her own fortune by illegal means.

So part of me has always wondered... Is our money dirty?

Even if it was once, I'm sure Bradford Steel laundered it and laundered it until it was squeaky clean. I did some preliminary research, and I found no evidence of dirty money.

But still I wonder. So today, I'm going to ask my father.

Once we break for lunch, and the attorneys, Aunt Lauren, and Uncle Ryan go on their way, it's time.

"Dad?"

"Yeah, son?"

"Where does the Steel money come from?"

He cocks his head. "You know very well where it comes from. You've seen our financials."

I nod. "Right. But how did my grandfather build a ranch into such a thriving enterprise?"

"That started before your grandfather. Your great-grandfather, George Steel, who none of us ever met, took his father's ranch to the next level by doing things like investing in land that had rich access to water, which was crucial in the desert state of Colorado. He built solid infrastructure and made the decision to concentrate on beef ranching where his father had also added sheep and goats. The sheep and goats weren't profitable, so he stuck with beef based on the suitability of the land. His abundance of land and water allowed him to let the stock graze so they were grass-fed while most commercial producers offer grain-fed products."

"I know all that, Dad."

"It's all part of the story, Bryce." Dad continues, "George had beef ranching down to a science, and when your grandpa took over, he had even bigger dreams. He inherited everything, being an only child, and he knew the business because he'd worked alongside his father since he could walk. With all the abundant grasses, the first thing he did was capitalize on what was left after the stock was adequately fed."

"Hay," I say.

"Yeah. You could say this business was built on hay."

I can't help a laugh. "I guess it's better than being built on straw."

"The next thing he did was invest in the best technology to get things working with the best efficiency possible. Then, when the hay crop was a success, he planted the orchards."

"But they took a long time to grow, right?"

"Not according to Uncle Joe. He planted trees that had just hit maturity. It cost more, but he knew if he could get them producing, they'd pay for themselves, which they did."

I nod.

"What really took him over the top, though, was when word got out about the quality of the beef. Orders began coming in from all over the country, and he had to expand to meet the demand. That demand led to huge profits, and he began making outside investments. This was around the time Uncle Joe and I became friends. We were three years old. Your grandmother says we were friends before that, but I have no memories. But both your grandpas were friends"—Dad grits his teeth—"so I guess it was natural that we were thrown together. Anyway, Brad was a natural marketer, and soon the Steel brand was well known in national and international circles. At that point, he diversified into various stocks and bonds, precious metals, and the like. And then he invested in other areas of business. Hedge funds, art." Dad sighs. "You name it, and Brad Steel had his hand in it. He was a genius when it came to making money."

"Dad..."

"Yeah?"

I take a deep breath. "I worry about what went on here. On our land. With Wendy. Did any of her money get mingled with ours?"

Dad pauses, strokes his chin. "I've asked myself that same question many a time, Bryce. I understand your concern, and Uncle Joe and I share it. We've known for a while that Brad funded the Future Lawmakers Club, of which he and my father were members. They got into drugs and other illegal stuff before they got into human trafficking. Brad swore up and down he was out of the business by the time anything illegal was happening."

"And you believed him?"

Dad scoffs. "Hell, no. But Uncle Joe and I have been through these financials from as far back as we have records, and we've seen only clean money."

"So you trust my grandfather? Mom's dad?"

He swallows. "No. I don't trust him, Dave."

"But—"

"That's not to say that he didn't build this business ethically. The money isn't dirty, legally, but it wasn't necessarily won in the most wholesome of ways either. All we know is that your grandfather had no qualms about skating on ethics. Same with his father. There's a lot we don't know that died with them. A lot we can only surmise, but Uncle Joe and I have our suspicions that your grandfather got what he wanted in, shall we say, unethical ways."

"Like pointing a gun to people's heads?" I ask.

He says nothing.

He doesn't have to.

I already know Uncle Joe did that himself with Doc Sheraton and Brittany. Brock was there, and he told me.

But Uncle Joe didn't do it to fund his business. He did it to find out what kind of illegal activity was happening on his property.

"There are things about Brad Steel we'll never know," Dad finally says. "Things only he knew. Things that are only in *his* story. But Uncle Joe and I and our attorneys feel comfortable that our current fortune is clean and was obtained legally."

I scratch the side of my head. "It just seems like such a big feat, to go from a successful ranching business to having billions."

"It does. But both your great-grandfather and your grandfather were savvy businessmen as well. Yes, they cut a few ethical corners here and there, but they got things done. And in the end, the money was clean."

"But Wendy Madigan..."

His face darkens. "Wendy Madigan is another story. Nothing she did was clean. And unfortunately, her blood runs through some of the people of our family."

"And your father..."

"Yes, my father. Say what you want about Brad Steel, but he was a virtuous man compared to my father, Aunt Ruby's father, and your grandmother's brother."

"Do you ever worry about the genes that we come from?"

Dad shakes his head. "Not anymore, but all I *did* was worry about it for a while. My father was a complete psychopath, and your grandmother on your mother's side lived most of her life in a world of her own creation due to her mental illness. But you and the girls and Henry are all bright and healthy and intelligent. So are all your cousins. I'd say we escaped that fate, and I thank God for it."

"Thanks for explaining it all to me, Dad."

He raises an eyebrow. "Is there a reason you want to know all of it?"

"I've been curious for some time, but yes, there's a reason."

"Would you like to tell me what it is?"

I cross my arms. "Not just yet. But I will."

He smiles. "I'm always here for you, Dave."

I give him a hug. "I know, Dad."

I leave then, wondering how I'm going to break it to him that I want to work with Uncle Talon in the orchard...instead of at his side.

CHAPTER THIRTY

Maddie

Lunch with Grayson was fun and easy, so when he asked me to have dinner with him, I figured, what could it hurt?

But when he kissed me on the cheek and said, "Great, I'll pick you up at seven, and we'll go into the city," I wondered if I should have declined.

But I'm going, so we'll see how it goes.

He's very handsome, and he's smart. Of course, I've known him for all of five hours.

I have no idea where he's taking me in the city. It could be something as simple as fast food or something as elegant as the Fortnight.

No, it won't be the Fortnight. Grayson doesn't scream money to me. He's obviously working as a lab assistant, and he mentioned he was on scholarship as well.

Definitely no Fortnight in the cards for me.

Maybe Dave will take me there Saturday night.

I choose a pair of plain black jeans and a long-sleeved shirt that's clingy and shows off my breasts.

For shoes, I opt for black suede booties—my best pair. They saw a lot of Europe—well, not a lot. But they saw London, Edinburgh, Glasgow, and one day of Paris.

The tour is going very well. Jesse and Rory keep me

updated, and I'm so happy for them.

And I so wish I were still there.

I wish Dave were there too... And I wish I weren't going on this date.

But I am. Dave and I have been together for such a short time, there's nothing wrong with me seeing another guy.

Part of me feels like I'm cheating on him, though.

But I'll get over it.

I'm checking my makeup and hair when someone knocks on the door.

I look through the peephole, and there stands Grayson. He looks good. He's slicked his hair back with some glossy product, and he's wearing a red bowtie over a patterned button-down, all under a sleek gray cardigan.

The exact opposite of anything Dave Simpson would ever wear, but the look works for Grayson. Kind of nerdy sexy.

I open the door. "Right on time."

"I'm nothing if not punctual." He looks me over. "You look great. Are you ready?"

I grab my purse. "Ready."

I don't have a car, but he must, or he wouldn't have suggested we go to the city.

We walk toward a Honda Civic, and then I realize someone else is in the driver's seat.

"I hope you don't mind Uber," he says. "I never drink and drive."

He's smart, and he thought ahead. That's good.

He also wants to drink. Which means he may get flirtier later.

Guess I'll play this by ear.

"I don't mind at all." I slide into the back seat, and he

slides next to me. "Hi," I say to the driver.

He nods to me.

"I'm not a big drinker," Grayson says, "but to be honest, I don't have any wheels at the moment."

"Neither do I," I say. Seems I have a lot more in common with Grayson than I do with Dave.

The thought makes me kind of sad.

"You like Italian?" Grayson asks.

"Love it."

Although it makes me think of my last meal with Dave— takeout from Lorenzo's.

Not to mention the amazing lovemaking we did after the meal. I subconsciously curl my fingers into a loose fist.

"I know an amazing place. It's called Alfredo's. And it's not far."

I smile and nod. "Oh yeah, I've been there many times."

Many times with the awesome foursome and some of my other sorority sisters. Only if I can find a ride, of course. Angie, Sage, and Gina all have their own cars, but they still haven't returned to campus. Not that I'd want them knowing I'm on a date with a non-Steel anyway. Dave wouldn't be pleased if word about this outing got back to him.

Fifteen minutes later, we arrive and head inside. The place is kind of a dive, but the food is great. Red-checkered tablecloths and wine bottles in a basket with a taper candle adorn each table.

The hostess shows us to our table, and Grayson pulls out a chair for me.

A gentleman.

But Dave Simpson is also a gentleman. All the Steel men are.

"Can I bring you anything to drink?" our server asks.

I jerk my head upward. "Oh, hi Rosalie."

She smiles. "Hey, Maddie. I didn't even realize it was you. We're so busy tonight."

I gesture across the table. "Rosalie, this is Grayson George. Grayson, this is Rosalie Fortnight. She was a sorority sister of mine until she graduated last year."

"Fortnight?" he asks. "As in *the* Fortnight?"

Rosalie laughs. "You think I'd be working here if that were the case?"

Grayson returns her laugh.

"I'm working here while I go to grad school," Rosalie continues. "Sorry to be so abrupt before. What can I get you to drink?"

"I think I'll start with some water," I say.

"I'll have a glass of the house Chianti," Grayson says. Then he looks at me. "You think you'll want one with dinner?"

"Yeah, that sounds good actually."

"Bring a carafe then," he says.

"Awesome." Rosalie makes some notes on a device. "I'll be by with a breadbasket and some olive oil and balsamic."

Once Rosalie leaves, Grayson leans forward, eyeing me playfully. "So you're a sorority girl."

"I am. I was supposed to live in the house. I lived there last semester. But as you know, I got a late start to the semester."

He nods. "Yeah, why is that anyway?"

I bite my lip. "It's a long boring story."

"Boring?" He looks me up and down, smiling shyly. "I can't imagine anything about you is boring."

"I was in the UK, and in Paris."

His eyes widen. "That's hardly a boring story."

"I was with one of my sorority sisters. Brianna Steel. She graduated early."

His eyebrows fly up. "Another one of *the* Steels?"

"Yeah. She's engaged to my brother. He's a... Gosh, it feels even weird to say this now. He's kind of a rock star."

"Now I know there's a story there."

"Yeah, my older brother and sister are singers, and they have this rock band called Dragonlock."

He strokes his chin. "Oh my God, I've heard them. They're great. They played a bar here earlier last year."

"Oh yeah, they play at all the local bars."

"I don't remember there being a female singer."

"My sister only joined the band recently. Anyway, they happened to be in this one bar in Utah, and you won't even believe who was there."

"Who?"

"Jett Draconis and Zane Michaels."

He gasps. "Of Emerald Phoenix? No way."

"Yeah, and they totally loved the band. Their opener for the European tour had dropped out, and they invited Dragonlock to go on tour with them."

His jaw drops open. "You were following Emerald Phoenix on tour?"

"I was, until Brianna got called home for some family emergency."

He cocks his head. "Oh my God, is everything okay?"

I'm not sure how much I'm at liberty to say, so, "I honestly don't know that much about it myself. But Jesse and Rory were busy with the band, and I would've been all by myself."

"Yeah, but you would have been in *Europe.*"

But I wouldn't have been with Dave. Not that I can say

this, so I simply shrug. "I can always go back. I figured I'd just as soon come home and finish my semester so I wouldn't have to make it up later. This way I'll get to walk at graduation."

"I'd forgo walking at graduation for a trip to Europe anytime."

"That's what I had planned." I sigh. "But you know, circumstances sometimes change."

"I suppose they do." His eyes light up. "Now you get to study biology with me."

I chuckle. "So not my strong suit."

He places his hand on the table a half inch away from mine. "What do you want to be when you grow up, Maddie?"

His words hit me like a knife right between my eyes.

I frown. "I guess... I honestly don't know. I feel like an idiot even saying it, but it's so true. Part of me was hoping I'd find some kind of inspiration during this European tour, but now I'm back here."

"That's okay, I didn't know for the longest time, and then it hit me."

"What you were going to do?" I ask.

"With my biology major, I decided to go into nursing."

I smile. "That is a wonderful endeavor. What made you choose nursing?"

"A doctor was my first choice, but I can't afford medical school, and I didn't decide on this path until it was too late to get ready to take the MCAT on time anyway. So I figured I'd try nursing. If I like it, and if I still feel the drive to go to medical school, I can always do it later."

"That's an amazing outlook," I say. "But I still don't know what the hell I'm going to do with my life. Seems like I've spent it in my older siblings' shadows, and the shadows of some of my sorority sisters."

I don't mention the Steel cousins, but he may already know who I'm talking about.

"Maddie, you aren't in anyone's shadow. And you need to realize that."

I look down. "That's what my dad says too. I suppose I need to stop letting yesterday take up too much of today."

He widens his eyes. "Wow, that's really profound."

"Don't be too impressed. I didn't coin that phrase. Will Rogers did."

"That's okay. You pulled it out when you meant it."

Then something comes to me.

"I've always been so interested in finding people who inspire me," I say. "Maybe I need to start inspiring myself."

Grayson grins. "You've inspired me already."

I shake my head. "No, I'm being serious. I've read so many self-help books, and I end up feeling great after I read them. Then I go back into my old ways, but I always feel better when I'm helping someone else."

"You could be a therapist."

I shake my head. "No, definitely not a therapist. Clearly science isn't my thing. More like a... A life coach." I cross my arms. "I don't think I would be good at helping someone heal from past trauma, but I think what I could do is help them look forward and achieve specific goals. And my first client is going to be myself."

He smiles and takes a sip of his wine. "Did I just help you decide what to do with your life?"

I nod as a smile slowly spreads across my face. "I think maybe you did. It feels right. And nothing about where I'm going in my so-called career has felt right...like ever. It's funny.

When we were in Europe, Brianna told me that my gift was empathy, helping other people with their feelings. I think she may be right. I could use those skills as a life coach."

"Sure you don't want to go into therapy?"

"No, I don't think so. I like to focus on the future rather than the past. It's like Will Rogers said. Don't let yesterday take up too much of today."

Rosalie returns to take our orders.

"I'm so sorry, Rosalie," I say. "I haven't even looked at the menu."

"I'm having the lasagna," Grayson says, "with a Caesar salad."

"You know what?" I put down my menu. "I just had lasagna yesterday, but it still sounds good. I'll have the same, Rosalie."

Rosalie smiles and collects our menus. "Great, I'll get these right in."

I smile at Grayson, and he gives me a wide grin back.

I'm happy.

Happy to be here, and happy to be sharing a meal with a nice man.

Even though I'd much rather be looking across the table at Dave Simpson.

★ ★ ★

By the time we get into the Uber to go back, I'm just giddy. I feel like a giant weight has been lifted off my shoulders, knowing now what I think I can do.

It's like I've been training for this my entire life, looking for inspirational quotes, helping myself feel better about my situation.

And the funny thing is? I feel better about my situation right now in this moment than I have for a long time.

We get to the dorm, and Grayson walks me to my door.

"I had a great time, Maddie."

"I did too, Grayson. Thank you."

He leans down to kiss me, and I let him brush his lips against mine, but when he probes between them for entrance with his tongue, I pull away.

He blinks. "What's wrong?"

I take a deep breath and sigh. "I don't want to give you the wrong idea, Grayson. I'm involved with someone else. It's new, but it's exciting, and the two of us have been through a few things. I don't want to screw that up."

He frowns. "You could've told me that before I took you to dinner."

I drop my jaw. "Seriously? You want to go there?"

Maybe he's not such a nice guy.

But then he rakes his fingers through his hair. "God, no, I'm not that guy. I don't know why I even said that. It's just that you're so pretty, and I haven't found anyone I've clicked with in a long time."

I cock my head. "How's that possible? You're smart, good-looking."

"I don't know." He looks at his feet. "But it's not your problem."

"Maybe it is. You want to talk? It might be good practice for me."

He looks at my door. "I suppose it would be too much to ask to talk in your room."

I laugh lightly. "Probably not a good idea. We can go down

to the lounge. It's still early on a Saturday night. I doubt too many people will be down there."

A small smile creeps over his face. "You know what, Maddie? I think I'd like that."

CHAPTER THIRTY-ONE

Dave

"Hey," I tell Maddie on the phone early on Friday, "I can't wait to see you tomorrow."

"I can't wait to see you either," she says. "I've got some amazing news."

"Yeah? What is it?"

"It's something I want to tell you in person, Dave. I'm just so excited."

Her voice is jubilant, and I'm not sure I've ever heard her sound quite as happy as she does right now.

I'm happy as well—happy that I'm going to be seeing her tomorrow evening.

Not happy that my uncle is fighting cancer.

He's heading toward some nasty chemo and radiation, and he and Aunt Melanie have pretty much gone into seclusion.

I'd probably do the same thing if I were him.

I'm not happy about the talk I'm about to have with my father, either, where I'll tell him I want to leave the position I've trained for my whole life and work with my uncle instead.

But all that matters right now is that Maddie is happy about something.

"Whatever it is, I'm glad about it because you sound ecstatic."

"I totally am, Dave. I just have so much to share with you."

"And you're sure you don't want to tell me any of it over the phone? I could use some good news."

"No, I totally do not. It's just too much excitement."

I chuckle. "All right. I'll see you at six o'clock sharp. Dress nicely. I'm taking you to the Fortnight."

"Oh my God, that's so funny. I was just thinking about that place."

"Were you?"

"Yeah, I was out with this new friend of mine, and he—"

"*He?*"

"Yeah, he's just a friend. He helped me make up some biology labs—"

"Sounds like a date to me, Maddie."

"Oh, no, it wasn't." She pauses. "Although I think he thought it was."

"Oh my God... Did he try anything?"

"Just a kiss."

Fury consumes me. The jealousy. It's like a green madness has overcome me.

"Maddie..."

"He's just a friend. I promise. I made it very clear when he tried to kiss me that I was seeing someone else. We ended up talking until one a.m. in the dorm lounge, and I actually helped him with—"

A fist of darkness closes around my heart. "Maybe we shouldn't go out tomorrow."

"Dave, don't be like that."

"If you're going out with other guys..."

"I told you, I'm not. Let's just talk tomorrow, okay? I have so much great news."

I take a deep breath and remind myself that I'm not that guy.

"Yeah, you're right. I'm sorry. I'm just a little on edge. With Uncle Joe and everything with my family. And Pat Lamone is my damned cousin."

All that plus I haven't even told Maddie I'm about to switch careers. Damn.

"I understand. I can't wait to see you, Dave."

"Yeah. Six sharp, Maddie."

I end the call, wanting to say I love you.

But she hasn't said it back to me yet, so I don't.

I don't think she's lying to me. The guy may have thought it was a date, and maybe she didn't. Or maybe she *did* think it was a date and—

I shake my head quickly to clear it. I can't go there right now. Too much on my mind, and I don't want anything to ruin tomorrow with Maddie.

Dad and I have been going over lots of documentation, getting the ownership all transferred.

I'm heading into town now to see Donny at his office as the city attorney. He'll help me get everything recorded accurately.

And then...

I breathe in.

I've scheduled some time with Dad. After talking at length with Uncle Talon and finding out he's thrilled for me to be on board, I knew it was time.

I draw in a deep breath and let it out slowly. *Maddie was not on a date with another guy, I tell myself. And she has exciting news.*

Embrace the excitement for her. It will help you get your mind off your own damned problems.

Even though I know I don't have any problems. Uncle Joe is the one with the problem, and damn... He's not just my uncle. He's Brock's father. And Brock is closer to me than my own brother is.

I draw in another breath.

Time to focus on the task at hand, see Donny and Callie, get these damned new deeds recorded.

And then...my father.

★ ★ ★

I stand at the door to my father's office for a solid five minutes before I finally gather up enough courage to knock.

"Come in."

I open the door slowly. The hinges squeak.

Dad looks up and smiles. "Dave. How are you doing?"

I stand in the doorway. "Not bad." I clear my throat.

Dad gestures to one of the burgundy plush wingback chairs facing his desk. "Take a seat, won't you?"

I nod and slowly sit down in the chair.

I open my mouth, but nothing comes out.

It should be easy to say. *I want to change careers, Dad. I want to work with Uncle Talon and Brianna in the orchards.*

And then he'll burst into tears, asking me how I could do this to him right as he's about to lose his best friend to brain cancer.

I swallow. My dad won't do that. I'm just imagining the worst possible scenario.

"So, you've probably noticed that I've been a little...*off* since returning to the States."

Dad clasps his hands together on his desk and nods. "Of

course. We've all been affected by Joe's news, and I know you were still a little shaken from that trouble on the plane to Paris."

I take a deep breath in. "Yes. And I've had a hard time readjusting to work since getting back. But last week, a thought struck me. I called Brianna and asked if she could use any help in the orchards that day."

Dad cocks his head. "You worked in the orchards?"

I nod. "Surprised the hell out of me. But for some reason, in that moment, I was craving manual labor, and by a twist of fate, Bree was working outside because one of her foremen called in sick. I needed something physical to help my mind iron out some of the kinks. And the weird thing was that it worked, Dad."

Dad strokes his chin. "The mind and body are one and the same, so that makes sense on a certain level." He looks over at me. "But why did you need to tell me this, Dave? Surely you're leading up to something."

I run my hands through my hair. "Yeah, Dad, I am. When I was working with Brianna, everything just fell into place. Several hours passed, and I didn't even realize it until the sun started to set."

Dad frowns but doesn't say anything.

"And it got me thinking," I go on, "that maybe *that* is what I should be doing for the family business. Working in the orchards, doing the work, getting my hands dirty. Instead of sitting behind a computer screen all day."

Dad narrows his gaze. "Are you saying that what I do isn't noble work?"

I put my hands up in front of me. "Of course not, Dad. It's just... I don't think it's how *I* want to spend my life. Anyone in the family can do what I do, and they can do it better. But I think I can make a real difference in the orchard, especially once Uncle Talon decides to hang up his hat for good."

Dad closes his eyes and takes a slow breath in.

This is it. He's going to explode on me.

So I keep talking, trying to stave off the blast. "In the orchard, I feel alive, connected to nature. I love the fresh air, the scent of the soil, the sound of the leaves rustling in the wind. It's peaceful yet invigorating. I found joy there, and it's where I see my future. Plus, with my business background, I'll be a valuable asset to Uncle Tal when he's working on that end."

He opens his eyes, and I brace myself.

But he doesn't explode. "Dave," he says calmly, "I won't pretend I'm not disappointed. I love working with you on the admin side of things."

"I know, and I'm so—"

Dad holds up a hand to quiet me. "That said, I would be a horrible father to deny you the opportunity to try a new path if you think it will lead you to happiness. I'll miss having you around, but you have to do what you have to do. Have you talked to Talon about this?"

I nod. "I have."

"Then it seems to be settled."

I get to my feet. "Thanks, Dad. I know you won't regret this."

Dad laughs softly. "It's funny. Your sister was in here not an hour ago asking if there was a position for her with me once she graduates from college."

"Angie? No. She's got her heart set on medical school. It must be Sage."

Dad smiles. "Yes, Sage. This whole thing with Uncle

Joe got her thinking about her future in a way she never has, I think. You know Sage. Always up for a good time. I told her that of course I'd find a place for her."

I scratch the side of my head. I guess sometimes things *do* come together.

"That's great, Dad. Someone as charismatic as Sage would be perfect working the business end."

Dad nods. "I think she will. And training her will give me something to keep my mind off Joe." His face twists for a moment, but he regains focus. "It sounds like this new position in the orchard will do the same for you."

I grin from ear to ear. "I think it will, Dad. To try new things." I rise and turn to the door. "Thanks again for understanding."

My hand is on the door when my father clears his throat. I turn back around and face him. "Everything okay?"

Dad's head is cocked, and his eyes have a slight sparkle to them. "This change of heart wouldn't have anything to do with Madeline Pike, would it?"

I widen my eyes. "Why would Maddie have—?"

"Because I had a very interesting conversation with Frank Pike earlier today. He seemed to be under the impression that the two of you are something of an item."

My cheeks warm. "We kind of got together in Europe. And we've been seeing each other here and there since getting back here."

Dad chuckles. "I think this is the first time I've heard of you going out with a girl for more than an hour. Sounds serious."

"It is, I think." I hesitate a minute, gathering my thoughts. "I'm in love with her, Dad. That plane ride really jolted my priorities into place. I think she might be the woman I end up marrying."

He crosses his arms. "Poor Maureen Pike. Four Steel in-laws. God help her whenever she hosts a family dinner."

I laugh. It feels good to laugh with my dad. I can't remember the last time we were having such a cheery conversation. Certainly not since I came home.

I turn back to the door. "Is that all, then?"

Dad holds up a singular finger. "One thing, Dave. If it's true love—and it sounds like it just might be—don't you ever let it go."

"Don't worry, Dad. I won't." I head out of his office. All of this talk about Maddie has my head in the clouds.

I'll call her and tell her how things went with Dad. I would love to hear her voice.

The phone rings a few times, then I get Maddie's voicemail.

I end the call. She has good news she wants to tell me in person, so I'll save mine for when we get together as well.

* * *

The next evening...

I'm driving along the winding road, the soft hum of the engine providing a comforting background to my thoughts. The sun is setting, casting a warm, orange glow across the landscape. Tonight is the night. The night I've been eagerly anticipating for several restless days. The night I'll see Maddie again.

Uncle Joe is still sick, but Dad and I are good with my change of career. And Maddie... Maddie and I are...

In love, I hope. At least we are on my end. I can't wait to say those three words to her again tonight. Maybe she'll say them back this time.

As I steer through the gentle curves of the road, I can't help but smile. It's funny how life can take unexpected turns. I remember the first time Maddie and I talked when we were younger, how her laughter was like music, and her eyes held a spark of curiosity that drew me in. There she was, all this time, right in front of me.

I glance at my rearview mirror, checking my reflection. I want to look my best for her, even though she's seen me at my most ordinary. Now that Dad is behind my change on the ranch and Uncle Talon has welcomed me aboard, the puzzle pieces are clicking together.

Maddie is the final piece.

A smile tugs at my lips again as I imagine her smile, the way her eyes light up when she sees me, the warmth of her touch. This is it, the real deal, and I couldn't be happier.

I close my eyes for a moment, dreaming of the life we'll forge tog—

A deafening roar.

A massive truck swerves into my lane, its blinding headlights flooding my vision. Panic seizes my heart, and I grip the steering wheel, trying to swerve out of the way. But it's too late. The truck barrels into me, and everything goes dark.

My consciousness slips away as if it's been stolen. Time stops, and...

Silence.

Nothing but silence.

Then, a rush of sensations—the taste of blood, the throbbing pain in my head, the metallic smell of the twisted wreckage that used to be my car.

I try to move, but I can't. Fear grips me.

"Maddie!" I call out her name, but my voice is weak, barely a whisper. All I can think about in this moment is her.

The girl I've fallen in love with.

The girl I was supposed to meet tonight.

As the darkness closes in around me, I cling to the hope that somehow, some way, I'll see her again. I want to tell her how much she means to me, how my love for her burns brighter than anything I've ever known.

But for now, all I can do is hold on...

Pray that fate will give us another chance.

CHAPTER THIRTY-TWO

Maddie

This is so not happening.

I will not cry.

I'm dressed to kill, in a little black number that accentuates my curves. The Colorado winter is mild, so I even forwent wearing pantyhose, and I've got some gorgeous patent leather pumps on my feet.

My hair is down, falling around my shoulders in a dark-brown curtain. I even straightened it, so the natural waves are gone.

I wanted to look sleek and classy tonight for my date with Dave.

My makeup is done just so—a natural look but with a bit more eyeshadow than I normally wear.

And if I do say so myself, in this moment, with this anticipation, I look every bit as beautiful as Rory or Callie.

So I won't cry.

I won't mess it up.

I'll make sure someone sees me tonight.

Even though David Simpson is an hour late.

A whole hour.

I've texted him several times, but no response.

He called me earlier but didn't leave a voicemail.

The coward didn't have the courage to even leave me a message.

He'll probably give me some excuse. His family needed him for some other crisis. Or he lost track of time doing God knows what in the orchards again.

Maybe I should have told him I loved him back. Maybe this is *my* fault.

Or maybe he got pissed off that I went out with Grayson. I told him that we were just friends going out for dinner, and that—

No. There's no excuse.

If he no longer wanted to see me, he could at least have texted me before I spent the whole afternoon dolling myself up.

But no.

Something else stole his attention away from me tonight, away from the date that I've been looking forward to all week— that *he's* been looking forward to all week, according to the texts and phone calls we've shared.

But when the moment of truth came, he ghosted me.

He's no doubt wishing he hadn't said those three fateful words so soon.

My appetite is gone, of course. I'm too upset to eat. But I have to do something.

I don't know the girls on my corridor yet. I just moved in a week ago. The sorority girls are all at the house or already have plans for the evening.

I could go over to the house, see if any of them want to go out.

But I'm not in the mood to be a bubbly sorority girl tonight.

No. I'm in the mood for something else entirely.

If Dave wants to blow me off? Then I can blow him off right back.

Where to go?

I don't have a lot of money in my purse, but I look the part, and I want to go somewhere classy and elegant.

The Carlton. The bar at the Carlton. I have enough money to buy myself a drink, and after that I can start a tab on my credit card.

My credit card with its tiny limit of five hundred dollars.

My credit card that I never use except for emergencies.

Yeah? Well, tonight is an emergency.

I call an Uber, and because it's Saturday night in a college town, many drivers are out, so I get a ride quickly.

I drape my black trench coat over myself and walk out of the dorm to meet my driver.

"Going to the Carlton tonight?"

"Yep."

"You working?"

"No, I don't work there. Just looking for a night out."

"Oh."

By the tone of his voice, I see what he is insinuating.

He thinks I'm a *working girl*.

Now I feel worse than ever.

I don't talk to the driver the rest of the way.

And I also don't give him a tip.

When he drops me off at the Carlton, I murmur a quick thank you and whisk quickly into the hotel, turning toward the bar area.

I've stayed at the Carlton once before, back when Dad had his heart attack.

I was entranced then, and I'm entranced now.

Except tonight I'm on my own financially.

I walk into the bar. The lights are dim, and already an aura of elegance and sophistication surrounds me. Rich, dark wood paneling lines the walls, contrasting beautifully with the soft, warm lighting, which casts a welcoming glow over the space. The bar stools are plush leather, and the bar counter is a polished marble masterpiece, gleaming under the soft lighting.

Soft jazz music plays in the background. It's early yet, only half past seven, so I find a seat at the bar fairly easily.

A handsome bartender—his name tag says Garrett—strides up to me. "What can I get you tonight, beautiful?"

"Sidecar, please."

Then a low voice next to me rumbles as someone slides into a seat. "You can put that on my tab."

I turn and face an amazingly handsome man. His hair is blond, with some silver at the temples. His eyes are sparkling blue—though not quite as sparkling as Dave's.

But I'm not here to think about Dave. Dave stood me up.

"That's kind of you," I say.

He holds out his hand. "I'm Logan Templeton."

"Madeline Pike." I take his hand.

He lifts mine and lightly brushes his lips over the back of it.

I feel a slight spark but nothing amazing. More the fact that an older and obviously accomplished gentleman is paying attention to me.

"Do you come here often?" he asks.

"Only once before." When my father was in the hospital with a heart attack and the Steels treated us to dinner here, but Logan doesn't need to know that.

"Are you waiting for anyone?"

I narrow my gaze. "Maybe I'm waiting for you."

My cheeks warm. Did those words just come out of my mouth?

"That's what I like to hear. What do you do, Madeline?"

"I'm a life coach." It's not a lie so much as a statement of my future. That's what I tell myself, anyway.

He raises an eyebrow. "Really? That's interesting."

"Yeah, I really enjoy my work. It's very inspiring. What do you do?"

"I'm here on business," he says. "I'm an attorney in Denver."

"Really? My sister's studying to be an attorney. And my soon-to-be brother-in-law used to be with a downtown firm. Now he's the city attorney for the town of Snow Creek."

Garrett raises his eyebrows. "Don Steel?"

"Yeah. He's engaged to my sister Caroline."

I'm not sure why I'm not using our nicknames. All I know is that I'm talking to a guy who's probably in his late thirties or early forties, so telling him my name is Maddie seems kind of infantile.

"Interesting," he says. "So you have a connection to the Steel family, then."

"You wouldn't believe how many connections I have to the Steel family."

He cocks his head. "More than one?"

"Yeah," I say dryly. "Apparently you don't read the society pages."

"I can't say that I do."

"My sister Aurora is engaged to Brock Steel, and my brother Jesse is engaged to Brianna Steel."

"But you're still unspoken for, I hope," he says.

"I am free as a hawk soaring above the sunlit sky."

Where did *that* come from?

"And like the hawk, are you looking for prey?" His eyes dance.

Garrett slides my drink in front of me, and I take a sip of the sour liquid before I reply to Logan.

"I'm always looking for something," I finally say. "What it is depends on how the evening progresses."

I'm so not being myself.

This man is handsome, but he's way too old for me. Jesse had a conniption about the difference between Brianna's and his ages. Logan could easily be twenty years my senior.

"May I ask how old you are?" I ask bluntly.

"I'm forty-one. How old are you?"

"Thirty-one."

I purposefully place myself ten years below him. If he knew I was only twenty-two, he'd probably run for the mountains.

Not that I'm expecting anything to happen, but he's good for my ego at the moment.

"Thirty-one?" He looks me up and down. "You must have some good genes. You don't look a day over twenty."

"Thank you." I take another sip of my drink.

"Garrett, I'll have a scotch, neat. Macallan if you have it."

"Anything for you, Mr. Templeton." Garrett gets to work on the drink.

Logan's not wearing a wedding ring, which doesn't surprise me, given how strong he's coming on. But if he is out of town on business, he may have just taken it off.

"Are you married?" I ask blatantly.

He lifts his left hand. "You see a ring on this finger?"

"No, but that wasn't the question."

He chuckles softly, a low rumble. "I'm not married, beautiful. Are you?"

"Do you see a ring on this finger?" I hold up my hand in front of his, allowing our fingertips to barely touch.

No ring, but I am wearing the pendant Dave bought me in Paris. Right now it's burning as if it's branding my flesh.

Logan grins. "No, I don't."

I take another sip. "I'll be honest with you, though. I just got out of a relationship."

"Now that is interesting." He trails his finger over my forearm. "Because I did too."

Again a tiny spark skitters across my flesh, but it's nothing compared to the fireworks that erupt inside me when David Simpson is near.

But Dave Simpson *isn't* here. Something came up—something clearly so important that he couldn't even bother to text me and tell me he had to break our date.

Garrett slides Logan's scotch in front of him.

"Thank you." Logan slides a hundred-dollar bill across the table.

Maybe I've been hanging around with the Steels too much, but the hundred-dollar bill doesn't even make my eyes widen.

"So you want to get out of here?" Logan asks.

I swallow, tamping down the nervousness erupting in me. "I think I'd like to finish my drink."

"Okay. Let's finish our drinks." He looks out a nearby window. "The night is young, after all."

"What are you suggesting?" I ask.

"Maybe some dinner?" he says. "And then who knows?"

"Dinner sounds nice," I say.

"There's a great restaurant here in the hotel. Would you care to join me?"

I glance at my drink, which is still three-quarters full. "Maybe after our drinks."

As thrilling as it is to have an older man pay attention to me like this, I don't want to be the person who falls in bed with a stranger because I'm angry at another man.

But dinner? Dinner I can handle.

As long as he's not expecting anything beyond that.

I take another sip of my cocktail, the sweetness of the sugar on the rim tamping the sour a bit. "What kind of law do you practice?"

"Corporate," he says. "When you mentioned Don Steel, I took note because I had just become partner when he started at our firm."

This time my eyes do widen. "Really? Wow."

"He was an up-and-comer too. We were ready to make him a partner when he left."

"Yeah. To take the job as a favor to his mother, who was retiring."

"Right. I never understood why he gave up such a lucrative spot in the law firm."

"The Steels aren't exactly hurting for money," I say.

He takes a drink of scotch, and a small moan vibrates from his chest as he swallows. "True enough." He gestures to Garrett. "Garrett, could you call over to the restaurant and see if they can take this lovely young lady and me for dinner?"

"You got it, Mr. T."

I smile and take another drink.

CHAPTER THIRTY-THREE

Dave

I'm trapped inside a hazy, fragmented reality, drifting in and out of consciousness. My senses are overwhelmed by the discordant symphony of sirens wailing, voices shouting, and the distant thud of my own heartbeat.

The world around me blurs and distorts, like a fever dream. Shapes and colors meld together in chaotic patterns, and I struggle to make sense of what's happening. There's an intense burning sensation in my chest, each breath a laborious effort. I taste blood, metallic and acrid, as it trickles down my lip.

A touch on my shoulder sends a jolt of awareness through my foggy mind. I can vaguely discern the silhouette of a paramedic. His voice is a distant echo as he and his team speak urgently, trying to keep me tethered to this precarious reality.

Someone moves me, and my body protests with a dull, throbbing pain that pulses in rhythm with my erratic heartbeat. The world outside is a whirlwind of flashing lights, blinding and disorienting.

Through half-closed eyes, I catch glimpses of the remnants of my car, twisted metal and shattered glass. My vision blurs further, and my eyelids feel like lead, pulling me back into the murky abyss of unconsciousness.

But I fight to stay present, to cling to the fragments of the world around me. I hear snippets of conversation, snippets of hope. The paramedic's voice reassures me that help is on the way, that they won't let me slip away.

The hum of sirens draws closer, growing louder and more urgent. I'm cocooned in blankets and straps. The world outside is a swirl of motion as they load me into the ambulance.

Not again...

Please... Not again...

CHAPTER THIRTY-FOUR

M a d d i e

The hotel restaurant's interior is pure elegance. Crystal chandeliers hang from the lofty ceiling, and velvet drapes in a majestic violet adorn the windows. The tables are dressed in crisp white tablecloths, and the plush, high-backed chairs are upholstered in sumptuous crimson fabrics. Some tables are nestled in secluded alcoves, offering a romantic dining experience, while others are positioned to capture the best views.

I've been here once before, when Donny treated us all to dinner while my father was in the hospital. Jesse was scowling the whole time.

Tonight I'm determined to enjoy myself. Have the nice meal that I should be having with Dave. I excuse myself once we're seated to go to the ladies' room.

I touch up my makeup and force a smile on my face. This guy is going to buy me an expensive dinner, so I at least need to be good company.

On a whim, I pull my phone out of my purse and take a look.

Still no response to my many texts and phone calls.

Fine.

I'm still going to have a nice dinner tonight anyway.

I smile at the woman next to me washing her hands and then exit the restroom, walking slowly back to the table, trying to look confident.

"I took the liberty of ordering some champagne," Logan says.

"How nice," I say.

"Only the best for a woman of your stature."

The sommelier comes by with a bottle of Dom Perignon. He shows the bottle to Logan, who nods. Then he expertly uncorks the bottle. I stare at the smoky condensation that drifts up from the bottle opening.

The sommelier pours a small amount into a flute and hands it to Logan. Logan peers at the flute, swirls it a bit, inhales, and then takes a drink.

"Excellent," he says.

"Good, sir." The sommelier fills my flute expertly, not a bit of foam going over the top, and then fills the remainder of Logan's flute. He then bows and leaves us.

Logan picks up his flute and smiles. "To a wonderful evening."

I clink my glass to his but say nothing and then take a sip of the champagne.

It's surprisingly good. I've never had real champagne before. I've had the Steel sparkling wine at their parties, and it's delicious. And then of course I've had cheap California sparkling wine, but I wasn't in France long enough to actually taste real champagne.

And now here I am, in Grand Junction, Colorado, having real champagne with a strange man.

He seems like a kind man, but he's a strange man nonetheless.

And I begin to feel guilty.

He's probably expecting a little slap and tickle tonight after spending all this money on such a beautiful dinner for me.

I should probably tell him I'm not interested in that.

But I don't.

I take another drink of my champagne instead.

Our server comes by, dressed in a white blouse and simple black pants. "Good evening, I'm Charity, and I'll be taking care of you this evening. I see you're already set with your cocktail selection. Would you care for any appetizers?"

I blink. "I'm so sorry. I haven't even looked at the menu."

"Bring us a selection of your best oysters on the half shell," Logan says. He looks at me. "You do like oysters, don't you, Madeline?"

"Of course."

I've only had oysters on the half shell once, and they were kind of slimy, but they tasted good.

"Right away, sir."

He narrows his eyes at me. "You know oysters are an aphrodisiac."

I swirl the champagne in my flute and wink at him. "So I've heard."

Again I'm tempted to tell him this evening will go nowhere, but then I think, why not? Why not have some indiscriminate sex when I got stood up by the man who professed to be in love with me?

"Tell me a little more about yourself," he says. "How long have you been coaching?"

Right. I lied.

But it's not technically a lie, is it? I do plan to become a life coach. I feel very certain in this endeavor. More certain than I felt about any path in my life—other than Dave Simpson.

And obviously that's gone up in flames, so why the hell not?

"Not long," I say.

"I find it very interesting. My sister worked with a life coach and said the results were amazing. It really helped her map out her goals."

"I'm so glad to hear that. What does she do?"

"She's a novelist. But she had trouble setting daily goals that she could make happen. The coach helped her realize what was holding her back and got her on a schedule that works for her."

"That's wonderful. I'm so glad to hear that. What kind of novels does she write?"

"She writes romance novels. If you read romance, you've probably heard of her. Leah Templeton."

"I don't have a lot of time to read for pleasure," I say. "But the name rings a bell."

"She's very good. Several of her books have been bestsellers."

I smile. "I'll definitely look them up. But enough about me. Tell me about the work you do with your firm."

"It's mostly corporate work," he says. "We represent big businesses, keep their contracts in order."

"What businesses?"

"I can't give you the names of our clients. Attorney-client privilege and all. But you would probably recognize them if I did."

I nod. We've effectively run out of things to talk about.

I take another sip of my champagne and then glance down

at the menu.

I jerk when my phone buzzes in my purse.

"Excuse me," I say. "I'm actually expecting to hear from someone."

I grab my phone.

But my heart sinks. It's not Dave.

It's Brianna.

I rise. "Would you please excuse me for a moment?"

"Of course."

I walk away from the table as I pick up the call. "Brianna?"

"Oh my God, Maddie. Thank God you picked up."

"What's wrong?"

"It's Dave. He's been in an accident. He collided with a truck on the road to Grand Junction."

My heart drops to my feet. Chills coarse through my entire body. I have to fight to keep from toppling over.

Brianna didn't just say what I think she said.

Dave. My Dave. The man who told me he loved me.

In an accident.

He could be dying.

For all I know, he could be...

And here I am, acting like a child, out on a date with the first man who looked my way. Acting like a complete slut. Not once did it cross my mind that there might be some other explanation. I was so in my head about Dave not wanting me anymore that it never occurred to me that something awful could have happened to the man I—

"Maddie, are you there?"

I bring the phone back to my ear, my hand shaking. "Y-Yes. I am."

"He was on his way to Grand Junction. Was he going to

see you?"

My God, this is all my fault.

A tear runs down my cheek.

"I... I thought he had stood me up. Is he...?"

"He's in rough shape. Thank God someone was coming the other way and called 9-1-1. He's at St. Mary's. Uncle Bryce and Aunt Marj are on their way there, along with Henry and the girls. You should go."

I say nothing, my thoughts tumbling.

"Maddie?"

"Yeah, I'm here. I'm... I'm on my way."

I rush back to the table. "I'm so sorry. There's been an emergency. I have to get to the hospital."

"Which one?"

"St. Mary's."

"I'll come with you."

"Please, don't bother. It's..."

"It's what?"

"It's a man. A man I care about." I bury my face in my hands. The tears are coming. "I shouldn't have led you on like this. I thought he stood me up this evening, so... It was immature of me to allow you to take me to dinner. I'm so sorry, Logan."

He rises. "Don't be sorry. I enjoyed our time together. It would have been nice if it were more, but right now, we need to get you to the hospital." He pulls out his phone. "I'll contact my driver."

"Really, you don't have to."

"Please, let me do this for you. Consider it my good deed for the day."

I fall against him, giving him a quick hug. "It is definitely a good deed. Thank you so much, Logan. And whoever left you? Big loss on her part."

* * *

I slam the door to Logan's town car harder than I mean to.

"Sorry!" I yell back at him.

He waves me away amiably.

I run quickly to the ER, stopping at the volunteer at the front desk.

"David Simpson?" I say breathlessly.

He looks up from his computer screen. "You family?"

"Isn't his family here yet?"

He taps on his keyboard. "I'm not showing any visitors so far. But I can only give information out to family."

"I'm his...girlfriend," I say.

He shakes his head. "I'm afraid only legal spouses count as family, ma'am."

"Then fine. I'm his wife."

He mentioned a possible honeymoon, so what the hell?

"Ma'am, do you think this is the first time someone has said they were someone's significant other and then *corrected* themselves when they found out we can only release information to spouses? Please take a seat. When a family member of the patient arrives, we can give out information."

"Fine." I turn around in a huff, glancing around the room.

No Bryce, no Marjorie, no Henry, no Angie, no Sage...

But a moment later, they all come rushing in.

And they don't look good. Marjorie and Bryce are both wearing combinations of pajamas and jeans. They must have been planning an early night at home. Henry's face is sheet white, and the girls' eyes are streaked with mascara.

Angie runs into my arms and sobs. "Oh, Maddie. I'm so glad you're here. I can't believe this, on top of everything else going on with our family. Is he okay?"

"I don't know what's going on. They won't tell me anything because I'm not family."

"Mom and Dad will get the information." Tears stream down Angie's face. "I can't believe this is happening. How much more can we be expected to go through?"

I feel so bad for her. This is her brother, after all. If something like this happened to Jesse, I would be devastated.

I'm devastated now. This is the man I love.

And I can't lose him.

Why didn't I say it back?

Why didn't I do so many things?

I was so worried about stupid stuff.

Bryce and Marjorie talk to the volunteer and then return to us in the waiting area.

Bryce's face is pale, and Marjorie doesn't look much better.

But it's Marjorie who speaks to us. "All they know is that he's in surgery. He's had some abdominal injuries. They're sending someone out to talk to us."

I gulp and sit down next to Angie. Sage and Henry sit across from us, looking worried. Bryce and Marjorie are still standing, pacing back and forth.

A man in scrubs comes out. "Mr. and Mrs. Simpson?"

"Yes?" Marjorie rushes to him and brings him back. "These are our children and a family friend. Please speak freely."

He nods curtly. "Of course. I'm Dr. Amos, and I was the

attending physician when your son was brought in. He suffered soft-tissue injuries, lacerations on his face and neck."

"Did the airbag deploy?"

"It did," he says. "But he was hit head-on by a pickup truck. His Jaguar couldn't compete."

"Where's the asshole who hit him?" Henry asks.

"Henry," Marjorie says.

"That driver didn't make it," Dr. Amos says. "His airbag didn't deploy."

"Good on him," Henry says.

"*Henry.*" His mother again.

But I can't blame him. Someone put Dave in this position. He's a good driver, and he loves that car.

"Our imaging studies show several broken ribs and a hairline fracture in his collarbone. Your son is young and healthy, so these will heal quickly and easily." He flips through some documents on his clipboard. "However, the studies also show blood in the abdomen. That means he probably has internal bleeding, and that's why he's in surgery. We need to find and repair the damage to the organs that are affected."

"I see." Marjorie slides into a chair.

"What can we expect?" Bryce finally asks, his voice low and sad.

The doctor takes a deep breath. "We just don't know yet, sir. He may also have brain trauma. He was in and out of consciousness when he was transported here."

Oh *God*. Brain trauma? So even if he recovers physically, he could end up a vegetable for the rest of his life.

I would still love him anyway.

I want him back in whatever form, as long as it means he stays on this planet.

"What else do the scans show?" I ask.

"No bleeding in the brain, thank goodness. But he will probably have a concussion. He may have some amnesia. We just don't know."

"I don't understand," Marjorie says. "Why can't you tell us more?"

"I'm not the surgeon," he says. "I'm an ER doctor. But we have the best trauma surgeons taking care of him right now. Drs. Lucas and Montgomery. One of them will be out to speak to you as soon as they can."

"My sister-in-law practiced here for years," Marjorie says. "Dr. Melanie Steel."

He nods. "Yes, I know Dr. Steel."

"Can't you get us any information quicker?"

"We know your family is a huge benefactor to this hospital," he says. "But I can't make the surgeons work faster, ma'am. I'm sorry. They will do their best, and your son is in the best hands he could be in."

"My God..." She rises and falls against Bryce.

"We'll do everything we can, Mr. and Mrs. Simpson." Dr. Amos nods and walks back through the doors.

CHAPTER THIRTY-FIVE

Dave

I'm floating. It's an odd sensation, like being suspended in a dream. I can see my own body lying on the operating table, still and lifeless. Doctors and nurses are huddled around, their voices muffled, their faces obscured by masks. They're working with a sense of urgency, but I can't make out their words.

I want to reach out, to tell them that I'm right here, watching everything they're doing. But my voice doesn't work, and my limbs won't respond. It's as though I'm a mere spectator to my own existence.

I look down at my body, and it's a strange sight. Tubes and wires are attached to me, and the monitors beep rhythmically, a reminder that there's still life within me, even if I'm floating above it all.

The room seems to shimmer with an otherworldly light, and I see an aura of energy surrounding the medical team. They're focused, determined, and skilled. I wonder if they know that I'm here, that my consciousness is observing every detail.

As they continue their work, I'm overwhelmed with a sense of detachment from my physical self. It's as though I've stepped into a different dimension, one where time and space don't quite behave the way they should. I'm neither here nor there, but somewhere in between.

I watch as they make incisions, work to mend what's broken inside me. Worry is in their eyes, the furrowed brows, the occasional glance exchanged between them.

A surge of emotion washes over me. Fear, hope, uncertainty—they all swirl together, creating a turbulent sea of feelings. I want to tell them that I'm rooting for them, that I trust them with my life. But my words remain trapped.

Time passes, though it's impossible to say how long. The room begins to blur, and I feel myself being drawn back toward my body. The sensation is disorienting, like being pulled by an invisible force. I want to resist, to stay here in this ethereal realm where I can witness everything without being bound by the limitations of the physical world.

But the pull is too strong, and I find myself descending, back into my body. As I re-enter, I feel the weight of it all—the pain, the vulnerability, the fragility of life.

Another chance.

I have another chance.

CHAPTER THIRTY-SIX

Maddie

Hours pass. Or minutes. I'm not really sure which.

One of the surgeons, a younger woman with blond hair, comes out twice and updates Bryce and Marjorie, and I try to listen.

Going well. No answers yet. We're doing all we can.

Damage to kidneys. To liver. To spleen.

All I can think about is Dave—the man I love—lying on an operating table, his life depending on these doctors.

Totally without his control.

Totally without my control.

Without the control of his parents.

Angie and Sage have fallen asleep, Henry is pacing, and Bryce and Marjorie sit together, holding each other.

How much more does this family have to go through?

Jonah is sick, and now Dave...

I can't let my mind go there.

A volunteer comes to me. "Can I get you anything, miss?"

I shake my head, though my mouth is dry.

Not even a drop of water would stay down.

She asks the same of Henry and Bryce and Marjorie. All three of them shake their heads.

Both doctors come out then.

I rush over to Angie and Sage. "You guys, wake up? Both the doctors are here."

Angie gasps. "Is he okay?"

I don't reply, just run toward the doctors and stand with Marjorie, Bryce, and Henry.

"He's not out of the woods yet," the doctor is saying, "but we were able to repair the damage to his liver and his spleen. Unfortunately, the damage to his left kidney was too invasive. We had to remove it."

"What about his other kidney?" Marjorie asks.

"His other kidney was much less damaged and we were able to repair it," the doctor says. "So if he recovers, he'll have full kidney function."

Marjorie breathes a sigh of relief.

"But you said he's not out of the woods yet," Bryce says.

"The next twenty-four hours are crucial. We'll be monitoring him in the ICU."

"Can we see him?" Marjorie asks.

"One at a time," she says, "and only family."

I swallow.

That means not me.

"You go first, sweetie," Bryce says.

Marjorie heads back with the doctor, and Bryce turns to me. "You may as well go home, Maddie."

"No," I say adamantly. "I'm not leaving."

"You need to get some sleep."

"Don't you get it? He was coming to see *me*. This is my fault."

Bryce's face twists as if he's angry but then falls into sheer exhaustion.

"I'm not leaving. I love your son."

He raises his eyebrows weakly. "Do you? Then please stay." His lips twitch upward. Were the circumstances different, I think he'd be smiling right now. "You're a lovely girl. And my son seems to be quite taken with you. I hope you can have a future."

Dave's father, usually so strong and assured, seems like a shadow. Dave told me how Jonah's illness is affecting him. They've been best friends their whole lives.

And now this.

He can't lose a best friend and a son.

And damn it, I can't lose Dave.

Henry walks up to me. "I'm taking the girls over to the Carlton. We're going to get a suite. You're welcome to join us."

"I'm not leaving," I say.

"All right." Henry nods. "Keep us posted. Please."

I nod.

I'm uncomfortable. I feel conspicuous in my black trench coat with no pantyhose and black pumps.

But that's the least of my worries.

I'm not leaving.

Not leaving until I can see Dave.

Until I can talk to him.

Until I can tell him that I love him.

* * *

Twenty-four hours later, Dave is still in the ICU.

But I heave a sigh of relief when Bryce and Marjorie tell me his prognosis is good.

I still haven't been able to see him.

"When can I see him?" I ask.

"He's awake now," Marjorie says. "And he's asking for you."

I don't bother to thank them or say anything else. I simply run toward his room in the ICU.

As soon as I enter the room, the blood freezes in my veins. I have to use every muscle in my body to not burst into tears at the sight of him.

He looks so pale and weak lying in the bed, his body attached to so many machines.

The beep of his pulse.

An IV in his arm.

I have no idea what I look like. And I don't care.

I'm still wearing the dress from our supposed date. I guess he'll see me in it after all.

I walk in tentatively. "Dave?"

He turns his head slowly. He's not smiling, but why would he be? He has a bandage over one eye, and some other scratches and bruises on his face.

But to me he's still the best-looking man in the world.

I sit in the chair next to the bed and take his hand. "I was so scared."

"Sorry about our date," he croaks out.

I shake my head, sending a tear flying off my cheek. "Please don't worry about that."

He twists his lips into a crooked smile. "You look... beautiful."

I can't help laughing. "I've seen myself in the mirror. I have raccoon eyes, a swollen red nose. I'm a mess."

"I've never seen anything more beautiful." Then he closes his eyes.

I cup his cheek. "I know you need your sleep, but I need

to tell you something. I need to tell you that I love you, Dave Simpson. I should have said it last week. I knew it. But I... I was scared. I was trying to figure so much else out. But I love you. I love you so much."

He smiles wider, sort of. His lips are cracked and chapped. "That hurts."

"Then don't say anything."

"I'll say only this..." He reaches his hand out.

I grab it.

He squeezes it lightly. "Marry me, Maddie. Please."

I gasp as my jaw drops. I'm stunned, overwhelmed. Sure, he mentioned a honeymoon, but...

We've only been together a short while, but every moment with Dave has felt like stepping into a dream I never want to wake up from. I race through our short romance in my mind—the laughter, the shared trauma, the ridiculously amazing sex, and best of all, the way he looks at me like I'm the only person in the world. It's been a short time, but it's been the most intense and beautiful time of my life.

I look into his eyes, those deep pools of sincerity and warmth that are bloodshot and haloed by lacerations.

In them, I see love. I see promise.

I see my future.

I take a deep breath, let the fluttering butterflies in my tummy settle, and smile. "Are you sure?"

"It hurts to talk, so don't make me say it again."

I lean down and brush my lips over his. "Of course I'll marry you."

"We'll have to wait a while. Until I'm fit for human eyes again."

I kiss him again. "I'd marry you today if I could."

"No," he says. "We'll wait. Wait until Jesse and Rory get back from their tour. Until you and Brianna walk for graduation. Then we'll have the most lavish, exciting wedding in the whole world."

He closes his eyes then.

And I sit with him, holding his hand. I brush my lips over his dry, chapped ones yet again.

"I love you so much," I say. "I love you so damned much, Dave."

CHAPTER THIRTY-SEVEN

Nine months later...

The Steel Family
and
The Pike Family
*request the honor of your presence
at the marriage of their children*

Brianna Brooke Steel
to
Jesse Francis Pike

Aurora Maureen Pike
to
Brock Alistair Steel

Caroline Rose Pike
to
Donovan Talon Steel

Madeline Jolie Pike
to
David Steel Simpson

*Ceremony and Reception at the home of Talon and Jade Steel
Steel Acres Ranch
Snow Creek, Colorado*

Special performance by Dragonlock

CHAPTER THIRTY-EIGHT

M a d d i e

In all my life, I never dreamed of such a fairytale wedding.

A quadruple fairytale wedding at that.

Dave, Brianna, Donny, and Brock asked Ava and Brendan to take part to make it a quintuple wedding, but they decided to get married quietly a month earlier at Ryan and Ruby's house. A very Ava ceremony, no frills and no fuss, and she is happily Mrs. Brendan Murphy.

Today is truly a merge of the Pike and Steel families.

And for once, I'm not the odd woman out.

It's fall on the western slope, and our theme is rustic elegance. We used the autumn color palette of greens, rusts, and browns accented with gold—the elegance part.

Talon and Jade's land has gorgeous views of the Rocky Mountains, and they brought in a wide gazebo where we'll all take our vows. It's adorned with orange and yellow flowers and harvest fruits. Wrought-iron chairs are set in rows for our guests, arranged in a round so everyone has a good view of the gazebo.

The reception area is set up with round tables with fine green linens, gorgeous ivory china, crystal glassware, and sterling silverware. The centerpieces are cornucopias containing fruit from the Steel orchards. Brianna handpicked each apple herself.

The weather cooperated fully, so we didn't have to set up the tents.

Off to the right is the stage where Dragonlock will be performing after dinner. Their encore of all encores.

Fairy lights and lanterns are strung throughout the trees and around the perimeter of the reception area. They'll light up after darkness falls.

All of this is paid for by the Steels, of course. Dad finally came around. In the end, he decided that if his children could have the wedding of their dreams, he shouldn't stand in the way.

All the men are dressed in white button-downs, black pants, and cowboy boots, but we women all went for flare.

Always the cowgirl, Brianna chose a white mid-length gown made from lightweight cotton, featuring a flowing prairie-style skirt. The bodice has delicate lace detailing and subtle beading, but the true star of the show are her white leather ostrich cowboy boots.

Rory chose a strapless white cocktail gown, reminiscent of the dresses she used to wear when she sang opera. The fabric is satin, and it shows off her figure beautifully. On her feet are silver sandals, and her toes are painted black—an homage to her new status as a rocker.

Callie's choice surprised me. I figured she'd go for some kind of understated elegance. Nope. Her dress is white with orange trim to match the fire diamond on her left hand. It's a tea-length gown with a dramatic low back and asymmetrical neckline. Her shoes are simple pumps dyed to match the orange trim, but the true standout are her eyes—her light brown works perfectly with the color choice. It also works great with our autumn palette.

Then there's me.

Madeline Jolie Pike, soon to be Simpson.

My dress is the skimpiest of the bunch—a spaghetti strap sheath in white stretch satin. It hits me mid-calf and fits like a glove, and I love it. For shoes, I went with simple white slides accented with a few rhinestones.

Four brides, four different looks.

Four ecstatically happy women.

With four handsome men waiting to meet us after we walk down the aisle.

My father is talking to Callie out of earshot. He's dressed identically to the grooms, except he insisted on a black jacket and tie. He took Rory aside and then Callie. He returns a sniffling Callie and meets my gaze.

"Madeline," he says.

"Yes, Daddy?"

"Come with me. Let's walk together for a minute."

"You may need to have your makeup redone after," Callie whispers to me, wiping her nose with a cotton hanky.

I follow my father to a secluded spot. "What is it, Daddy?"

He sighs, shaking my head. "My baby girl. You're all grown up."

I nod. "That's what baby girls do."

"I was ready for Rory. Even Callie." His lip trembles. "But you, Mads. This one hurts."

I raise my eyebrows.

"Not in a bad way," he clarifies. "It's just... Once you're done having children, the baby is always the baby. No one comes along to replace her."

I smile.

"That's part of what makes you so special to me," he continues. "Your brother and your sisters are amazing, all three of them, but you, Maddie... You are the one I never worried about."

My eyebrows nearly pop off my head. "You didn't? Is that a good thing?"

"I had my normal parental worries, of course. But a father always worries about a son. Boys go through puberty with a vengeance, take risks they shouldn't. I know because I was one. As for Rory—and Jesse too, for that matter—choosing a career in any creative field can lead to so much heartache. It did for Rory, until she committed to rock and roll. It did for Jesse too until the band made it. Then my Callie." He shakes his head. "I worried for her because she asked so many questions. Was always looking for answers. Wanted to make everything logical, and life, as you know, princess, isn't always logical. I was worried she might never find a true companion because she was so caught up in her head over her heart."

I nod, swallowing.

"But you, Maddie," he says. "You were the one I knew would find her way."

I cock my head. "I don't understand. When I came home from Europe, I told you I didn't know what I wanted to do with my life. And you know how I've always felt like an oddball, how I cried when the Steel girls left me out of their plans. How can you say I was the one you never worried about?"

He smiles. "Because you know how to feel, princess. You don't hide from your feelings. You let them out, and you grow. You draw inspiration from others and from yourself. It makes a person feel good just to be around you. I always knew you would find your way. It just took a little longer."

Damn. A lump forms in my throat. "Why didn't you ever tell me any of this before, Daddy?"

He places a gentle hand on my cheek. "You weren't ready to hear it, Madeline. You had to find it for yourself. When you came home during spring break and announced you'd found your calling and you wanted to learn to be a life coach, I was never prouder. It's the perfect choice for you."

Tears pool in my eyes, and despite my best try, one falls down my cheek. "Daddy, you always believed in me?"

He wipes the tear off my cheek with his thumb. "I always believed in all four of you. That's what a father does. But I worried the least about you, baby girl." He takes a step back and gazes at me. "And look at you now. You're a beautiful young lady marrying a good man, and you're starting your life coach training next month. You're going to change the world, Maddie, and I thank God every day that He saw fit to heal me from that heart attack so I can see you do it."

I rush into his arms and hug him hard.

"I love you, baby girl," he whispers. "Now let's go get you married."

CHAPTER THIRTY-NINE

Dave

It's time.

I walk with the others to the gazebo and take my place. Henry stands next to me as my best man. Brock's best man is his brother, Bradley, and Donny's is Dale. Jesse's is Dragon Locke. He's been out of rehab for a few months now.

All of the wedding guests are dressed to the nines, some opting for black tie, while others have donned western formalwear. Lots of cowboy hats, lots of bowties, and even a few bolos. My throat catches ever so slightly when I see Uncle Joe, who's making one of his first public appearances post-surgery and post follow-up chemo and experimental treatment. He looks remarkably good with no hair, and he's opted to not wear a hat to conceal his baldness. He's lost some muscle mass in his chest and his face is a bit gaunt, but according to Aunt Melanie, he's been fighting his cancer like a champ, and we're all optimistic that we'll get to hold on to him for a little while longer.

I'm glad he'll at least get to see Brock get married. His face has been lit up since he got here.

The string quartet is done warming up, and finally, Mozart's *Wedding March* begins.

First comes Brianna on the arm of her father, Uncle Talon.

Then Rory with Frank Pike.

Once he's deposited Rory with Brock, he turns and says to the guests, "Be right back."

Laughter fills the yard as he goes back down the aisle. He returns with Callie, and then again with the most beautiful of all.

My Maddie.

He gives her to me with a stern look.

"I'll take good care of her," I tell him.

He smiles and takes his place next to Maureen in the front row.

"Welcome," our officiant says. "Ladies and gentlemen, family and friends, we are gathered here today in the beauty of nature to celebrate not one, but four incredible unions. It is a rare and wonderful occasion to witness the coming together of not just two hearts, but eight, all intertwining in the bond of love and commitment.

"As we stand under the open sky, surrounded by the beauty of this Colorado day, we are reminded of the vastness and depth of the journeys these couples are about to embark upon. Today, we are not just witnesses to their vows. We are participants in a joyous celebration of love, friendship, and the shared dreams that have brought them to this moment.

"Each couple here today brings their unique spark, their individual stories, and their personal promises to each other. Yet they also share a common thread beyond their family ties—a belief in the power of love, in the strength of unity, and in the promise of a future written together.

"Let us open our hearts and minds to the beauty of this day as we join these four couples in celebrating one of life's greatest moments. To the couples, may this day be the beginning of a lifelong journey filled with love and laughter. To everyone here, thank you for being part of this unforgettable moment."

He walks to the first couple, Jesse and Brianna.

We all chose traditional vows, and as I listen to my cousin make hers to Jesse Pike, I think about the timeless words they're speaking. They resonate with me, reminding me of the profound commitment we're about to make. It's not just about the good days, but also standing together through life's challenges—and there have been many since Maddie and I got together. Soon, it will be our turn to speak these same vows, and I feel a surge of determination to live up to every word, to honor and cherish my partner through all the days of our lives.

Brock and Rory are next.

Donny and Callie.

Then—

"David Steel Simpson, do you take Madeline Jolie Pike to be your wife, to have and to hold, for better, for worse, for richer, for poorer, in sickness and in health, to love and to cherish, until death do you part?"

And it's absolutely no hardship to look into Maddie's beautiful brown eyes, cup her soft cheek, and say loudly and proudly, "I do."

EPILOGUE

Jonah Steel and family...

Jonah Steel will defy the odds and become part of the one percent. He will live fifteen years after being diagnosed with glioblastoma and will always live life to the fullest. And yes, his gorgeous hair will grow back!

Dr. Melanie Carmichael Steel, his wife, a retired psychiatrist, will mentor her niece, Angie Simpson, as she goes through medical school with plans to pursue psychiatry.

Bradley Steel, Jonah and Melanie's older son, will continue his work with the Steel Foundation, the Steels' charitable arm, as its chief executive officer. He is not in a relationship.

Brock Steel, Jonah and Melanie's younger son, will continue his work with his father, Jonah, on the beef ranch side of the family business. He is married to Rory Pike Steel. Rory is one of the lead singers of the band Dragonlock, which, after opening for Emerald Phoenix a few more times, will embark on its first headlining tour across the United States. Brock and Rory are also expecting their first child, a boy to be named Jonah Francis after his two grandfathers. He will be called Little Joe.

Talon Steel and family...

Talon Steel continues to lead in the Steel orchards but will retire soon and leave his beloved fruit trees in the hands of his daughter Brianna Steel Pike and his nephew David Steel Simpson.

Jade Roberts Steel, Talon's wife, is the retired city attorney for the city of Snow Creek. Now she works with her best friend, Marjorie Steel Simpson, putting together elaborate Steel parties that the whole town looks forward to.

Dale Steel, their oldest son, is married to Ashley White Steel, a sommelier, and they are expecting their first child, a girl. Dale and Ashley run the Steel winery together, and they will continue to take it to further success.

Donny Steel, the city attorney for the town of Snow Creek, is married to Callie Pike Steel, who's currently in law school. Once she finishes law school and passes the Colorado bar, she will take her place at her husband's side as the assistant city attorney.

Diana Steel finished her internship in architecture and is now a full-fledged architect at a downtown Denver firm. She is not currently involved with anyone.

Brianna Steel is married to Jesse Pike, co-lead singer for the band Dragonlock. She will continue to work with her father and cousin Dave managing the Steel orchards.

Ryan Steel and family...

Ryan Steel is retired from the wine business but still keeps his hands in the barrels when he can.

Ruby Lee Steel, Ryan's wife, does freelance private

investigative work and will continue to do so.

Ava Steel, their older daughter, is married to Brendan Murphy. They live in downtown Snow Creek and run Ava's Bakery and Murphy's Bar together.

Gina Steel, their younger daughter, is pursuing a master's degree in visual art. She will become a sought-after artist with gallery showings in New York and London. She is not currently in a relationship.

Marjorie Steel Simpson and family...

Marjorie Steel Simpson, the youngest Steel sibling, is a gourmet chef who, along with her sister-in-law and best friend, Jade Steel, spends most of her days planning Steel events. They also plan the galas for the Steel Foundation.

Her husband, Bryce Simpson, is the chief financial officer of Steel Enterprises and works in the office. He will groom his daughter Sage to take over when he retires in a few years.

Henry Simpson, their older son, works with his cousin Bradley at the Steel Foundation as the chief operating officer. Henry is not currently involved with anyone.

David Simpson, their younger son, will begin working with his uncle Talon Steel and his cousin Brianna Pike in the orchards. Dave's wife, Maddie Pike Steel, completed her training as a life coach and has begun taking private clients. Before that, she and Dave took a two-month honeymoon to complete their tour of Europe.

Angela Simpson, one of their twin daughters, is in medical school. She will choose psychiatry for her residency and will become nearly as renowned as her aunt, Melanie Carmichael Steel. She is not currently involved in a relationship.

Sage Simpson, their other twin daughter, will take over as chief financial officer of Steel Enterprises when her father retires. She is not currently involved in a relationship.

Lauren Wingdam Steel and family...

Lauren Wingdam, now known as Lauren Steel, works with her new sister-in-law, Ruby Steel, doing freelance investigative work. She has a knack for it, and as an ulterior motive, she wants to find out the truth behind the death of her younger son's adoptive parents and make sure her late mother, Wendy Madigan, hasn't hidden anything else. Lauren is not in a relationship.

Jack Murphy, now known as Jack Steel Murphy, her older son, has taken his place in the Steel empire working as a real estate investor. Jack is not in a relationship.

Pat Lamone, now known as Patrick Steel, her younger son, has begun learning the investigative business from his mother and his aunt/sister, Ruby. He also wants to find out the truth about why his adoptive parents changed their names and learn more about the circumstances of their deaths. He has vowed to make up for the pain he caused the Steels and the Pikes. Pat is not in a relationship.

And yes, Wendy Madigan is dead!

ACKNOWLEDGMENTS

Where do I begin?

Do I tell you how many tears I shed writing this book? *Many.*

Do I wax poetic about how much this series has meant to me over the years? So much.

Do I thank all of you for your emails, your kind words, your devotion to this series? *Thank you so much! You have no idea how grateful I am.*

Part of me can't believe this is the end of the saga. These characters have been a part of my life for nearly ten years now. I wanted to give you a true encore with this book—an extra couple in Dave and Maddie so we could have the quadruple Steel/Pike wedding. I hope you enjoyed their love story as much as I enjoyed writing it!

The Steels aren't gone forever. We'll see some of them again in future books, but the Steel Brothers Saga—the series—ends here. It's been a wild ride, and I hope you've all loved it as much as I have.

So many wonderful individuals have helped make this series a success.

First and foremost, Scott Saunders—this series benefited so much from your editorial direction. You've made the process easy and fun, and I've learned so much from you.

Meredith Wild—who knew, when you emailed me twelve years ago to edit a book called *Hardwired* that we'd both become bestselling authors? Thank you for your belief in me and my work, and for your friendship and loyalty.

Thank you to the rest of the team at Waterhouse Press—Jon, Jesse, Kurt, Haley, Audrey, Chrissie, and Michele. Your help has been invaluable, and the books are better because of your input.

To my readers and superfans at Hardt & Soul—you keep me going! Thank you so much for your unending support.

To my family and friends—especially Mr. H and my boys, Eric and Grant—thank you for always believing in me. A special shout out to Eric for his help with the first draft of this novel.

Most of all, thank you, my readers, for letting the Steels and me be a part of your lives for so long.

But don't go anywhere... You will love what's coming!

ALSO BY HELEN HARDT

Misadventures Series:
Misadventures with a Rock Star
Misadventures of a Good Wife (with Meredith Wild)

The Temptation Saga:
Tempting Dusty
Teasing Annie
Taking Catie
Taming Angelina
Treasuring Amber
Trusting Sydney
Tantalizing Maria

The Sex and the Season Series:
Lily and the Duke
Rose in Bloom
Lady Alexandra's Lover
Sophie's Voice

Daughters of the Prairie:
The Outlaw's Angel
Lessons of the Heart
Song of the Raven

Cougar Chronicles:
The Cowboy and the Cougar
Calendar Boy

Anthologies Collection:
Destination Desire
Her Two Lovers

STEEL FAMILY TREE

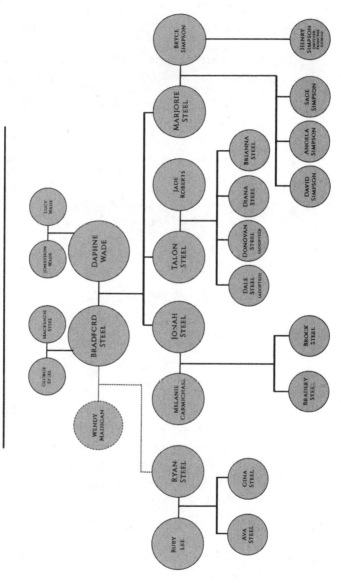

PIKE FAMILY TREE

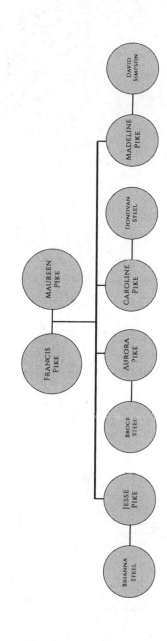

MADIGAN/STEEL/MURPHY FAMILY TREE

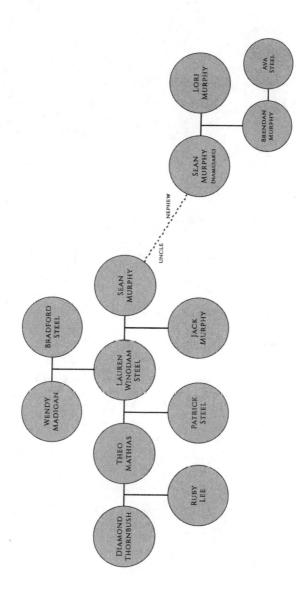